PILAR RAMIREZ
AND THE ESCAPE FROM ZAFA

PILAR RAMIREZ

AND THE ESCAPE FROM ZAFA

JULIAN RANDALL

SQUARE
FISH

Henry Holt and Company

New York

SQUARE
FISH

An imprint of Macmillan Publishing Group, LLC
120 Broadway, New York, NY 10271 • mackids.com

Square Fish and the Square Fish logo are trademarks of Macmillan and
are used by Henry Holt and Company under license from Macmillan.

Our books may be purchased in bulk for promotional, educational,
or business use. Please contact your local bookseller or the Macmillan
Corporate and Premium Sales Department at (800) 221-7945 ext. 5442
or by email at MacmillanSpecialMarkets@macmillan.com.

The Library of Congress has cataloged the hardcover edition as follows:

Names: Randall, Julian, author.
Title: Pilar Ramirez and the escape from Zafa / Julian Randall.
Description: First edition. | New York : Henry Holt and Company, 2022. |
Summary: While doing research for her documentary about her cousin
Natasha—who disappeared in the Dominican Republic fifty years ago
during the Trujillato—twelve-year-old Pilar Violeta Ramirez is transported to
Zafa, an island where Dominican myths and legends come to life and where
her cousin is being held captive in a sinister magical prison, and Pilar must
defeat the Dominican boogeyman if she hopes to free Natasha and return
home to Chicago. Includes author's note.
Identifiers: LCCN 2021023055 | ISBN 9781250774101 (hardcover)
Subjects: CYAC: Folklore—Dominican Republic—Fiction. | Missing persons—
Fiction. | Memory—Fiction. | Animals, Mythical—Fiction. | Family life—
Fiction. | Magic—Fiction. | Dominican Americans—Fiction. | LCGFT: Novels.
Classification: LCC PZ7.1.R36665 Pi 2022 | DDC [Fic]—dc23
LC record available at https://lccn.loc.gov/2021023055

Originally published in the United States by Henry Holt and Company
First Square Fish edition, 2023
Book designed by Aurora Parlagreco
Square Fish logo designed by Filomena Tuosto
Printed in the United States of America by Lakeside Book Company,
Harrisonburg, Virginia

ISBN 978-1-250-86606-6
1 3 5 7 9 10 8 6 4 2

Dedicated to the de la Oz women:
my tías and especially my mother for showing me
what our magic has always looked like

ONE

I'M PAID TO BELIEVE IN what I can see.

Okay, I don't actually get paid, pero it's the principle of the thing, entiendes? Anyway, all I'm trying to say is that I'm mad observant—it's kinda my thing.

Pero that place I saw last week was nuts. Straight tontería, you feel me? I was just trying to finish my movie, inform the masses, and maybe score some extra credit to start off the eighth grade . . . but now? Everything is upside down. And I mean that last part literally.

Wait. I'm doing that thing that I hate in other people's films—starting in the middle. So, let's rewind and run the whole thing back.

It was all good just a week ago. I woke up in my usual bed in the house with yellow walls and a blue fence on Talman Avenue. Now, I'm saying blue fence because it's been passably CTA blue my whole life, but it hasn't ever been all the way blue. Ever since I can remember, we've lived here, behind this chain-link fence with peeling paint that Mami always means to repaint but never actually does. Even when I was super little it had tiny nicks and cuts in it from where mi hermana, Lorena, would jump over it to ride bikes down the block. Or, from the dents we made playing baseball.

All my life, through this fence, I've been watching people from the block ride down the street. People like our neighbor Manuel, driving by between his gigs playing guitar with a bachata band and his job making lightbulbs at the local factory. According to Mami, our family and Manuel must be the only Dominicans in all of Chicago. Most folks here are Latinx—that's the gender-neutral version Lorena learned in college. I like the word, and it's pretty easy to say once you get the hang of it. But most people here are Mexican or Puerto Rican like my best friend, Celeste.

That reminds me, my name is Pilar Violeta Ramirez— *that's Pee-LAR*—say it right or don't say it at all, entiendes? For twelve years straight everybody and their mom, even their cousins, have been mispronouncing my name. As a result, the vice principal of my grammar school told Mami I have "patience issues." Which is slander. I'm super patient—a good director has to be. I'm just not patient with people who think my family would ever name a lil' Dominican girl "Pillar" and send her out into the world. Because when I say it that way, it doesn't make any sense, right?

Speaking of things not making sense, let me bring it back

to the day my whole life changed. I woke up one morning in Chicago and went to sleep that night on a magic island.

That morning, my best friend, Celeste, wasn't around. Her family had moved to Milwaukee because the rent in Chicago had been going up and up since I was a baby. Most of the people I'd grown up with were gone. Some live in cheaper parts of the city, some got new jobs in another state . . . but no matter the start of the story, the end is the same: They ain't here no more.

It feels like the music has been leaking out of our block a bit more each month with each dweeby-looking white kid who moves into the buildings that used to be Marcelo's crib or Vanessa Martinez's apartment. Developers even tore down the old factory—the one where Lorena hit her first home run on the roof (which was super cool, even for her)—to build a medical insurance building (boring, no character, no story at all).

It's basically just us now, me and Abuela and Mami, bracing behind our shabby old blue fence, facing new building after new building. Under their breath, the invaders say *we're* the immigrants. Pero as long as I've known what home is, we've been right here. They're colonizers who use credit cards to put their name on things they don't even understand. One day the colonizers are going to be the subject of my next documentary—them and the America they built on top of mine.

That morning there wasn't any music and there wasn't any Celeste, but I had a job to do and I was gonna do it. You see, Abuela brought Mami over from Santo Domingo, the capital of the Dominican Republic, back in 1957, when this real slimeball, Trujillo, ran the whole island. We don't really talk about him in history class, but that dude was a special kind of evil. Murder, torture, genocide on Haiti, and violence against women that makes Mami and Abuela flinch when they talk about it. You name a bad thing and Trujillo and his goons were up to their eyeballs in it.

Abuela lived through twenty-five years of that porque she's basically a superhero. She can go almost invisible when she wants to, stay real quiet and wait for the right moment to strike. She's where I get my patience from on the real. When I'm waiting for the perfect shot to enter my lens, I try to be like her, as observant as possible. The city is never fully quiet, but sometimes I can be and that's when I do my best work.

One day back on the island, Abuela got her last warning shot that it was absolutely, without a doubt time to bounce from the Dominican Republic. The details were sketchy, because nobody liked to talk about them, but after I interviewed a bunch of people for the documentary I'm filming (working title: *¿Dónde está la virgen del Trujillato?* copyright pending), a couple of facts started to line up.

The story goes that Mami had a cousin named Natasha and they were closer than sisters. Natasha's mom had been

4

jailed for "stoking insurrection," which basically meant she wanted to be free. Trujillo and his goons weren't about to let that happen, so they made her disappear. Natasha then moved in with Mami and Abuela in a little house while they waited for Trujillo to die, hoping the world would right itself.

But when both cousins were thirteen or so, Natasha just vanished. No warning, no warrant, no scary men at the door, no arrest. She just went out to get groceries one day y se fue. Vanished into thin air. The more I researched, the more I learned that apparently this happened all the time back in the day. Trujillo didn't mess with you, y ya. You were gone and just like that, people stopped mentioning you. Like being gone was contagious.

Abuela ain't need no further warning. She dried her tears, snapped Mami up, and they ran. Left behind almost everything. Sold the jewelry for plane tickets, and Natasha became just a name Mami whispered sometimes while shaking her head. Pues, she always said it with the same sadness. The irony is wild when you think on it honestly: Natasha was her true North, but Mami only immigrated North when her own personal North was nowhere to be found.

I've always wondered what happened to Natasha, even before I knew who she was. Mami only has one picture of them together, from when they were kids. They're wearing simple church dresses and standing beside Abuela and her sister. Only Mami is smiling in the picture. Sometimes, Mami just stares at the photo and cries—and Mami doesn't cry easy at all. Natasha's image in the photo is so faded it's like she's barely there.

I started my documentary as a summer project so I could finally get to the truth about Natasha. Maybe if I could find out what actually happened, no matter what it is, Mami could be at peace. Besides, I needed something to do now that Celeste wasn't around.

The morning my whole life changed, I hopped out of the shower and rubbed some coconut oil into my hair—like I did any other day. I threw on my light purple track jacket, a comfy Bulls shirt that Lorena stole off one of her boyfriends that I then stole off her (she wasn't going to wear it anyway), an old pair of jeans, and my worn pair of Adidas Boosts. I like shooting in them because the arch support is fire and they're this super fly shade of purple, like the sky right before the sun clocks out. Purp, just like my nickname was *supposed* to be. And then my phone buzzed, but not with the special three quick pops I have reserved for Celeste.

Turned out it was Lorena hitting up the family group chat, which is really just me and her and Mami, because Abuela doesn't rock with technology like that.

Oye, hermanita, are you still doing your little movie?? Lorena texted.

A frown slashed across my face immediately. This was a big part of why me and Lorena aren't that close anymore. She never took my work seriously, but I had to take everything she does seriously porque she's a nerd and goes to

U Chicago—like how is that fair? Fun goes there to die. Hard pass!

Yeah. I'm finna ride my bike to the library to see if that book I requested came in so I can do some research, I replied.

Mami started to type a message on the screen: three dots flickering in and out of sight. Her replies take longer when she's feeling the overtime. Since Papi died, our only income comes from Mami's job as a shift manager at the restaurant and whatever Lorena kicks back from her campus job. Lately, Mami's been working later and later, and today she's typing extra slow, no doubt having to fix spelling errors in her second language, starting and stopping like Lake Shore Drive traffic.

YAY!! I was hoping you'd say that! CANCEL ALL YOUR PLANS!! Lorena texted.

Mami's text indicator dropped cold and didn't pick up again.

Y would I do that? I texted back.

Because I got you something even better! Hay un professor who came into the dining hall today, Lorena said.

Typical Lorena. I love her, but the minute she accomplishes something, the whole world just gotta stop and recognize? Give me a break.

Lorena continued to type. **And we got to talking and he's a Doctor of Caribbean Studies who, wait for it . . .**

A GIF of a bunny doing a drumroll appeared. I rolled my eyes so hard I nearly dislocated an iris.

. . . studies all the disappearances during the Trujillato!!

Oh.

Isn't this exciting?! I got his office number and everything and he wants to meet with you!! Es perfecto!!

I wrote back: **Word, mil gracias. I'll be over in a bit.**

I didn't want Lorena to know how well she'd done, but she really had knocked it out of the park this time, farther than she had on that old factory roof back in the day. If this was true, then it was the biggest break for the documentary since Mami finally agreed to go on camera and give more than one-word answers.

I grabbed my video camera and placed it delicately in my backpack, cushioning it with old sweaters (also stolen from Lorena), and swung the raggedy black straps over my shoulders. I hustled down the stairs and rushed past the kitchen, almost too fast to catch the mixed scents of purple Fabuloso and arroz con pollo on the stove. My hand whipped for the door. I was the wind, I was the light, I was a waiting arrow of truth!

"Pilar Violeta Ramirez!! ¡¿A dónde vas?!"

I was . . . a twelve-year-old with a curfew and mad chores.

"Pero, Mamiiiiiii . . ."

"¡Ven aqui!"

When I entered the kitchen, the Fabuloso smell took a back seat to the sharp butter-and-adobo scent of the arroz.

Something about the way Mami cooks makes me feel like there should be music accompanying it. She turns rapidly between dishes, una media vuelta that never betrays how heavy and swollen her feet are after a shift. She was grace personified, and if I were lighting the scene, I'd use only the softest pinks. For the score, I'd choose some bachata with a lot of guitar, an overly sweet love song like the kind you can only find on Mami's old CDs.

"¿Pilar, a dónde vas?" she asked without looking up, as if she could smell that I hadn't done any chores and I wouldn't be back for a long while.

"Did you see Lorena's text? I'm going to meet with her professor."

"¿Sobre qué?"

"For the documentary. The one on—"

"Ay, Negrita, por favor, why can't you just accept that some things are what they are? Some things, they just—can't be changed. A veces people are just—" By accident she dropped her stirring spoon, sending a few undercooked grains into the sticky kitchen air before the utensil clattered to the floor like a clave. Even when she dropped things there was music.

"Pero, Mami," I said, reaching for the spoon. "I just need to learn a few more things and shoot some B-roll. And then we'll be in postproduction."

Mami sighed while she picked up the spoon, then cupped my face with a sadness in her eyes, which are the color of old brick.

"I'm just saying, mijita, you have been out of the house a lot when I need you here. This neighborhood"—the room was quiet except for the soft bubbling of the pot—"it's changing. I–You can't just come and go anymore. You're changing, too, entiendes? Things are different now."

"I understand, Mami, pero . . ." While trying to come up with the best response, I cast my eyes around the kitchen. Finally I tossed down Lorena's signature get-out-of-jail-free card: "Just think of the opportunity, Mami. A professor wants to meet with me! Maybe I could go to college where Lorena goes. Wouldn't you like that?"

I hoped lying wouldn't give me cavities, even though technically what I'd said wasn't a lie. I do want to go to college, but film school, not Lorena's Nerdtopia.

Something softened in Mami's round brown face and she pushed both hands over her thick graying curls. Mami's hands are always like birds, jittery and soft and fast. They skimmed over her hair like gulls flying across Lake Michigan when the streetlights are about to cut on.

"You be home before dark. Or else El Cuco will get you." She grinned sadly, like she could still see the little girl I used to be, the one who was afraid of El Cuco, the Dominican Boogeyman.

It wasn't a question, but I nodded anyway. She waved her hand toward the door like she was too weary for more words. Maybe she didn't approve, or maybe we were both learning that soon I would be too fast and she would be too exhausted to stop me. Either way, I was already out the door and unlocking my bike from the gate. I rode hard and fast toward the Blue Line and out of my neighborhood where everything was changing—and right into the day that would change me forever.

TWO

MY RIDE OUT SOUTH ON the Blue Line passed as it always did, with me trying to do like Abuela and melt into my seat while the city whizzed by the window. I don't know where you're from, but Chicago has the best summers anywhere, entiendes? The train took me south with the sun chasing us and only a few wispy clouds in the sky, like graffiti too high up to erase all the way. I loved Chicago more than anything, even in the winter, when it gets so cold the black ice coats the curb like plaque.

Looking around the train, I saw the average mix of folks: all ages, many in Cubs hats and sleeveless tees. Including this tall blond kid who lived in one of the town houses at the end of the street and never waved hello. He was boring, and sometimes boring people called the police like it was customer service if you looked at them too long. Maybe they don't want witnesses to notice how dull they are. Either way, I stopped staring at the blanquito, just to be safe.

I started counting tattoos instead. Only one was somewhat interesting: A dude had half a wing on his shoulder, but his shirt hid the rest. My favorite director, Josefina "Mira" Paredez, shot a documentary on the stories behind a bunch of people's tattoos. It turned out they were all connected to one another in the wildest ways! Mira is my idol, a badass Colombiana with silver glasses—rectangles just like mine— and ocean-blue streaks in her hair. Plus, when I looked her up, I found out we have the same birthday: October 24!

As I walked to my transfer for the Green Line, I patted my backpack every couple of steps just to make sure the camera was still in there. When I was four, maybe four and a half, Papi had given me an old broken cell phone so I could use it as a pretend camera. I knew I was at home the minute I looked through the lens. I went everywhere with that phone, polishing the screen with my Power Rangers shirt, which lowkey just made the screen blurrier, pero like, points for effort, no?

In the year leading up to my eighth birthday, Papi had worked even longer hours than usual. I hated those days when he was gone before I woke up and was still missing at night when I'd finished brushing my teeth. I knew he was out because his shoes weren't by the door, between Abuela's and Lorena's. He always claimed that he kissed my forehead when he finally got home, but I'd be asleep by then.

On my eighth birthday, he gave me a real video camera. It had a little screen that flipped out y todo! No more fake sound effects—I was a true director for the first time. Years later I looked up the price of the camera; it must have cost him hours of overtime.

The day of his car accident, I sensed something was wrong. It had been another missing-shoes night. But this one was different: Abuela was slumped on the couch con su rosario; Mami was by the landline, shaking her head and staring out into nothing. Lorena was out in the yard—she was the one who told me what had happened.

I remember not believing her at first. But that little gap between Abuela's and Lorena's boots was never filled again. That's how Papi transformed: como una mariposa in reverse. One morning he was a man who laughed and smelled like bread even on his off days from the bakery, and just like that he was a gap where his feet used to be.

I think he'd have been proud of how long I kept that first little camera alive. I only recently got the one I use now, on sale, so I could make the documentary. I bought it with some money Abuela gave me—the money I feel like all abuelas have stashed in some kind of secret vault only they know the code to.

Lorena had texted me while I was on the Green Line that she had to go to a different professor's office hours, so I was on my own. When I got onto the U Chicago campus, it seemed so alien with its Gothic buildings set against modern ones that looked like they were made of glass and light and donation money we didn't have. At every corner there were security guards looking for somebody, something, pero when they saw me, they just waved.

I wasn't worried about the guards, though. The students were the ones bugging me. With every other glance I felt like someone was pitying me, or angry that I dared to walk on their campus, like I didn't belong here—the stares wouldn't stop. I didn't understand why Lorena had chosen this place.

Back on the block, she was reina del barrio—everybody knew her, and everybody loved her. Perfect grades, fluent in Spanish (better than me, but she overenunciates everything, so annoying!), and a thousand-watt smile. She was so dang perfect I got a whole other name: Lorena's hermanita. I'm growing, but in Spanish it feels like the words always keep me the same size when Lorena's around: small.

Anyway, I was making my way past a bunch of buff blanquitos who were giving me the stink eye, and I was giving it right back. Maybe I should have let it go, but Mami ain't raised me to be looked down on by six people named Chad. Just when I thought one of them was finna say something, I finally found the building I was looking for.

I caught a lucky break, because there was a big group of girls walking out and laughing loudly. Real casual, I slipped inside before the door closed, and even laughed the same kind of high honking laugh to blend in. Then I looked back through the window at the Mean Mug Chads and gave them the evil eye. I don't think they saw me, but I hope they felt it.

Professor Dominguez's office, according to Lorena's texted

directions, was the door closest to the east stairs on the fourth floor. Outside the door was a slightly crooked little placard that read,

PROF. RAMON GIOVANNI DOMINGUEZ, PH.D.
VISITING PROFESSOR
DEPARTMENT OF SOCIOLOGY
OFFICE HOURS: T–TH 12–2, W 1–3

Seemed legit, though I couldn't help thinking that when Lorena became a professor, she'd never allow her name card to be off-center. Pues, knowing Lorena, she would probably iron it every Wednesday before office hours.

The office door was open a crack. I knocked softly three times.

No answer.

I waited a beat, porque Abuela always complains that I knock like I'm the police. I've got biggish hands for my age—blame DNA or puberty. Then I knocked three more times, louder, like I was trying to wake Mami after one of her double shifts.

Nada.

"Well, now what?" I mumbled to myself, looking up and down the empty hall.

Thinking back, maybe a different person would have called their older sister about the strange professor she was supposed to meet with. Maybe another person would have asked for help. And maybe that other person wouldn't have gotten trapped on a magic island as a result. Pero, I wasn't that girl.

I peeked inside the office and when he didn't answer, I did what my favorite director, Mira Paredez, would do: I went inside with my camera on, ready to find my story.

"What's the worst that could happen?" I asked myself, mad ignorant of exactly what was the worst thing that could happen. "If the dude comes back, I'll say I heard something and walked in."

I laughed a bit at my own excuse. You might be able to fool teachers with that, but Mami? She would already have the chancla in hand, porque she can smell a fib six miles away.

"And if El Profe doesn't come back"—I swiveled the camera around, getting a good pan of the office to use later—"at least I'll have some fly B-roll for postproduction!"

I really thought I was a winner either way. Payasa.

Looking around Dominguez's office, it was no mystery why his nameplate was crooked—everything in there was a mess. I'm not the neatest girl on the planet, but *sheesh*. The room was covered floor to ceiling in papers and files.

Did all these files have to do with disappearances during the Trujillato? I flicked the light switch y nada. This dude was a whole professor in an office with no electricity? So much for hospitality.

I turned up the flash on the camera by 80 percent and did some slow zooming in on various stacks, figuring I could narrate over it later. Mira Paredez once said in an interview on YouTube, "I always keep an eye to background, to setting, entiendes? People are as much about what they surround themselves with as about what they say. I've taken interviews that were never about the person. The person was just a door to what they were sitting in front of—that was the real story."

Mira couldn't have known how right she was, porque while I did that shot of the office, I found something I couldn't believe. Something that would change my life completely. In the middle of one tall stack of yellowed papers was a manila folder that had a slightly bent name tab. Written on it in faded blue ink was:

NATASHA ANTONIA DE JESUS (1957)

I nearly dropped the camera. I never drop the camera.

That was Natasha's name. *My* Natasha! And 1957 was the year she had disappeared. My heart immediately went into overdrive until its pounding was all I could hear. I didn't even have time to be kinda mad that Lorena had been right about me needing to see the professor.

My palms went slick, and between that and the loud pulse in my eardrums, it was like I was doing everything in slow motion. I gently set the camera down on the desk, almost like I was apologizing. For what? Nearly dropping it? For being in this office without permission? Who cared!

I was staring at a major, earthshaking break in my documentary!

I pulled the file out carefully, like a Jenga piece, and squinted at it like it would disintegrate if I looked at it too closely. I swear it hummed. I turned the camera toward me, careful to make sure it was recording, and opened the folder, eager to see what was inside.

Y nada. Nothing. Zip. Zilch. Except one blank sheet of paper.

Disappointment surged through my body. I could have cried. I probably would have if I'd made it out of the office, but that's when everything went absolutely nuts.

The piece of paper I was stroking with my right hand began to glow. And then, the next thing I knew, I was elbow deep in the paper, like it was quicksand, and the page was starving for me.

I yelped and tried to drop it, but the paper stubbornly hung on to my right arm! I swung my arm wildly, like I was trying to wrestle my way out of a winter coat, and almost tripped on a stack of folders. I had to be hallucinating. Another yank from the paper and I was in up to my shoulder. I tried to pull free again, heaving back and grunting.

Pero nada.

I saw the winking light of the camera. No chance I was leaving it behind.

I hurled myself with all my might toward the desk and ended up knocking over the files. The papers spiraled upward in tiny hurricanes, causing other stacks to topple to the ground. One envelope even zinged across the office, shattering a picture frame, but I didn't care. I managed to grab the camera with my left hand, maybe by magic or maybe by luck, quién sabe? Maybe those are two different words for the same thing.

Whatever, I had the camera. De verdad, I'd never hyperventilated before, pero I could barely get a full breath in while I tried to keep my grip on it. Heart pounding and arms shaking, I fixed the camera to my eye as the last of me was sucked into the page. Wherever I was going, I would need a record.

With that last thought, I fell down, into miles of white.

THREE

CELESTE'S MOM USED TO DELIVER window fittings when me and Celeste were little. Before her mom set us straight, we thought windows came fully set up, like they grew on glass trees or something. Her mom laughed one of those huge Latinx mom laughs; you know the one I'm talking about. They stop what they're doing, throw their head and wrist back at the same time, like they're shooting a fadeaway. My math teacher, who also runs the theater class, says laughter is beautiful because it doesn't have a language; but he's wrong. When Mami laughs like that, it's in Spanish, and I know for a minute she feels like she's back home in DR.

After she stopped laughing, Celeste's mom told us windows are made of sand, that every grain is like a tiny window that becomes the big one.

When I hit the beach inside the page, I was pretty sure I'd be spitting up tiny windows for the rest of my life. I stood up real slow, shook my hair, and half a sandbox fell out of it. Thankfully nothing was broken, which only freaked me out more. I turned my head up to the sky. Pero nada, no Pilar-shaped hole, just a long stretch of sun and blue, all innocent-looking. My pulse quickened as if it were saying wrongwrongwrong.

Look, I'm no scientist, but everybody knows if you fall out of the sky, it's supposed to hurt. I was a little dizzy, but that was it. No scratches. Nothing broken—

"THE CAMERA!"

I sprinted up the beach, sand flying up on either side of me. A little knot of dread swelled in the pit of my stomach.

I finally spotted the camera a couple yards away, where the beach began getting grassier. The muzzle and the lens were sticking out of the sandy grass. I breathed a big sigh of relief; the lens wasn't cracked. I pulled the camera out of the sand, running my fingers over all the grooves. I clutched the camera to my chest saying "Sorrysorrysorry."

Then, thunder. One of those huge cracks when the rain is mad, entiendes? When there's enough rain coming to fill all the potholes on Lake Shore Drive.

Perfect, I thought. *Just my luck.*

Pero when I looked at the sky again? Nada. The same perfect late July blue like my fence. No dark clouds. There weren't even any birds. Then the thunder stampeded all over my eardrums and a shiver rushed up my spine.

I looked out at the water for the first time and saw a white ocean. Not white frothing—the water itself was hospital-sheet white! The ball of anxiety in my stomach swelled even larger.

This wasn't right. But there it was, a whole ocean that looked like toothpaste. I felt dizzy. The world was spinning in and out of focus just like when I'd fallen from the sky. Where was I? I must have hit my head back in the office. The world kept spinning, clean blue sky over bleach-white ocean. I kicked the sand hard and screamed in frustration as it drifted back down. I was sweating a lot. How hot was it here? Where was "here"? I was so confused!

Mami said the whole world was changing. I thought she was just avoiding talking about boys and gentrification, not the ocean turning white!

"Mami!" I burst out. "I can text her and wake up from this nightmare!"

I whipped out my phone and entered my passcode so fast I messed it up the first three times. I got it on the fourth try. No service. I stared at the phone's background picture, tears pricking my eyes. It's me and Celeste and the boys sitting by The Lake last summer. Celeste was making this weirdo face and wearing our friend Carlos's hat backward. I'm at home in that picture. I wanted it to last forever.

I looked out at the bleach-white waves, light wind churning the sand. Acid climbed in my throat, burning until I thought I was finna throw up all over the sand.

"Where am I?" I whispered to myself, turning the phone off and tucking it back into my pocket between dry heaves. Hands on my knees, I looked out at the ocean. No boats, no people, not even a seagull. Alone. I was all alone.

BOOM!

A third wave of thunder crashed so hard that it felt like the world was shaking. I tore my eyes away from the ocean and looked behind me. Y pues, that's when I knew this place didn't make any sense at all. Just beyond the grass, I heard rain coming from a thick green forest. Rain . . . inside the forest, and *only* inside the forest.

"No," I muttered. "Uh-uh, no way. Nope. I am not going in there."

And I didn't . . . for a while. I stayed right on the beach. I shook sand out of my shoes. I filmed some pan shots of what I was seeing. I looked back through the film I had already shot to see if anything jumped out.

My stomach growled the whole time I combed the beach for food. I went east, I went west and not so much as one plátano! No matter how far I walked in either direction, there was the forest, looking straight out of a horror film for real! You know that kind of horror movie. The ones where a family moves to a mysteriously cheap house in the middle of a swamp, and then has the nerve to be surprised when they get attacked by a ghost whose hair is always wet porque I guess there are no towels in the demon world.

Pero like, there was nothing to eat. Plus, I was getting curious. I can't help it, I'm a director. I wiped the camera lens on my shirt, took a deep breath, and walked under the vines.

Inside the forest all the light was a gloomy blue. I tripped immediately porque I could barely see where I was going. The cover of the tallest trees reached almost too high to see. The bottoms of the trees were spindly like somebody had started drawing hundreds of them but never finished the sketch. Their roots arched above the ground. When the wind passed, the trees moaned like lost children.

My seventh-grade English teacher said we should *never* start a sentence with "in conclusion." But Dr. Johnson wasn't facing monster-size trees that sounded like they were going to fall any minute. In conclusion, the place gave me the creeps in a big way.

I generally don't like wearing my hair up (people say I got a big forehead, which is slander if you ask me), but after twenty minutes of walking in the rain my curls were getting in my eyes. I pulled my hair into a loose ponytail. I was so focused on my hair that I splashed my kicks in a big puddle beneath one of the trees.

"Ay, today just is not my day," I grumbled. I glanced at the mud on my kicks and sighed. It's not like they were the nicest kicks in the universe, but they're my favorite shoes to shoot in, and seeing them all messed up . . . It just wasn't fair, entiendes?

I just wanted to know the truth about Natasha. So I could give Mami some answers, so she could finally be at peace. Lorena ruined everything by sending me to her stupid made-up professor.

The forest got darker and a gloomy mist settled in the trees. After a while, I picked out a spot in the forest with the least creepy roots and laid out my jacket underneath it to try to get some rest. The darkness of the forest was messing with my mind. I had no idea what time it was.

I settled in with my head on my backpack and the camera in my lap. I hadn't been planning to fall asleep, but that's exactly what happened. Which, in retrospect, is where the trouble really began. Porque nadie sleeps easy in El Bosque de las Tormentas, nobody.

I couldn't have been out for longer than an hour, hour and a half tops, when a huge roar of thunder shook the Ceiba tree I was resting under. It was like waking up inside a circus cannon. My head rang and I shot up immediately.

Lightning bleached all the treetops out of sight. As my eyes adjusted, it looked like seven little balls had fallen from a nearby tree, like coconuts, but pitch-black. They hit the ground with soft pops, as if they hadn't fallen at least eight stories.

"But that can't be right," I mumbled, trying to rub the flash out of my eyes. "Ceiba trees don't grow coconuts."

I was right. They don't. Pero, in *this* forest, the trees do grow little monsters who try to kidnap future Academy Award– winning directors who just want to go home.

When those *things* started to unravel from their ball form, my nose was filled with the smell of a wet dog pulling along a cart of curdled milk. Or like old gym socks that got thrown away and are now out for revenge on their former masters. I started coughing immediately, tears in my eyes y todo.

At that point they didn't look like coconuts anymore. Try two rows of yellowing, drool-covered fangs and weepy-looking eyes with two little crooked horns at the top of the head. Oh, and throw in a surprisingly jacked torso, like bodybuilders with thick fur, and you've got it about right.

"Ummmm," I groaned, heart quickening as I wondered if these things even spoke a language, let alone English. "Is this about the tree? Because I can just—"

One to the left hissed and all of them roared and charged toward me on all fours. Cool, guess negotiations were over. Boring conversation anyway.

The first of the Evil Coconut People leapt almost eye level with me from the center of the pack, which caught me off guard because it wasn't any taller than my knee. I freaked out and stumbled backward over a root as it narrowly missed me but tore a slice of my jacket. My pulse went from quick jog to full-on sprint. What was this thing and why was it so ticked at me?

"Perfect." I rolled my eyes, hating the quiver in my voice. "Bad smell, razor-sharp claws, and y'all got hops? Are you sure y'all aren't eighth graders?"

They didn't laugh. Sue me—that was funny! Plus, I make jokes when I'm in mortal peril. Speaking of which . . .

Another leapt from the right, howling and slobbering mad gibberish. I caught it in the chin with a right hook. It yipped and fell to the side. I didn't even have time to reset before another two came running toward me from the right. I kicked one full in the face while the other leapt over me and charged straight into my thigh. I stumbled but managed to bat it away, my left knee throbbing like I got hit with a thick chancla.

My ears thumped so loudly that I could barely hear the rain. All my muscles tightened. Bright spots popped up in my vision. I hadn't realized I was holding my breath. Whatever these things were, they were fast and vicious. And coordinated.

Two of them threw a third into the air, high enough to plant its feet on a low-hanging branch and relaunch toward me like a nasty torpedo. I rolled out of the way just in time. Its wet dog smell mixed with dirt and rainwater as it hit the ground. So, they were launching each other now? What was this, the Evil Coconut Troll Black Ops Squad?

That lift-and-jump maneuver was clearly a favorite, because another three tried it again. A narrow miss.

"Another! Another! Another!" one of them chanted. The others joined in until the forest rang with their cheers. It got so loud I wasn't sure if it was just those seven screaming their little furry heads off or if sixty more were waiting nearby to jump me.

I hauled myself up and tried to make a run for it, but the bruise on my thigh was throbbing. I tripped and fell over a root curling out of the ground. I got back to my feet as quickly as I could. Another little smelly troll bounded toward me, keeping up the chant of "Another, another." I threw an elbow to the temple and left it cradling its head.

But by that point four, then five—no, six of them were on me. They grabbed me, two per leg and one on each of my arms. They dragged and pushed and hauled me. They were strong and moved like one putrid unit, chanting over and over. I couldn't get a thought straight in my head. I looked up and saw something flit between the branches.

"Great, more of your friends?" I called out, trying to sound brave while struggling to wrestle myself free from their grip.

In a blur, a foot collided with the back of the troll's head that was clutching my right arm. Where had the foot come from? A punch landed and two of the creatures on my legs slammed into the trunk of a nearby Ceiba tree. The chant stopped, replaced by a roar of fury from the creatures who were currently getting rocked by . . . well, I didn't know who exactly. Pero the enemy of my coconut troll is my friend, or something like that?

Whoever she was, it was clear she was ready, because ella was fighting como una bachatera. Rhythmic and graceful, ducking under the little savages' attacks like it was rehearsed. I didn't get a good look at her face, but her hair was a pitch-black mane of curls that danced along behind her. A strange sound was coming from her and it took me a moment to identify it as a laugh. Who was this girl?! She looked at those ugly little furballs and laughed as she casually whooped their butts? I was impressed.

After the fifth or sixth time she backflipped over one of

the creatures, while punting another deep into the trees, they realized they were out of their league. The tallest troll gave three quick barks like a dog and the others hightailed it out of there.

"Awww, leaving so soon, boys?!" the strange girl called out. She jumped into one of the trees, hands on her hips, still laughing.

Pues, ella had a laugh you never forget. It's hard to describe, pero she laughs like summer. You feel warmer, like things will all work out eventually.

With all the creatures gone, I dusted myself off and unzipped my bag to check over the camera. I let out a sigh of relief, sending up a quick prayer to Mira Paredez! Miraculously, it was still in good shape, though some of the paint was scuffed.

Just as I was tucking the camera back in my bag, one last coconut troll came hurtling down out of the branches with a high-pitched wail. I put up my fists and got ready to fight another wave. But it wasn't attacking—it'd been thrown. It smacked down into a puddle with a huge splash. The strange girl came flying down. Homie scrambled up and scurried after its ugly friends.

"¡Ven aquí feíto!" she yelled after him in quick Spanish. "Hijo de la gran—"

And then she stared at me full-on for the first time. She looked about Lorena's age. She was beautiful, with a devious smile framed by her long pitch-black curls. She had on a white sleeveless shirt that shifted subtly in the light like it was actually smoke. Her pants were olive green, almost like jeans, but also weirdly smoky in quality. I gasped, not at her outfit or even at the fact that she'd randomly appeared and rescued me. Pero none of that was the weird part. Given the day I was having, that was tied for seventeenth weirdest thing, tops.

Her feet were pointing all the way backward.

¿Qué te dije? That's when the real trouble started.

FOUR

"OMG WHAT HAPPENED TO YOUR feet?!" I said, scrambling backward on all fours in a crab walk. Sue me, you see somebody feet pointing backward and you'd freak out too, entiendes?

The girl with the backward feet looked at me mad annoyed. She had a deep crease all up in her forehead as her curls shook on either side, wet from the rain and catching the light from somewhere. Freaked out as I was, I had to admit she still looked pretty badass with the rain falling all dramatic y todo.

"WhAt hApPeneD to Ur FeEt?" she mocked back at me.

Y se fue. I felt my cheeks prickle hot with annoyance, and I blew a muddy curl out of my face. Boom, admiration over.

"Look, lady, you're the one with backward feet. I'm just tryna see if you good, you ain't gotta catch a whole attitude with me, entiendes?" I said, dusting dried mud off the elbow of my jacket.

"Oh, I'm good." She laughed, a mischievous lilt settling across her lips. "Then again, chica, I wasn't the one who got captured by a troop of Cucitos, so . . ."

She let her voice drag off into the distance. Lorena does that sometimes, leaving the room before her voice does. It drives me nuts, every single time. Pues, I felt my hands ball into fists.

"Cucitos? What is a . . . Look, you sure you didn't hit your head flying through them trees?" I said, putting my hands on my hips before muttering, "Ol' Family Dollar Tarzan lookin—"

"I didn't hit my head." She huffed, and all her hair bounced with her, her white sleeveless blouse shimmering like smoke fanning away from an open flame. "And my name isn't 'Lady.'"

She tilted her chin up and I felt a little bad. She seemed lowkey offended. Like, don't get me twisted, I'd have been down to try and kick her butt. Pero like, she had saved me from those Evil Coconut People she called "Cucitos." Mami always says I need to pick my battles more carefully. So y'know, growth.

"Hey," I started, pero she flashed a haughty look at me, gold-flecked brown eyes gleaming in the twilight. I started again. "I'm sorry, pues, today has been"—I gestured around at the forest, pointed at my (now definitely ruined) kicks—"a lot. Can we start over?"

Her stance slackened a bit and she turned her eyes back

toward me. She was softer now but still, shawty was no push-over. Her soft was the soft of a curl after the rainwater gets in, entiendes?

"My name's Pilar, sorry I ain't ask yours first." I thumbed away some soggy grass from the logo on my jacket, not want-ing to look at her.

"Carmen."

"That's your name?"

I turned the *r* in her name over in my mouth. In her voice, the whole word purred like an engine. Carmen shot me a "duh" look, which reminded me so much of Lorena's face whenever she says, "Well, hermanita, let's think this through," that I thought about fighting her anyway. Pero another flash of lightning screamed across the sky. It illuminated the tops of the trees, the branches harsh against the light. It would have made for a really dope shot.

I tore my eyes away from the sky and a look of concern rippled across Carmen's face. Pues, now I knew we were in trouble porque cocky as she was, I had to give ella credit where it was due; she kicked some coconut troll butt. So any-thing that could have her looking that shook was bad news.

"Yes, Carmen's my name. And we're not safe here . . ."

Before I had a chance to ask any more questions, she faced me and grabbed me under the arms.

"What the—" I blurted, but before I knew it she'd launched us up into the trees.

Carmen was incredibly strong and she had hops forreal.

34

The wind sang sharply over us as we hurtled upward. It was highkey very scary, pero like I wasn't going to scream if Carmen wasn't screaming.

"Also, you roll your *r*'s weird." She laughed as we surged toward a high branch. I glared at her. "Pilar," she added.

She said my name right on the first try, a soft note in her tone; almost an apology, almost a song.

We swung clunkily between a few branches—apparently Carmen wasn't used to doing this while carrying someone else. Pues, that back-and-forth tontería was really making me wanna hurl. Thankfully we eventually landed gracefully, but I was still mad; it's the principle of the thing.

"Do. Not. Ever. Do. That. Again." I flapped my jacket back up over my shoulders.

Carmen scoffed and held up both hands.

"Okay, well, you carry me next time." Sarcasm dripping from her every word. "We can trade off until either we get back to Minerva or you get eaten by the Cucitos. Your choice!"

She clapped her hands at the end. I just scowled and undid my ponytail, squishing water out of a few curls. Wait . . . did she say *eaten*? My pulse thudded in my ears.

"Nah, I got questions! I'm not going to Minnesota with you?!"

"¿Qué es un 'Minnesota'?" Carmen slowly tongued the word like she was trying to get some half-cooked rice out from between her teeth. Abuela does the same thing sometimes, chewing on a word until it makes sense. "I said we're going to Minerva!" She punched each syllable in "Minerva" and finished off by kicking at something invisible with her backward feet.

Which, of course, set me off all over again.

"And another thing!" I said, knowing I was finna mention *way* more than one thing. "Where the heck are we? Is Minerva a person or a place? What were those things you fought? Do they all smell like that? Porque that was gross!" I counted off questions on my fingertips. Carmen looked like she wanted to interrupt, but I held up a hand just like Mami does when she can't be bothered to say "Ya." "What happened to your feet? How do I get home? Are there more of those things? Is that why we dipped?"

I would have gone off for another hot sixteen, but a massive bellow of thunder slammed and the rain picked up even harder.

"And. Why. Won't. It. Stop. Raining?!"

I took off my jacket, the cold drops of rain sprinting down my arms as I shivered. I crouched down and draped the jacket over my backpack. I looked up at Carmen and she looked back at me, half irked, half sympathetic.

"Okay, okay, tranquilo, chica!" She held out a hand. "I know a spot a little farther into El Bosque that has good cover from the rain."

I opened my mouth, but this time it was Carmen's turn to hold up the "ya" hand. "And I will answer your questions when we get there, entiendes?"

I giggled a bit. She said "entiendes" just like I did. I still didn't know if I liked Carmen. I didn't know if I could even trust her. Pero like, it was trust her or get soaked and eaten by coconut trolls. Rock, meet Hard Place. Hard Place, meet Rock.

"Okay, fine." I bit my lower lip. "Is there like any way that we can go without you carrying me?"

"Not really," Carmen said. My shoulders slumped and my cheeks burned. "It's pretty high up. Most of the other ciguapas don't even go there anymore. It'd probably take you a couple days to climb up from the ground."

Ciguapa. Of course! A mix of understanding and anxiety danced beneath my skin, like my whole body was a foot that fell asleep and was prickling itself back awake. I had heard stories about la ciguapa from Abuela. Pero none of them were happy stories. Carmen's voice cut in on my thoughts/anxiety storm.

"Pilar, Pilar, hello?" She dragged out the *o* with an "anybody home" look on her face. "You ready to get going? Or you want to spend the next few days getting soaked trying to climb un árbol?"

She stuck her hand out again, the palm turned up like a question. I wiped a mix of sweat, mud, and rain off my jeans and stared into her eyes. The gold flecks gleamed like old coins.

La ciguapa was a notorious trickster.

I took a deep breath and looked around at the rain

slapping against branches in the distance, trickling down the bark in spiderweb patterns.

No man has ever seen her and lived, I heard in Abuela's voice. But Carmen was my best option, and I was no man. I took her hand and we swung down, east and farther into the belly of the storm.

FIVE

THE GROVE CARMEN GUIDED US toward was beneath a tight knot of branches that laced together like ancient knuckles. Above us, the branches formed a roof like one of those yurt houses you see on TV.

I figured Carmen had some kind of wild ciguapa magic working to avoid slipping on the slick moss that stretched along the branches. I mean gasoline shimmering in the middle of the street type slick, weirdly pretty but you would absolutely bust your butt if you weren't careful. And Carmen landed on a branch a level below the top ones, graceful as a cat. With no shoes. Show-off.

She let me go as I muttered a thanks and we walked beneath the roof-like branches. I was still clutching the backpack to my chest. I sat down, heard a squish, and immediately wished I had put the jacket down first. Now my pants were wet all over again, fantastic! Carmen, for her part, tried not to laugh. I mean, I could still see chica giggling behind her hand as she crouched, but I guess it was nice that she tried.

"Okay," I said, shifting awkwardly to mimic her crouch and not think about my pants. "Where are we? What's going o—"

"Pues, chica, I gotta hand it to you, you don't give up. Da me un minuto."

Carmen stretched her arms and then fished around in her pockets. I narrowed my eyes at her warily. I thought about checking on the camera, but Abuela said you could never afford to take your eyes off la ciguapa. Not even for a minute. Pues, that's why la ciguapa was born with her feet backward; at least according to the story. It makes her impossible to track because wherever she walks it looks like she went the opposite direction.

I stared at Carmen intently. She was still fishing around in her pockets, her tongue sticking out to the left with one eye closed. She looked goofy honestly, but Celeste makes the same expression when she's trying to remember which pocket she put her keys in. My chest warmed a bit thinking about Celeste and then I thought about how I may never see her again, especially if la ciguapa herself had lured me to a high place to destroy me. The warmth in my chest went out.

"Victory! I knew I didn't leave it behind in Minerva!"

The ciguapa did a dorky little dance with her arms holding a shiny orange stone. I cocked my head to the side, heart thumping.

"What the heck is that thing? Are you going to use it to kill me?!" The question was out before I could help it.

Carmen cocked her head to the side now, a look of utter confusion on her face. "Kill you? Payasa, this is just a hot stone." She looked at me for confirmation, but all I had on my face was a blank stare. "Have you . . . never seen one before?"

I shook my head. Carmen huffed in annoyance and grumbled something that sounded an awful lot like "Do everything my dang self," and pressed both her palms onto the little amber stone. An orange blade of light pushed out from between her knuckles, then two more followed until the whole grove was full of its glow. Carmen placed the stone between us and it warmed the whole space as if it were a roaring fire.

"See?" she said. "Totally harmless. Nobody likes being interrogated *and* sopping wet. And you seem pretty dead set on the whole interrogation thing, so we might as well be warm." She grinned and laughed that high, summery laugh.

I hate to admit it, but I did instantly feel a lot better. I held my hands out to the pulsing heat of the stone and felt some of the wet starting to come out of my clothes already.

"Yeah, it was a gift from Minerva. Pretty simple enchantment, pero like it's super useful porque—" She gestured around. "None of this is going to catch fire. Only downside is the glow is a big giveaway, pero it's fine because the Cucitos like to get the jump on people from above and this is way too high up for them."

She shrugged and right as I was about to finally get some

answers, Carmen cut in. "So . . . why did you think I was going to kill you?"

"Ummm . . ." I wasn't really anticipating having to explain that.

"I mean, I'm not going to!" She chuckled.

"Well, um . . . like you're la ciguapa." Carmen cocked an eyebrow suspiciously at that. "And like, I don't know . . . your reputation . . . kinda precedes you. You lead men to their doom and like I guess eat them or whatever." I petered off at the end. I know she *said* she wasn't going to kill me, but like . . . quién sabe?

Carmen was quiet for a moment. Then she burst out laughing. Short breathless bursts that shook the rain from the branches overhead.

I crossed my arms. Pues, it wasn't that funny.

"Me? Eat a man?!" Carmen slapped her thigh, shaking with laughter. "Absolutely not, boys would taste so gross! Ha, wait until I tell the others." She put her hand over her heart, smiling. "I solemnly swear by the grace of the Galipote Council that I will never eat you, especially considering I am a vegetarian."

"I'm just saying those are the stories I heard from my abuela," I grumbled.

"Chica, your abuela probably heard that story from a MAN. Me and the other ciguapas don't eat men."

"Wait! There's more of you?!"

"Well, as you can see"—Carmen flashed a thousand-watt smile and did some silly model poses—"I'm one of a kind, pero like, yes, there are other ciguapas. Like sixty of us, back in Minerva."

"So Minerva *is* a place!" I pumped my fist.

"I mean . . . yeah. It's the capital city of Zafa and . . ."

"What's Zafa?"

Carmen looked dumbfounded, her jaw hanging slack like she'd never been asked that question before. "Pues, you're standing on it."

I blinked at her so many times that it was almost as if Carmen were moving in stop-motion.

She continued on with her story. "All of this is Zafa. The whole island is Zafa. El Bosque de las Tormentas, where we are now. Minerva, la capital, where we're headed. Even este atrocidad La Blanca, it's all Zafa. We've lived here for as long as Dominicans have had stories to tell. Even the stupid ones where apparently there's only one ciguapa." She laughed at the end, but softly this time.

"Also like, rule of thumb kid, anytime a man tells you there's only one of something . . . mentiroso!" We both laughed at that one.

"Oh, and if you'd let me finish." She glared at me, looking irked. "Ciudad Minerva is the capital and we call it that porque the leader of the Galipote Council is also named Minerva."

43

"What's a Galipote?" I hadn't heard of that one before.

"Ugh, do they not teach you anything wherever you fell from?" I was finna argue with her, but Carmen was finally getting somewhere with my questions, so I elected to fall back.

"Rare shapeshifters with deep magic. The sisters protect the city from our friends back there . . . and *worse*." Carmen cracked her knuckles, then started counting off on her fingertips. "There's Dede, Patria, Antonia Maria, and Minerva." Carmen's tone went grave, all the laughter sliding out of her eyes. "They're our leaders in the fight against El Cuco."

I shivered and felt my chest grow tight. What had I gotten myself into?

"Wait, what?!" I yelled. "Like from the story? Ay dios, are you kidding me, fam?"

The whole world was spinning. And I still had no idea how I'd gotten here or how to get home. Pues, and now folks are talking about a *fight*?! Against the dang Boogeyman? I didn't sign up for a war.

Carmen stood up and grabbed the hot stone, whispering into the little glowing orb, and just like that it took all the heat with it. Like shawty just whispered and *bam* the sun clocked out.

"Pues, afraid not, chica. We're in a fight and we been losing big-time for as long as I can remember. We have to move now if we want to make it to Minerva before Second Light. Anyway, the Galipotes are better at telling the full story. And I'm sure they will be over the moon to see you."

I cocked my head up. Pues, Carmen was tripping if she thought I was going to just take that on faith.

"Me? Why me?"

"What part of mythical island of monsters and legends is confusing you? We don't exactly get a lot of visitors!"

SIX

THE RELENTLESS MOSS AND THICK mud smell of El
Bosque began to fade as we swung between branches. According to Carmen, it rains in other parts of Zafa, pero like it is
always raining in El Bosque de las Tormentas. The rain blocks
out the light most of the day, so trying to measure the hour
by the sun was for payasas. But for a brief stretch of the day,
the light creeps back through the branches, and they call this
strange time "Second Light." The downside to Second Light
was that you lost the cover of darkness normally found in El
Bosque—so it was easier to be hunted.

As the clotted purple at the top of the trees shed layer
upon layer of dark to reveal a shroud of amethyst-colored fog
(which would have made a great time-lapse shot, but I was
afraid to drop the camera while swinging between vines), I
began to hear a howl shaking through the trees, a sound alive
with teeth.

"Ay dios, I thought we'd have more time!" Carmen grunted.

46

Another horrible scream pressed in from all directions and left my ears ringing.

"When is today going to be over?!" I huffed.

Carmen hauled me up like I was a backpack. It was mad undignified, pero beggars can't be choosers, especially if the choice is to be left behind to be eaten by something howling through the rain.

The trees thinned out even more and a new scent wafted in, like charcoal. I bucked from side to side on Carmen's back, trying to suss out where the smoke smell was coming from. Maybe if I could find the source, it'd lead us to the howler. The noise was louder now and swelled over us from all sides. Pues, I was just so useless, like a baby riding along through a hurricane. I looked below as Carmen sprinted the length of a branch and saw something that looked like a pack of dogs.

Were there dogs in Zafa too? Why would dogs smell like charcoal? What did they want with us?

The ciguapa landed hard on a branch, y pues, she barely broke stride. It was some wild, *American Gladiators* type of balance; she'd win that show easy if she ever came to my world.

"Almost . . . there." She grunted as she sprinted along a narrow tree limb. With nothing in front of it. "Hang on tight!"

And then she jumped.

"WHAT ARE YOU DO—" The breath shot out of me before I could complete my thought.

We dove straight down, the gravity pulling tears out of my eyes. Pues, I have never been so happy I'm not afraid of heights like Lorena. She never even took me to Six Flags because just looking at the roller coasters makes her sick. But yup, we swan dove and I gripped Carmen's neck as tightly as I could. A small wheeze escaped her and probably an annoyed glance.

Carmen seized a springy branch and swung us powerfully up out of the dive-bomb. As we zoomed up, a massive charred gray bird swooped low over our heads. Each flap of its wings was accompanied by a spray of soot that drifted like thick black snow. Everything seemed to slow in response.

Pues, that was no Cucito, pero like also not a bird. Carmen clearly saw it too and I heard a sound like a gasp come out of her. The Not-Bird opened its coal-black beak and inside there was a mass of red that swelled up and down as if something were burning inside it. It let out a harsh scream. Pero not the scream of a bird, something not quite human that settled in my blood.

My pulse was racing, a vicious bass that felt like it was tearing me apart. I held on even tighter, my palms slick with sweat. The scream was joined by others, a horrifying choir. Was this bird the dogs' leader?

I can still hear that call now; I'll never be able to unhear it.

Carmen kicked at the Not-Bird, but it dodged away. She hopped off one final branch and we were out of El Bosque, greeted by a warm breeze. We landed in a small stretch of pitch-black sand that glimmered under the moon like oil. In the distance I could see a skyline of white buildings, domes, statues, and balconies that glowed almost blue against the dark of night.

It was gorgeous—nothing on the Chicago skyline, pero still, it was beautiful just like Abuela's old pictures of Santo Domingo. When she takes them out at Christmastime, the small brown hills of her shoulders settle lower and she laughs sadly, but like she's somewhere with better weather.

I climbed off Carmen's back as she rubbed the sides of her hips.

"Anybody ever tell you that you got real bony knees?" Carmen grumbled.

"You said to hang on!" They are pretty bony, but I was just following directions, so this slander seemed pretty uncalled-for. A near-death experience ain't just a hall pass to be rude, entiendes?

"Shhhh!" Carmen hissed, her neck tilted up to the sky.

My number one pet peeve? You guessed it, being shushed. Especially by someone who looks only a few years older than me.

"Oye, don't you shush me! I am a gro—"

"SHHHHHHH!" Carmen glared at me. "Do you smell that?"

Her glare gave way to wide-eyed confusion, then a crease in her brow as she looked at the ground.

"No, they can never come this close. It can't be . . ."

I tried to follow where her eyes were going. Smelled the night air, which was balmy with a hint of salt and . . . smoke. I looked toward El Bosque. Standing on that beige sand a few feet away were sixteen snarling gray-black dogs. They sat in a perfectly straight line, dark red eyes narrowed, the tips of their yellowing fangs dark in the moonlight. Something dripped from the ends of their teeth.

Was that blood?

"We gotta go," Carmen said from behind me.

I didn't even question it. We turned in unison with each other y se fue. I didn't even care that nobody in the history of the world has looked graceful running with a backpack on. Not to catch the El and not to escape a pack of Hell Dogs and their weird bird leader, who let out a final shriek.

Our feet touched dirt road as we reached the end of the black sand, huffing, hands on knees, and found the city asleep with only a few windows lit. Wild how anyone could sleep through all that tontería we just ran from.

"Well, at least some of the city's defenses are holding up." Carmen straightened and put her hands on her head like she'd just run the mile.

"What happens if they fail?" I asked.

Carmen gave a nervous glance at the ring of black sand and the demon dogs pacing at its edge, like the sand was all that stood between them and their dinner.

I wiped sweat from my eyes to get a better look at the city for the first time. In the moonlight, the blue-white buildings almost hummed with how sharp the colors were. I reached out to lean against the wall of a nearby building. It was a stucco-type material, the little hills of plaster pressing into my palm like blunt needles. Black flowers rustled in the breeze, hanging from balconies like elaborate scarves.

It was a perfect night. I sat down in the dirt of the road porque my clothes were definitely already dirty beyond anything I could imagine. I pulled out the camera from my bag and slid the lens cap off its one dark eye.

"¿Oye, Pilar, qué es eso?" Carmen panted. She was still pretty out of breath but doing way better than I was. I'm in the forty-eighth percentile for mile time in gym class, so, you can do the math.

"Oh, it's my camera. I'm filming a documentary on my cousin Natasha."

Carmen still looked mad confused.

"What's a documentary? ¿Y quién es su prima?"

I was about to tell Carmen about the girl fading from the picture on Mami's shelf. How I'd spent hours tracing the unsmiling lines of her face, mining the silence around what happened. How exactly does a girl become thin air? How exactly does someone's name become a kind of quiet? Like the quiet that comes after the El goes underground and your ears are full of pressure, in the space between popping and the roar of the tracks. I was going to tell Carmen that all I wanted was to know what had happened to the only person I've ever seen Abuela cry over. How somewhere in that quiet was the truth. And how that led me here, somehow. Through miles of white and into another world entirely.

And then two more ciguapas landed quietly in front of us, eyes trained on Carmen.

They were carrying machetes.

"Carmen, the Galipotes are expecting you."

SEVEN

AT LEAST THE CIGUAPAS LET me keep my bag, so the camera was safe.

Whether I was safe from the business ends of their machetes was still up in the air.

The stars seemed to bristle as we walked below them, the sky as black as that ring of sand around the city. I winced as the ciguapa holding my arm tightened her grip and nudged me forward. I stepped on one of the rocks in my shoe and stifled a gasp.

Pues, with every step I took, the more distance there was between me and those demonic perros and that creepy bird. AKA you don't have to push hermana, I was already going!

Carmen looked pretty guilty, but she kept her thoughts to herself as we moved in stony silence. I figured it was best to follow her lead and stay quiet. The moon pulsed down onto the buildings, that blue-white glow beaming from every surface. It was like the city itself were a star, a star full of dozing streets and people sleeping in a time of war. I noticed as we walked that wherever the avenues and side streets of Zafa didn't end in a building, they led straight back to the black sand.

"¡Oye, Señora Gray Locks, tengo una pregunta!" I couldn't help it, I had to ask.

The grip on my arm tightened from "Come to the principal's office immediately" to "Blood pressure sleeve in the Target pharmacy." She made no move to respond. Whether you are captured or not, it is never a good idea to call your always half-frowning 6'3" muscular "guard" "Señora Gray Locks," even if it is super accurate.

Carmen snorted. It was the first sound she'd made in five minutes and I smiled despite ciguapa Gray Locks giving me the evil eye. I'm not really sure why I wasn't more afraid of the ciguapas; for all I knew they were basically Zafa Cops.

Pues, don't get me wrong, my pulse was going bonkers. But they hadn't bound our wrists. They hadn't hit us like the CPD did to Manuel last October. Or our next-door neighbor Javier in May. Or last year to Katerina, who sings lead for a local punk band me and Celeste love called "Second Chance Lobster." We don't know why the band is called that, pero everybody knows why Katerina, with the blue-dyed tips of her curls hanging in her face, cried the whole time as the cops put her in the car. She came back, but we were all worried, the whole block as quiet then as the streets of Minerva.

"Who lives in this city anyway? More kids who fell

through pages?" I asked, but was met with more stony silence. Tough room.

The ciguapa guards were armed with machetes but they stayed in their belt loops, the arc of their blades catching the curve of the moon. But if Carmen wasn't scared, I wasn't going to flinch either.

As a large domed building loomed in front of us, I swallowed a huge lump in my throat and looked up at the sky one more time. The moon was such a brilliant white that it made my eyes water. I felt like a baby, crying at the moon, pues, you see it every night and it's pretty but nothing special. Nothing special until you fall hundreds of feet out of the sky onto a strange island. And the ocean is white, and the forest is full of monsters and storms, and the only people who have spoken to you have machetes and backward feet. Then the moon is familiar. When that much changes in a day—I promise, familiar is the most beautiful thing in the world.

I almost busted my butt looking at the moon. As we made the final steps toward the domed building, the street changed from gravel to cobblestone. If it hadn't been for Gray Locks's vise grip on my arm I would have fallen flat on my face. When she hauled me back up I could have sworn she was smiling, but it was gone by the time I side-eyed her properly. Pues, Gray Locks was shady, but I give her credit for not laughing. She was quiet like Abuela.

The doors were huge and dark against the glow of the rest

of the domed building. They were inlaid with carved drawings of ciguapas and butterflies dancing across a cityscape. They were gorgeous and I ached to get a shot with the camera, but it didn't seem like Gray Locks would be down for a pit stop, entiendes?

The ciguapa holding Carmen briefly released her arm to knock quickly three times on the door. She was tall with long brown curls and a hard scowl; across her shoulders she wore an olive-green jacket with two gold stripes running down each arm. I chanced a look at Carmen, who was staring at her feet and massaging her elbow with a this-ain't-over expression. Was she in trouble? I tried to flag down Carmen while her guard knocked four more times, almost too lightly to hear.

"You know I can see you doing that, right?" Gray Locks's voice was deeper than I expected. And accompanied by another tight, painful squeeze to my arm, which I had expected.

"Yami, mija, what is taking so long?" said Gray Locks.

"Lo siento, Captain, I always forget the code midweek." Yami's voice was high pitched and tense like a tightly strung violin. A beautiful sound, but she also seemed like she could seriously use a nap.

"Try it again. ¡No tenemos tiempo para eso!" Gray Locks could have rivaled Mami's quit-messing-around voice if it came to it. Thinking of Mami sent a quiet chill over my skin that had nothing to do with the still balmy wind.

Yami nodded dutifully and resumed scowling at the door. She knocked once, then paused, knocked again, then paused, over and over eight times. And then? Nada. I was about to suggest that we should maybe knock harder when suddenly the door started *moving*. Not opening—moving. I *still* can't believe that I missed capturing that shot.

The jet-black inlay of the ciguapas and mariposas and cityscape all shivered. I was mad confused; I thought the door was stone. Pero what separates a good director from a great director, according to Mira Paredez, is listening and seeing at the same time. When I listened, the door groaned and made a sound like rain dragging itself over more rain—one of those wild Chicago storms in mid-July when the sewers overflow.

"SAND!" I called out triumphantly. "The door is made of sand!"

Gray Locks and Carmen both rolled their eyes at me in unison. Pues, sue me, I hate puzzles, but I love beating a puzzle! The sand at least seemed to appreciate it, because it moved more quickly, two waves of it separating down the middle and slithering to the edges of the doorway, leaving only the silver of the actual door behind. The sand retreated from the outlines of all the creatures of the door in great silver ribbons as it fled.

Yami cocked an eyebrow and muttered something that sounded like "Getting faster." But ultimately she shrugged as the sand parted, and an opening appeared as the doors swung open. She ushered Carmen inside but didn't grab hold of her again. Gray Locks was clearly feeling . . . less trusting and kept her vise grip on my arm as we advanced inside the building.

Pues, the interior didn't disappoint either! I was so stunned I had to pause and take it all in. A long hall led toward a circular cul-de-sac with four chairs on a slightly raised stage. Medium-size balls of light hovered along the sides of the hall, throwing a warm half yellow light over everything. The muted silver of the walls was engraved with intricate patterns traced by the same sand from the front door. It kept shifting in sinuous waves. The art showed humans and ciguapas holding hands, fighting what appeared to be Cucitos beneath a flag of three butterflies arranged in an upside-down pyramid. Some of the humans were being carried away to what looked like a faraway fortaleza in the distance made of white marble.

The details of the art were so precise, it must have taken forever to create: the wings of the butterflies on the flag, the thrill in one of the ciguapas' faces as she clubbed a Cucito with the butt of her machete, the anguish in a human girl's face as she was hauled off toward that strange marble fortress.

Long ropes of black sand swooped and danced through all of this in graceful loops like kites on a summer wind. Except near the marble palace, which they dove away from.

"All right." I heard Gray Locks's voice behind me, softer than before. "We don't want to keep the sisters waiting, do we?"

She gave me a prod, not like the half shoves of before.

Even though I guess she'd been in Zafa her whole life, maybe there are some wonders you just never get over.

I moved forward but kept glaring at that strange marble fort. I couldn't put my finger on what it was, but I felt ill just looking at it. It looked like an interruption. The black of the sand should have been able to span the whole mural, but here was this giant white scar on what, I began to understand, was a visual history of Zafa, of the island and its people. Nothing should be able to stand against that, not even the whitest of magic.

As we advanced I shot another glance at Carmen, who was looking more nervous than before. She kept braiding and unbraiding her two tight curls. She didn't look back. Yup, we were definitely in trouble.

Just my luck, accidentally transported to an ancient island of Dominican magic and I get linked up with the one ciguapa with disciplinary issues. Typical.

We arrived at the end of the hall to find four empty chairs made of polished rosewood, a deep brown like Abuela's skin in August. Each was engraved with a butterfly and a different letter: *M, P, D,* and *A.* We stood there for what felt like forever, and as we waited I got more and more nervous, the noise of the sand's movement almost drowned out by the thudding of my pulse.

"So . . . ," I said after a few minutes, trying to break the tension. "Is something supposed to be happening or . . ."

Nobody laughed. Pero it got results, because a few moments later, four silver butterflies drifted down from above.

I blinked and they turned into women!

Another shot I missed porque Gray Locks was on her "no flash photography" flow. But seriously, they landed and just like that they transformed. I guess miracles pass like that, blink y se fue.

The two wearing white silk dresses with fog-gray hems landed in front of the chairs marked *D* and *P*. The other two wore white short-sleeved blouses and dark brown pants. Also, apparently there were no shoe stores in Zafa, because they were barefoot.

Gray Locks released me and swung her right arm across her body, bringing it to her shoulder. She nodded a salute that Yami and Carmen mimicked, feet crossed left in front of right before swinging their right feet out in front as they marched in lockstep toward the little stage. They stood at attention at either side of the stage, machetes gleaming in the light that was emanating off what was unmistakably the sisters, the Galipotes, leaders and heroes of this city sleeping through its own war.

My pulse thudded even louder, and I felt my tongue go dry. Should I be doing that salute thing too? Was that only for people in this . . . I guess it was an army? I wasn't tryna appropriate anybody's cultural tradition, but if everyone here was a product of Dominican stories, was it my culture too? Sweat glazed my palms as I thought more about it. Pues, the arm part felt simple, pero what if I tripped and fell trying to do that weird foot thing? First impression, ruined.

Just like always, nobody was explaining anything even while it was happening in front of my face. Turns out being captured is not super different from being a younger sibling, quién sabe?

Before I had more time to freak out, the Galipote Sisters blossomed huge silver-and-purple wings. The one who stood serenely in front of the chair marked with an *M* waved her left arm in a lazy arc from east to west. Silver light trailed behind her every motion. Carmen slackened from the salute and exhaled loudly. Had she been holding her breath?

The Galipote standing in front of the *M* chair cleared her throat, the sound high and familiar like the first note of a song everyone knows.

"So, Carmen, where *exactly* have you been?"

EIGHT

ABUELA USED TO SAY THAT la ciguapa has perfect memory, and Abuela is never wrong.

Normally, Abuela's voice is warm and dancing at the edge of her accent, like no matter how long she's been in this country, part of her will never smooth out like she's been told. But as Abuela told the story of la ciguapa, her voice quivered, like when I would interview her about the Trujillato. Pues, maybe Abuela is always haunted by what she never saw with her own eyes; la ciguapa's hunt and Natasha's disappearance living side by side in the same section of her memory.

La ciguapa has a perfect memory, mija, she'd say. *La ciguapa remembers the face of every man she ever made disappear.*

So when the Galipote Sisters asked Carmen where she'd been, pues, I was curious too.

"Umm, I don't know," Carmen replied. She stared at the ground, kicking her right leg back and forth, toes pointing toward the door.

I smacked my palm against my forehead, mirroring Gray Locks. We were doomed, totally doomed, and I still hadn't eaten anything since dropping into this wild place. It's one thing to be in mortal danger, but having to die hungry is just insulting, entiendes?

"You . . ." The Galipote standing in front of the *M* trailed off.

"Don't . . ." Now the *P* Galipote.

"Know?!" The other two finished in unison, the sound bouncing up and down the hall.

Carmen half shrugged.

"You've been gone for two weeks!" Gray Locks groaned, dragging her hand down her face. "How can you not know where you've been?"

"Pues, I was doing reconnaissance."

"Por favor, be specific and don't waste the sisters' time."

"On . . ." Carmen shot me a glance.

I shook my head. Pues, I just got here! What did she want me to say?

"The enemy. In El Bosque," Carmen finished.

An awkward silence bloomed as I stared intently at the left-hand wall. The black sand wound through the long curls on a carving of a woman with both hands raised against . . .

Hold up, was that a werewolf? Are there even Dominican werewolves?

Before I could give it more thought, the Galipote who

stood in front of the *M* pinched the bridge of her nose and spoke.

"Carmen, you had *very* specific orders to observe and detail the movements of the bacas in the Northern region for *one* week. Did you complete your mission?"

"I did, Doña Minerva, pero then . . . I saw these Cucitos and it was an excellent chance to disrupt the enemy position."

My mouth dropped open and Carmen's muddled speech about troop positions faded into background noise. My eyes snapped from her to the Galipote, who was doing a wild good impression of Mami listening to me explain how I broke her favorite lamp.

So *this* was Minerva, leader of the rebellion; the woman who owned a city. Her dark lips cut a slash across her tan face, framed by the dim silver of her wings. Her hair fell to her shoulders in thick, raven-black waves. She looked about thirty-five, as did the two sisters with pitch-black hair standing in front of the *A* and *P* chairs. The fourth stood closest to me, hair as silver as her wings. I looked at Minerva again, y pues, her hair rippled slightly as if wherever she went the wind was on her side.

". . . And yeah, I intervened porque I had to take advantage of the opportunity," Carmen finished, biting her lip defiantly.

I snorted. Amateur, using the "opportunity" defense. I invented the opportunity defense. Pues, the opportunity defense was how I got there.

The Galipotes weren't buying it either, each sister sitting in silence while their wings twitched with how irked they were.

"Pues, mija, be that as it may—" Minerva started but the silver-haired sister cut in.

"Do you have any idea how irresponsible this was?" Her voice wasn't loud, pero it boomed in the hall.

"Dede, the girl's doing her best," said another of the sisters. "She just has . . ."

"A bit of a temper." Dede restrained a roll of her eyes. "Yes, Patria, we have heard it all before, pero the fact remains that she could have been captured. She could have died."

"Carmen is one of our best troops," Patria chimed in with a note of annoyance. "A soldier who made a tactical choice. She's two hundred, Dede, she can make her own decisions."

Wait. Two hundred?! Note to self: Ask Carmen for her skin care routine if we aren't both thrown in jail after this conversation.

"Not if she has nothing to show for it," said the fourth sister. "Our ranks are not large enough that Carmen can just take a joy ride in El Bosque for weeks at a time without *consequences.*"

Carmen slouched a bit and I felt bad watching. Weird how she seemed to stand so much taller in front of trees that stretched hundreds of feet high than she did in front of the four sisters who were maybe 5'8" *tops*. I felt a pressure building in my fingertips, the kind I always feel right before I have what

Vice Principal Guttierez calls a "disproportionate response to the situation."

"SHE SAVED MY LIFE, PLEASE DON'T KILL US!"

The words were out of my mouth before I could stop them, booming loudly in the hall like fireworks. Carmen gave me a "did you really just say that?" look.

It was my turn to look at my feet, staring down at the mud on my kicks, cracking at the toes. I could feel every eye in the building fixed on me. Did I really just shout at four shapeshifting sisters over some girl I met this morning?

When I tilted my head up, the first thing I saw was Gray Locks. Her eyes looked like they were about to bug out of her head, her left hand trembling with rage near the handle of the machete. But much to my surprise, she was the only one who seemed angry. Everyone was looking at me, shocked, as if they had just noticed that I was there.

Finally, Minerva broke the silence, her smirk a shadow in her dark lipstick. "Carmen saved your life?"

Her voice had a feeling to it, a power sleeping beneath its soft tones. I took a deep breath and nodded.

"Good! That is what we trained her for," Minerva said with a broad smile, that forever wind tossing her hair.

I was afraid to break eye contact with the Galipote, but I saw Carmen straighten up an inch in response.

"Now," Minerva continued, her smile dropping a quarter of an inch, "who exactly are you? And why has one of my best recon agents brought you into my city unannounced?"

NINE

FUNNY STORY: TURNS OUT, DESPITE knowing your name for twelve years and saying it correctly for eleven, facing up with an immortal shapeshifter makes it hard to remember. Finally, after a pause I brushed a stray curl out of my face (and some sweat) and said:

"My name is Pilar Violeta Ramirez! And umm . . ." Dang it, me and Celeste had rehearsed this intro before she moved away. "And I'm a director. Oh, and my friends call me Purp!"

I chanced a look at Carmen, who was pinching the bridge of her nose. The good news was that Minerva didn't look offended, more vaguely confused than anything.

"Pilar." Minerva turned the word over in her mouth like a piece of hard candy. "A beautiful name."

And then I swear I saw her mouth "Purp?" just once, like a question that soured on her tongue. Sounds crazy, pero I know what I saw y pues, everybody's a critic.

Gray Locks was flexing her machete arm now, eyeing me

as if at any moment I might unzip my suit and turn out to be a Cucito cleverly disguised as a tween Dominicana from a rapidly gentrifying neighborhood.

Thankfully Carmen came in to save me from an early death. "I found her being attacked by a troop of Cucitos." Carmen snapped into another salute, her tone clipped and professional. "She held her own for a while as I observed, but ultimately they overwhelmed her."

Gray Locks snorted loudly, sizing me up as if she couldn't believe that I had managed to hold off the Cucitos single-handed. Rude.

"She is . . . not of Zafa, not of our world," Carmen carried on, trying to be stiff like she was in JROTC or something. "She is from The Above . . . I believe she can be an asset against the enemy."

Gray Locks's mouth was open like she was about to be shady. And my mouth was open to tell her where she could stick that machete. But Minerva held up a hand for quiet. Each of the sisters' eyes flashed when Carmen said "The Above."

"She could be a spy sent by the enemy," Gray Locks said in a stage whisper. "You and the council could be in dan—"

"Gracias, Yaydil. That will suffice for tonight," Minerva cut in. "If this child—"

"Hey!" I piped up out of habit. I hate being called a child; it's just a way for adults to make you feel invisible.

Now Yami's hand was also on her machete. Why did I have to open my big mouth?

But Minerva's hand was up again, and silence fell. "Pilar is the first to fall to Zafa from The Above in hundreds of years. It's a risk I am willing to take."

"The Cucitos were chanting when they found her!" Carmen cut in. "They kept saying '*Another, another.*' And I'd never heard them speak actual words before, so naturally I brought Pilar back here."

The sisters exchanged a meaningful look at this. For the first time since the conversation started everyone was looking at me like I mattered, but I almost missed it because I was still reeling about "hundreds of years." How was I ever going to get home if there hadn't been another person in hundreds of years!?

"Curious, indeed," Patria said matter-of-factly. "That being said, the girl cannot be left unattended."

"She will stay with Carmen in the barracks tonight, then," Minerva finished. The other Galipotes nodded.

The whole time Carmen was explaining who I was, Minerva never looked away from me. Not once. I shifted uncomfortably as my stomach growled again.

"And Yaydil?" Minerva said, finally turning her head to look at Gray Locks. "See to it that these two eat before we reconvene at daybreak. It is late, and we sisters have much to discuss about what Pilar's arrival might mean."

Relief swelled in my chest. I hadn't realized how shallow my breathing was during the whole conversation. But at least for the moment it seemed like we were going to get to eat and we were *not* going to be executed. The day was ending better than I had hoped, entiendes? Pues, so of course I opened my big mouth again.

"¿Doña?" I squeaked out.

"Hmm?" Minerva cocked an eyebrow with a hint of amusement in her dark eyes.

"One: Do you know how I can get home? I promised Mami I'd be home before the streetlights went on. And two—" I looked at Carmen, who shot me a please-let-it-go expression.

"Speak freely, little one. You are in no danger," Minerva said with the ghost of a laugh. "Only our enemies execute defenseless people."

"El Cuco." I tried not to shiver thinking of the demon Boogeyman from Mami's stories. The clawed maniac who stole bad children in the night, when the lights were out. I tried not to shiver, pero I did.

"Yes, him and more. But we may speak on this in the morning. Rest for now." Minerva turned her back to me.

And it could have been that easy. I had a bed and a *much-*needed meal waiting for me. For the first time in hours, nobody was threatening me with a machete, there were no coconut trolls or a creepy bird chasing me. But . . .

"You know your sand's not working, right?" I replied, the words jumbling together like a Twista verse. "The sand that protects the city? Something's wrong with it."

Minerva looked back over her shoulder. In her eyes was a look of unimaginable sadness. Pues, the kind of weary I see in Mami after she's worked a double at the holidays, as if she's been fighting day and night for her whole life with no breaks. Minerva, invulnerable shapeshifting leader. Minerva, the only woman I had ever met who had a whole city named after her, looked like she couldn't possibly be more tired.

I panned my gaze to each of the sisters, how remarkably similar they looked with their glimmering silver wings and the sad slashes each of their mouths made on their faces.

"We know," they said in unison. And with a flash of wings, I blinked, and they were gone.

Later, I barely remembered walking with Carmen to the barracks, two different ciguapa guards flanking us on our way through the still quiet streets of Minerva. I felt a knot of guilt that I hadn't asked the sisters if they might know where Natasha was, pero I was so tired I could barely walk straight anymore; who knew what time it was in my world? Pues, I was so tired I barely noticed Minerva hadn't answered my question about getting home.

"The streetlights must be on by now," I mumbled to nobody in particular since Carmen seemed pretty zoned out too. "Mami will be so worried."

I thought of Mami and Abuela, sitting across from a full plate and an empty chair. Mami and Abuela taking turns on the phone, frantically calling anyone who might know my whereabouts. Were both of them looking, just like the day Papi died, at the space where I kept my shoes and wondering if I would ever come back?

TEN

DAYBREAK FELL IN SOFT PINKS and oranges through the Hall of the Galipote Sisters while me and Carmen waited for them to arrive like we were in the principal's office. Pues, what is it with adults and keeping people waiting? I was irked. I had to wake up mad early and leave the barracks with my hair looking a mess and mad eye boogers. Y también, they weren't even on time to a meeting in their own house? Only Gray Locks and another ciguapa were waiting. Mami would have flipped.

The only way for the Galipotes to redeem themselves for holding a meeting this early would be to start the meeting by saying, "Pilar, you're going home, also Mira Paredez called."

When the Galipotes finally arrived, each was rocking a simple black dress and I tried not to roll my eyes. If they were all going to wear the same thing why did it take them so long to get ready?

Minerva, who was also wearing a silver necklace, spoke first. "Pilar, how did you sleep last night?"

"Umm, fine, I guess. Do you know how I can get home from here?"

The Galipotes exchanged glances, the rising sun trickling gold down the deep black of three of the sisters' hair.

"We have some theories on that," Antonia Maria said.

"But first," added Dede.

"We need to know how you got here," Patria chimed in.

I ran my fingers through my hair to try and get my brain in order. I had been too tired to even think about showering last night and we'd been hustled out by the same ciguapa guards this morning. My hair felt filthy, my face went hot and sent pinpricks down my arms thinking how I must look like I've never been anywhere before.

"I, uh, well, I was working on my documentary and—"

"¿Qué es un 'documentary'?"

I was getting more irked now; I *hate* being interrupted. Pues, I don't even like when people pause movies. But I took a deep breath and started again.

"Well, I am trying to tell a story about my cousin—"

"Quién es su prima?" asked Patria. Y se fue, I snapped.

"I would tell y'all if you would stop interrupting me!! Pues, you can't be late to the meeting and not let people finish answering. It's mad unfair! Now do you want to hear the story or not, porque I woke up too early para esa tontería, entiendes?"

Pues, we were right back where we started last night, with several ciguapas waiting to pull machetes on me over my big mouth.

"Pilar, are you out of your mind?" Carmen hissed at me. "This is not how—"

But just then a huge musical laugh filled the hall, first trickling in like the sun but then louder, washing the whole room in its warmth.

"Pues, I like this little one!" Minerva beamed at Carmen. "She reminds me of you as a trainee."

"Doña, I would never—" Carmen stammered.

"Oh, save it." Minerva laughed, softer this time. "How do you think Yaydil went so gray? We need soldiers who question, who fight, who . . ." She turned her face back to me. "Fear nothing more than not finishing their story, apparently. Please, mija, carry on."

I looked around and took a deep breath. I had the floor.

"Pues, my name is Pilar and I'm from a place called Chicago. I was in Chicago doing research on my documentary about my cousin who disappeared before I was born. A documentary is kinda like a story, but with pictures that move, which I film on my camera. Which"—I paused and glared at everyone—"I am not giving to any of you, security concerns or no, entiendes? Pero I digress. My cousin Natasha disappeared years ago in DR during the Trujillato. And . . ."

I never finished that sentence porque everyone but the sisters took in a sharp breath at the word *Trujillato*. Pues, even the sand seemed to stop shifting, as if it was listening extra hard. At least Trujillo's name was dirt here too.

The sisters exchanged a look, the breeze in Minerva's wavy

hair moving faster and ruffling the mariposas' wings so they shimmered in the sun.

"We try not to say that name around here," Minerva said.

Great. More mysterious silences around Trujillo. This place was more like home than I thought.

Pero, I was wrong, porque Minerva continued talking. "But you didn't know that, mija, you have nothing to be sorry about. He was the greatest ally of our mortal enemy when he was alive. El Cuco and he, pues, you'd think they were brothers."

A million questions exploded in my brain. El Cuco . . . and Trujillo? Partners? Allies? When? How?

Now it was Minerva's turn to take a deep breath, as if she were shuffling an old, impossibly sad story into order. Y pues, she was.

"Mija, watch the sand. I'll tell you everything we know."

As Minerva began her tale, the dark lines of sand along the walls zipped and curled and dove through the silver carvings of El Bosque, a pair of silver eyes gleaming between the trees.

"For as long as Dominicans have had children, we have kept them away from El Cuco. You know what he is?"

I nodded.

"Pues, then you know more than most because not many have ever seen him y nadie knows where he came from. He shapeshifts like us, pero he could only move in the shadows back then. Como un boogeyman. Stealing children in the dark, it was how things have always been. Even we were raised to fear him."

"And Galipotes do not die," Antonia Maria added with a firm flap of her wings.

"Still," Dede continued, "in Old Zafa, everyone knew to fear El Cuco, pero he was still only one man then. Or rather, one extremely hairy troll who ate children."

"Y también, La Negra protected us," Patria chimed in.

I shot a look at Carmen, who was biting her lip, eyes shimmering sadly, like the story didn't have a happy ending.

Dede nodded gravely and continued. "But that was long ago. Before."

It grew quiet as the black sand snaked through an intricate drawing of what a blanquito might mistake for a yeti or bigfoot leaping down from a tree toward a group of terrified-looking kids.

"It used to be that the Hairy Ladrón stole maybe one or two kids a decade," said Maria Teresa.

"Despite the stories you may have heard, he doesn't actually need to eat them to survive. We know that much. He just does it . . . for sport." Patria frowned in disgust.

"Pero centuries ago"—Minerva's voice went deeper and sadder—"it all went wrong. Something changed."

The sand bolted through a carving that depicted many battles, and traveled toward an image of a faceless man shaking hands with . . . a man dressed in military uniform and covered in hair como un werewolf. Pero the scary part was that in the carving, the man in the uniform had teeth but no eyes. My pulse sped up. I felt sick just looking at him.

"El Jefe and El Cuco made a deal," Minerva pressed on. "Trujillo—" Another sharp intake of breath, but quieter this time. "Trujillo asked El Cuco to build him a prison for some of his worst enemies. And in exchange El Cuco was granted the power and muscle he needed to finally rule the island in the light, as he had dreamed since the day he was born."

"How?" I asked without meaning to. Pues, either nobody heard my question or they were too caught up in their story, porque the sisters went on.

"Once El Cuco and Jefe met, diablo." Minerva punctuated the sentence by spitting on the ground like Abuela does, as if it was bad luck to swallow the spit the name rode in on.

"El Cuco wasn't after just kids anymore; he sent his first and most wicked servant, El Baca, to The Above and stole all kinds of people for Trujillo. Men and women and children . . . all transported to Zafa and marched off to that awful prison," Maria Teresa said.

The sand surged through a carving of a line of scared-looking people marching toward that strange white marble fortaleza. The man with teeth and no eyes grinned sharply like a machete.

This conflict had nothing to do with me. But I felt desperate, furious, embarrassed, all these emotions swirling around me. I looked at the empty carving with the faceless man and felt sick all over again. Pues, I could taste the vomit in my throat, the acid sizzling back down into my stomach as I swallowed.

"That deal is where the Cucitos came from. We think they are children of the shadows, pero Cucitos don't talk, so quién sabe? Cuco used to be restricted to the dark corners, could only hunt at night. Since he met El Jefe, his strength has grown to the point he can move in daylight, toss grown men to the side with a flick of his wrist," Patria said bitterly, chewing on each word like old meat.

"How is he doing all this?" I shouted this time. "Where did he get this power? What prison? And okay, thanks for the info on the Cucitos, but I don't . . . I just don't understand."

My knees shook and a little sob caught in my throat. This was all just so . . . embarrassing. Why was I getting so emotional? In front of strangers? What was wrong with me? Why couldn't I just control my temper and be patient, like Abuela? She would have known what to say. She probably even would have known how to get home.

I wiped a tear from the corner of my eye and glared up at the sisters, daring anyone to laugh or pity me. Pero all I saw was grim understanding. I looked to my side and Carmen was wearing a helpless expression.

"El Cuco's power comes from one source. Unkillable, and never captured. El . . ."

But before Minerva finished answering, I zoned out because the sand zoomed once more and coursed through a picture of, pues, I wish I knew a better way to explain this. The biggest dog I had ever seen. Pero ese perro was standing on two legs, like a man. Even though the drawing was pure silver, I knew his fangs must be caked in blood. I could see it, like it was my own memory even though it wasn't. I shook my head and looked again; the carving was just a carving again.

The dog was massive, and the black lines swung through the drawing showing he was muscled like Thor. And slung over his shoulder was one smallish Dominicana. Her face was a mask of terror and confusion that I had never seen her make before.

But I knew that face, like I was staring at Mami's photo. The girl over his shoulder looked exactly like . . .

ELEVEN

"NATASHA."

The name stumbled out of my mouth, a whisper. Pues, I was so shook I barely noticed that the Galipotes were still talking.

"El Baca," Minerva said gravely.

It took me a hot minute to figure out they were speaking not of Natasha, but the hulking, ferocious dog holding her, forcing that terrified, confused look onto her face. I immediately felt hot, like I would throw hands at this monster if only someone would tell me where to find him.

Carmen coughed twice loudly in my direction. Could she see that I was lost in thought? Pues, I was being rude. I tuned back in as the Galipotes continued their explanation.

"When Trujillo and El Cuco forged their alliance, it birthed a baca, a demon contract from the depths of hell," Maria Teresa said, a frown pushing deeper lines into her face.

"But this," Dede added, "was no ordinary baca."

I heard everything, but I couldn't stop staring at Natasha every couple of words, my mouth too dry to form a question. It couldn't be, there was no way . . .

"Dominicans have made deals with the devil since the dawn of la isla. Y de verdad, there have always been bacas born to enforce those agreements," Patria said matter-of-factly.

"El Baca is a special case, though. Forged between two devils, he is the strongest of all of Cuco's allies, a bounty hunter who can pass between the worlds, and the most brutal enforcer we have ever seen. He is the source of El Cuco's strength, and the beast can't be killed so long as La Blanca, the prison El Cuco maintains for Trujillo, stands."

Carmen spoke for the first time in a while, a determined look in her eyes. "Which is why I still say we should launch a direct attack on La Blanca and El Cuco. We have been running and hiding—"

"We are not going down this road again," Gray Locks cut in, machete quivering in its sheath and throwing weak rainbows in the light. "We don't have the numbers, Captain. You will not question the sisters' leadership; they are the reason you are alive."

"How alive can we be when we hide in this city? Waiting for what? With all due respect to the sisters." Carmen threw a half-hearted salute in the direction of the stage.

The Galipote Sisters simply watched the fireworks between the two ciguapas play out. Even the black sand had stopped coursing, as if it were watching.

"We wait for the right time to strike." Gray Locks's hands were trembling y pues, she said each word like she was throwing punches. "We have responsibilities to the people of this city, but what would you know about that?"

Carmen rolled her eyes. She looked so much like Lorena; it was freaky, entiendes?

"I know we have a duty to win." Carmen huffed. Minerva nodded at that, but Dede put up a hand and the hall fell still.

"Carmen, we hear you, but we don't have the strength to launch an assault on La Blanca without also abandoning the city. We've been over this. Abandoning all the people that we have saved, who have built a life here. We cannot take such a risk on the hope that we can bring down everything in one shot."

"Is El Baca taking the girl in the carving to La Blanca?" I asked, trying to force the quiver from my voice.

"Yes." Minerva scowled and pointed toward the white marble fortress at the edge of the silver carvings. "The prison is an abomination we should have—"

"All we have been *able* to do"—Dede cut a quick side-eye at Carmen and Minerva—"since the war began is try to rescue some of the poor souls who Trujillo, El Cuco, and El Baca sent to that—"

"DOES THAT MEAN THEY HAVE MY COUSIN?!"

The question just surged out of me. Pero, you can't judge me. Wrestling with embarrassment at what felt like my nineteenth outburst in front of these strangers was something golden and warm. Pues, it was like hope, like stepping into a building after seven blocks of walking upwind in March. Natasha, the girl fading from Mami's picture. Tearstained Natasha, missing Natasha, might be alive and nearby. It was too good to be true, it was too good to keep inside, entiendes?

"What cousin?" said Minerva, eyes laser focused on me.

"The one from my documentary. Natasha. Kidnapped during the . . ." I sidestepped saying Trujillato and continued on. "During the dark times? That's her in the carving. Pues, I'd know that face anywhere!"

A look of understanding swept across the sisters' faces, their wings drooping in sync like dog-eared pages in a book. That golden feeling plunged out of my chest, becoming a heavy ball in my stomach. This was the look Mami had worn when she told me about Papi. I know bad news when I see it, even . . . pues, maybe especially when nobody is willing to say it.

How could I be so foolish? Look at that monster; nobody could survive that.

Then, the most unlikely voice, Gray Locks, stepped into the conversation. "I remember this girl. Y pues, mejor que nada, she lives."

A warm feeling sprung up in my chest again, but I pushed it down this time. Pues, you know that feeling when you're so desperate to know something that it's like you're outside your body, watching your mouth ask a question? Well, combine that with the rapid-fire tongue of an anxious Dominicana director and you get this:

"HowdoyouknowAreyousureHowcouldyouposs—"

"Because I was there," Gray Locks said, chin jutting out. "And all ciguapas have—"

"Perfect memory," I finished, my voice still wary. "Fine, let's say you're right, how do you know she's alive?"

Gray Locks seemed annoyed that I wasn't taking her at her word, pero like, would you believe someone who arrested you and wouldn't take their hand off their machete with good news? Exactly.

"I tell you she lives and that's the face you make? You dare question me?"

"I want to believe, but what if you're wrong? I can't lose her again!"

Pues, and I thought it was quiet before. No wind, no rustle of clothing or anxious whispers. It was that terrible silence that came when adults don't know what to do with you and they are all out of ways to hide it.

I closed my eyes to stop the prick of tears. I shut them so hard that little lights popped in the dark behind my eyelids. This was even worse than the quiet after the cops took away our neighbor Javier.

Eventually I heard the sound of footsteps. Carmen placed a palm on my shoulder as she said, "So there's good news y también bad news. The good news is that El Cuco never executes a prisoner. He brings all of them to La Blanca porque it's part of his agreement with El Jefe."

Through my closed eyes I saw the two diablos shaking hands on top of some high mountain and laughing like supervillains. Trujillo's pale face stretched like the world's ugliest balloon, his hands peeling and spotted with bleach. A shiver ran along my arms—was I imagining a nightmare or remembering history? It was very strange, entiendes? Knowing something I never saw.

"Pero the bad news is that if Natasha is in La Blanca, then she may as well be dead. Nobody has ever escaped the prison. And we can't get her back because—"

"Because it takes all our magic to keep this city safe." Minerva's voice was as warm and soft as the wind in July.

"But . . . what if we found you someone else to help defend the city?" Carmen said.

The ghost of tears was still swimming before my eyes, and I didn't want anyone to see me cry. It's been a firm policy for me since fifth grade and I wasn't breaking it for anybody, even four immortal shapeshifting sisters. But Carmen's proposal def made me cock an eyebrow and a tear spilled out through my eyelashes. I wiped it away quick, hoping nobody saw.

"Carmen, be serious." Gray Locks sounded just like Mami when I asked her for a new camera. "La Bruja hasn't fought at our side in nearly—"

"Six hundred years, I know," Carmen said back, excitement creeping into her voice. "But what choice do we have? Our defenses are weakening—La Negra retreats further still. We need to put this petty division aside and ask for her help."

"With our forces this thin?" Dede scowled at Carmen like she was a child—and not a two-hundred-year-old who happened to look like one. "You, a naïve spy, would go alone? Are you crazy? You are living in a fantasy world, Carmen."

Pues, it took a lot to keep my mouth shut and not point out that I was actually the only person there who *didn't* live in a fantasy world. But something was up; there was a chance to rescue Natasha.

"She wouldn't be alone," I said, breaking my silence. Pues, at the end of the day I'm not Abuela, I'm me. I'm Pilar and I was done talking and ready to kick some butt if it meant getting off of this tontería island with Natasha. "I will go with Carmen. We will raid La Blanca. We will rescue my cousin, because it was your job to save her and you didn't. And then you will send us both back to my world."

TWELVE

"ABSOLUTELY NOT," ALL THE GALIPOTES replied in unison, a burst of wind kicking dust into everyone's mouths.

Rude, pero I was determined.

"Look, if Carmen's right, then there isn't much time before your defenses fail, so I don't think y'all are in a position to turn down free help."

The sisters exchanged a look, but nobody interrupted me, so I kept going.

"Give us three days. If we can't convince La Bruja, we'll come straight back here . . . and Carmen will never trouble you about this again."

"I'll what?" Carmen exclaimed, her hand flying off my shoulder as her eyes narrowed.

"Now, do we have a deal?" I said, stomping my foot for emphasis.

The sisters looked at each other warily, pero I could tell they were thinking about it. They had the same look that

Mami had on her face when I convinced her to let me go to U Chicago to interview Professor No-Show.

I thought for a second about how in another world, pues, if I was another Pilar, I might have just stayed home and been washing dishes right now. I kind of envied that Pilar, who never got chased by a freaky bird or attacked by evil trolls.

But I'm not that Pilar, who's happy to just stay at home. So, I guess I'm the girl who occasionally falls out of the sky; pues, at least I'm not boring like Lorena.

"All I'm saying is that if you think I'm going to sit quietly through this tontería until that freaky bird comes back I—"

"You saw The Bird?" all the Galipote Sisters said at once, each of their mouths a grim slash.

"Yeah, it and those demon dogs chased us through half the forest! It only stopped once we got past La Negra. What is it?"

"El Baca's . . . pet." Maria Teresa spat out the last word, like the whole sentence was rotten.

"That bird is El Baca's scout. He commands all of the bacas on Zafa," Dede added. "But The Bird and he are unusually close. There are—were protections so that it couldn't come within twenty miles of the city."

I gulped and thought about that ring of La Negra around the city. The enemy wasn't twenty miles away; they were down the street.

"If the defenses are failing," I said, trying to sound calm, "then it's not much safer for me here. So what's the point in me staying in the city instead of trying to find La Bruja?"

"Fine," said Minerva icily. "Given the state of La Negra, we talked about this possibility last night. We've decided that these are desperate times and they call for imagination. And maybe having the perspective of someone from The Above will be—tactically valuable. But we are serious—we will give you three days. No more than that. If you can bring La Bruja back to the city, then we will use our magic to transport you back to your world."

"After the raid on La Blanca?!" said Carmen hopefully, trying to keep the excitement from her voice.

"Yes, after the raid." Dede sighed warily. "*If* you can get La Bruja to agree. *If.*"

"Yaydil will outfit you for the trip," said Patria, a sad smile pulling at the corners of her face.

I looked up at Gray Locks and for once she seemed less ticked off than usual. Pues, I thought at first that it was just that she was like those JROTC kids, a grim military officer who valued nothing more than order. Even if she didn't like where we were going, she'd go porque the sisters were her commanding officers and that's the way things were.

But looking in her eyes as she took us out of the building, I could tell it was more than that. She had that look that Abuela gets when I ask about the Trujillato and Natasha, a sadness that's been brewing for decades.

Meanwhile Carmen was basically skipping on her way back to the barracks. Could you blame her? Ella had walked into the hall expecting to get grounded and instead she gets to

go on a quest and maybe raid a prison, like she's been wanting to for centuries. Pues, if Gray Locks hadn't been there,
I'm sure she would have been doing backflips, entiendes? I
couldn't knock the hustle. Carmen was cocky and clearly a
pain in the butt prodigy just like Lorena, pero I was starting
to like her style. At least she was trying to fight for change.

As we made the final couple of steps toward the barracks,
Gray Locks cleared her throat. Carmen stopped walking
immediately, pero I didn't get the memo and nearly tripped
over my laces turning around. My face flushed in the hot sun
as I straightened up and tried to look like someone who had
just been entrusted with a secret mission to save the city.

"Carmen." Gray Locks nodded at her stiffly. "Pilar,
I don't think I need to waste much time telling you how
important this mission is. There will be danger." She looked
directly at me. "The likes of which you've never known."

Looking back at her, I saw a softness behind the trained
hardness of her glare. I realized I hadn't really seen Gray
Locks's eyes before, porque she was always glaring or yelling,
but they were a gorgeous deep pecan brown. In that way she
kind of reminded me of Mami. I've spent hours wondering,
who would she be if life hadn't always asked her to be so hard?

"Carmen, you've been preparing all your life for this. Go
get your things, you and I will talk after. I must speak with
Pilar. Tú sabes there are things that she ought to know."

Carmen didn't need to be told twice. She did that weird
salute thing y se fue. Now it was just the two of us. Me, Gray

Locks, and the sound of a city starting to wake up. I could hear distant voices carried by the wind. Shopkeepers and camperos yelping prices, a crying baby; it's mad weird that there are normal sounds in a city at war.

Gray Locks's eyes were closed, as if she were drinking in the sound. When she opened them, she half smiled and jutted her chin toward the barracks, and we started walking the final paces in silence. I wiped some sweat that was beading on my neck and chanced a question that I hadn't gotten to ask the sisters.

"Can you tell me who La Negra is?"

I'd been curious every time one of the sisters mentioned La Negra because that name comes from the same root as Mami's nickname for me, "Negrita." Pero I hadn't seen anybody darker than me in the room? And if La Negra was so important why didn't she speak?

Gray Locks didn't answer at first, and instead bent down at the edge of the road and scooped up a handful of that pitch-black sand. She held the little palmful out to me and put it in my hand, where it felt cool to my touch despite the thick heat that had me sweating through my Bulls shirt. I saw images flickering quickly through my mind: women dancing in a village between the huge trees in El Bosque, a city with silver buildings wreathed in smoke I could almost taste—more memories that weren't mine, pero whose were they? The sand sat humming slightly in my hand, a little palmful of shadows.

"That's La Negra," said Gray Locks, straightening up and

wiping dirt off both of her backward feet like a point guard. "She is la tierra, Pilar. She's our memory and our protector and the source of our power. Pues, without her we would have been finished centuries ago, entiendes?"

I nodded but still didn't really understand.

"What you need to know," Gray Locks said, casting her arm out in a wide arc, "is that La Negra is Zafa. She used to cover the whole island and El Cuco couldn't touch her without burning porque he was born out of a deep evil. Those were the good times, back when I was . . . how old are you again?"

"Fourteen," I lied, trying to look taller.

Gray Locks clicked her tongue and cocked an eyebrow and just waited.

"Okay, twelve."

"Well, back when I was fifty, which I guess is kind of close to how old you are now for a ciguapa, La Negra was everywhere. Pero once El Jefe and El Cuco founded their alliance, pues, the very day that La Blanca was built, La Negra started to lose her grip on Zafa. Porque what people from your world don't seem to comprehend is that the land is alive, it knows evil just as much as you or me, and La Negra fought off that powerful Fuku that surrounds that monstrosity they've built a meter at a time. Pero we are all . . . so tired, every curse wears you down eventually. This is one of the last places where La Negra's roots are deep. And even now, the enemy is squeezing in on us. Do you understand?"

I'd never been at war, but I understood what it's like to grow up somewhere and watch it be taken away from you an inch at a time. Tears pricked the sides of my eyes as I thought about the beach where I first landed, the bleached sea and soft white sand like a resort. How many centuries of suffering and sadness had Gray Locks been forced to sit through and watch her friends get captured or disappear? On the run from something not even the most magical beings alive knew how to stop. Pues, no wonder she was so gruff and edgy all the time.

If I've learned anything between my life before Zafa and my life after I fell from the sky, it's that you can only watch the land you live on be forced to forget for so long before it hurts something in you that can't ever be fixed.

At the door of the barracks, Gray Locks paused and cleared her throat. "Carmen is one of my best soldiers. She could have my job if only she would focus."

Gray Locks opened the door to the barracks and walked up creaking wooden stairs to her room. "Carmen was basically a child when her home, Ciudad de Plata, fell. She lost both her mothers in the chaos. She's taken it harder than most. That fire inside her can take over sometimes, pero so long as she is with you, you will be safe. Relatively speaking I mean. Why El Cuco's troops wanted you bad enough to speak, yo no sé, but I don't like it." She pushed open the door to a room full of yellow daylight. "I don't like it one bit."

"I thought that you said the Cucitos try to kidnap kids."

"Pero they don't normally speak actual words. Just kind

of"—Gray Locks wrinkled her nose and made a shooing motion with her hand—"slobber and fight."

Gross. So frickin gross.

"Like it or not, Pilar, they have plans for you. Are you sure that you want to go through with this? Please don't take this the wrong way, pero you're only human. Nobody has seen La Bruja in hundreds of years, and El Baca has hunted her since . . ." Gray Locks trailed off. "Just take a moment, and if you tell me you're certain, Pilar Ramirez, I'll never ask again."

With the sun at her back, Gray Locks was outlined in gold. I was kinda annoyed by the "only human" comment. I'm not weak; I had been holding my own in that fight with the Cucitos before they started hitting me multiple Cucitos at a time. I didn't come all this way just to sit around like I was scared. I could help too! Pero I could also hear in Gray Locks's tone that she was genuinely worried for me.

Before I could answer, Gray Locks crossed the room and opened a huge closet. Inside arranged neatly on shelves was what appeared to be, no offense, a bunch of very random junk. Old keys, wallets, a bunch of mismatched leather shoes. There must have been hundreds of items in there. What was Gray Locks doing with all this stuff?

"Here. You should have this," Gray Locks said gloomily.

She handed me something without looking away from the closet. It was a small brown leather journal no bigger than my hand. The lower right corner of the journal's cover was dog-eared, and a little tattered leather string wrapped around the journal in a messy bow. As I tugged the little knot loose, I noticed that some of the yellowed pages were starched and fanned out like they had been dropped in water.

Page after page was full of cramped handwriting with what looked like a dull pencil. I was very interested, except there was a problem.

"I . . ." Beads of sweat slithered down my neck. "I'm sorry, I don't read Spanish super well."

I expected Gray Locks to laugh. All the old people I tell this to either laugh or say Mami should be ashamed. Who raises a Dominicana who can't read Spanish, they say, and that's why all grown-ups can't be trusted. Pero Gray Locks didn't laugh, she didn't even look at me.

"I think if you try again, you'll find everything makes sense if you give it time."

I sighed and flipped to a random page. Y pues, Gray Locks was many things, pero never a mentirosa. As I looked at the words on the page they shifted from Spanish to English like magic. I nearly dropped the book, entiendes? What kind of Harry Potter tontería was this? And why wasn't I capturing this shot for the documentary??

On a gut feeling I turned the journal back to the first page. The letters shimmered. On every other page, the letters slouched into each other like abandoned buildings. Pero on this page, the letters were clean and meticulous. Right in the middle of the page was a date: 3/26/57.

As the letters shimmered into English . . .

ESTE DIARIO ES LA PROPIEDAD DE NATASHA
ANTONIA MERCEDES DE LA CRUZ

...BECAME...

THIS JOURNAL IS THE PROPERTY OF NATASHA
ANTONIA MERCEDES DE LA CRUZ

THIRTEEN

"WHA-HOW-WH-WHERE DID YOU?" I sputtered like a payasa.

"These were all somebody else's once." Gray Locks gestured at the closet. "Things that slipped from the pockets of people we couldn't save. I keep them as a reminder of why we fight, who we have failed, and who we might yet save. This is war y también a war not all of us were born into, pero we got pulled in anyway just like you, nena. Your cousin dropped that when El Baca took her."

She tapped the journal with a long brown finger like an orchestra conductor.

"El Baca came for her personally. I forget nothing, pero even if my memory was like yours, I doubt I'd ever forget the day. I tried, please believe me I tried, but he was too strong. He carried her off, this poor frightened little niña who probably had no idea what she'd done to deserve such a fate. Pues, sometimes it's the not-knowing that hurts worse than the machete."

I didn't know what to say. I nodded and gripped the diary a little tighter in my right hand.

"I think you should have it. Maybe it will help you understand. If you're determined to go on this journey, then you deserve to know more about who you are rescuing. It's the least I can do."

"Mil gracias," I said. "Pero why can I read this?"

"Zafa is made of myths that go across languages. Dominicans don't just speak Spanish. Pues, it's not even our oldest language. So anything written or said here arrives in the language of the beholder, entiendes?"

I had to give it to them: Zafa may be dangerous and full of dictators, monsters, and bad-smelling trolls, but an auto-translate feature? Pues, pure genius.

I gave Gray Locks a quick hug and she stiffened before relaxing a bit and patting my back. I looked up at her and understood all over again how tired centuries of war must have made her.

"I have to go talk to Carmen now," said Gray Locks. "There are things that she and I should discuss about the mission. We'll meet downstairs in ten minutes. Your bag is waiting for you on your bunk."

And with that Gray Locks spun on a heel and walked to the doorframe. Then she turned and threw that across-the-arm salute. I did my best to mimic it. Gray Locks gave me a small smile and descended down the stairs leaving me alone with the journal.

I flipped it open to a random page near the front and began to read those claustrophobic letters. Pues, the magical translation was cool, but it still did precisely nada for Natasha's handwriting. Typical.

3/12/1957
Dear Diary,
This is my third time writing since I filled up the last notebook. Y también the one before that. Mami says I have to slow down before the island runs out of trees! Pero it's not my fault that I have a lot to say. Blame the island and especially El Jefe. Mami says to never write his name down because he's the devil and he'll know and nothing but bad magic can come from a man like that. I know he's a bad man because bad men love him; all his soldiers and spies waltz around the island like they own the place. Mami is the bravest woman I've ever known, though Grecia may tie her when we get older.

I sat in the room with my eyes unfocused, staring at the little golden frames that poured across the edge of the bed. Grecia, Mami's name. And I pretty much only know that from permission slips porque to me and Lorena, she's Mami, and to Papi she was always "Mi Amor," and Abuela always calls her "Mija." And she's the bravest person I know too.

Pues, it's so strange to read something from her cousin,

my cousin, her only real friend. Despite every weird monster, ally, and machete I'd come across in Zafa, this was definitely one of the top three freakiest things yet. The day before I would have sold everything I owned (and some of Lorena's stuff that she wouldn't notice) to just know something like this even existed. I kept reading.

Mami is the bravest woman I've ever known, though Grecia may tie her when we get older. But right now Mami's the bravest and even she gets scared of the SIM. It stands for Servicio de Inteligencia Militar, but really it's just a bunch of letters to spell Bastard. Mami says they're El Jefe's secret police and that's why we never make eye contact with them when we walk to the market. If they see you, they might make you disappear. Nobody knows what happens to the people they collect for Jefe and his minions, but girls like me go missing all the time and nobody makes a sound.

I wondered how often those disappeared folks had been taken by the SIM and how often they were stolen away by El Cuco. That's the frustrating thing about the Trujillato—him and all his cronies didn't keep records of even half the evil they were up to on the island. The Trujillo era was kind of like a floor full of roaches in the dark; once the lights got turned on, they scattered. It became almost impossible to know how terrible things had really gotten.

Mami says not to say this to anyone, but she promises that one day we will be free. We'll live in a better Santo Domingo where people aren't always so afraid. She won't tell me how, though, no matter how much I ask. I might ask Grecia if she knows anything. Her mami knows someone whose cousin works in the presidential palace. Maybe El Jefe is sick? Pues, who am I kidding? Devils never catch fevers.

I wanted to keep reading for hours, but it was time to meet Carmen, so I reluctantly closed the journal and made my way down the stairs toward our bunk. On the bed I found my backpack, a pair of fingerless green leather gloves, and some folded olive-green clothes. I opened the backpack with my heart thumping in my ears and carefully removed the camera, checking all the curves and switches to make sure nothing was broken. The battery was riding at only 60 percent. And of course, there's a lot of downsides to a magical island in the middle of nowhere, pero none hit as hard as the fact that there are no outlets when you need them. Luckily I always carry a spare battery, so I still had plenty of time, but it meant I would definitely need to pick my shots carefully.

I sat down on the bed and held the camera toward me with one hand while holding Natasha's journal with the other. Once the red light flicked on, I looked directly into the camera and tried my best to summarize everything that had happened. My wild fall through the blank paper, my scuffle with the Cucitos in El Bosque de las Tormentas, the Galipote Sisters, and Carmen and Gray Locks. It all sounded so wild, like a super specific sci-fi movie.

A light knock sounded and I saw Carmen standing in the doorway. She'd changed outfits, though her clothes still had that weird smoky quality. This time it was a dark green jacket over a black tank top with a small gold necklace. Her pants were matte black, and the material scrunched like sweats above the ankles of her backward feet. A small army-style hat sat precariously on top of her mane of curls, looking like a gentle breeze could easily knock it off.

"Oye, G.I. Jane." I smiled. "You look like you boutta shoot an early 2000s rap video!"

"Shoot a what?" Carmen cocked her head to the asked, army hat leaning dangerously far to the right. "¿Y quién es 'Jane'? Pues, you better get it right, Pilar, I'm an original, entiendes?"

She did a model pose and we both laughed.

"So, you ready to go find ourselves a bruja?" Carmen asked, wiping a tear from her eye. One second she was laughing and the next she was all business. "It'll be kinda dangerous, pero La Bruja likes me, so I don't think it'll—"

"Wait, you know her?"

"La Bruja and I go way back," Carmen said, a cocky grin splitting her face like a half-moon. "Where do you think I got this outfit?"

"Pues, how would I know?"

Carmen waved her hand in the air like she was shooing smoke. "Moral of this story is that we should be able to get to La Bruja in about a day."

"I thought we needed three days." Now it was my turn to tip my head to the side in confusion.

Carmen just responded with a grin and started walking out the door before looking over her shoulder like a cover model. "That's what the gloves are for. It takes three days if you go the boring way. Pero me? I'm an original."

FOURTEEN

LONG ROPES OF RAINWATER SLAPPED my face as me and Carmen swung through El Bosque side by side. Pues, you read that right—I said side by side!

It turns out what Carmen meant by the *not*-boring way was that she snuck a pair of climbing gloves out of the armory alongside the rest of our gear. The gloves could stick to nearly anything and doubled the strength of their wearer, which allowed me to keep up with Carmen. Well, almost keep up. I'm not exactly breaking any school records back home in the mile, entiendes?

The rain continued to streak past, the occasional strike of lightning making the streams glow like neon exclamation points. Pain crept through my shoulders as we made our way toward the spot where Carmen had last seen La Bruja. At first, the swinging had been kinda fun, trying to match Carmen dive for dive, pues, it was like flying and being Tarzan all at once. But after an hour or so it felt like hustling through a set of monkey bars that stretched for miles. And, as curious as I was to meet a real-life bruja, I also was anxious to spend some more time with Natasha's journal. It's not every day a long-lost family member's literal diary from the year they were kidnapped falls in your lap.

What if there's a clue in there about how to defeat El Cuco?

But I was determined to stay the course and not slow down. And if I'm being honest, I felt a way about knowing where the gloves came from. Porque the ciguapa army use them to train very young ciguapas (turns out sixty-five is basically a fourth grader to them) on how to move between branches until they're strong enough to do it on their own. Though, of course, Carmen had never needed them.

Between Lorena recommending the professor whose messy office transported me to Zafa and Carmen of the Jungle swinging through El Bosque so casually, all I knew was that these show-off prodigies were going to be the death of me.

My form got sloppier as the burn in my shoulders built into a fire that nearly ran me into a tree like a payasa. Carmen looked back over her shoulder and called out.

"Left! Left!"

I coughed up what I hoped was part of a leaf and followed her lead. Carmen isn't great at giving directions, but eventually I found the spot and dropped down in a heap, my chest heaving. Meanwhile, Carmen set up a small tarp on the low branch where we were perched.

"You lasted longer than I thought you would." She smiled encouragingly. "Most of the trainees would have quit three miles ago."

My chest was still ablaze. I tried to wheeze out a thank-you, pero my lungs were not having it, so I nodded and held my mouth open, hoping some rain would fall on my tongue.

"You might not want to drink that." Carmen laughed.

Was the rainwater yet *another* deadly feature of the forest? Would it melt my guts? Or worse, did Cucitos bathe above, and I was drinking coconut troll bathwater?

I swallowed and gasped out a "Why?"

"Porque we have clean water in the bag, Pilar. Here!" She lifted a flask and took a swig, a few stray drops raining from her lower lip.

My shoulders screamed at the effort of pushing myself up into a seated position, then I reached out for the flask before drinking heavily.

"So," I said after what felt like five minutes of uninterrupted drinking, voice still a little raspy, "how far away are we?"

Carmen ignited a hot stone and set it down under the tarp. She beckoned me with a hand and sat down, angling her palms toward the orange light. I stripped off the gloves and held my sweaty palms over the hot stone. Carmen had her eyes planted firmly on the hot stone, though I wasn't sure why.

"Pues, we're like maybe seven hours away if we push

through. That would put us at La Bruja's by Second Light."
Carmen looked up at me. "How are you feeling? You look
exhausted."

I felt like I might collapse at any minute, but what did I
say? "Me? Pssh. Never been better."

Carmen raised an eyebrow. "Well, let's wait it out. It's
bad news to arrive at Second Light anyway. For some reason
the Resistance has never figured out, El Cuco's minions seem
to be stronger and more vicious at Second Light than at any
other time. So if they're monitoring La Bruja's hideout, then
we would be in deep trouble, make sense?"

"Good point," I said, wincing and working my shoulder
around some more.

"Here, I think I packed a balm that should help," Carmen
said. "First couple of months are always pretty rough on the
joints as you learn how to shift your weight into the swings,
entiendes?"

She pulled out a little purple jar and shuffled behind me.
It smelled suspiciously like Vaporu. Pues, that sharp medic-
inal smell that seemed to make the air sizzle around it was
very welcome, almost like home. Honestly, after everything
I've been through and everything I've seen, the idea that
Vaporu cures all injuries is still my favorite Dominican myth,
entiendes?

"Is it okay if I put this on for you? It's also fine if you want
to do it yourself," Carmen said.

I thought about it and shrugged my green Resistance jacket down my shoulders. "You got it, pues, I don't think I can raise my arms to do it, hermana."

"I hear you. Back when I was a trainee, I started showing off flips during a swing-and-retrieve drill and Yaydil made me flex-arm hang off a branch for the rest of practice."

I sighed in solidarity. "Dang, that's so harsh. How long were you up there?"

"Two hours. The general said if I wanted everybody to look at me, then I might as well hang there like a statue. Pues, my shoulders killed for days, te prometo!"

Carmen laughed bitterly as she rubbed the Zafa Edition Vaporu on my shoulders. It reminded me of back when I was little and Lorena used to braid my hair while she sat on her bed and I sat on the floor between her knees. She was kind of annoying even then, talking all the time about school and homework, pero she was gentle as far as older sisters go. I never let anyone braid my hair besides her.

The pain eased as the balm settled into the knots of muscle and relaxed to a dull, sore thud rather than the electric tension that I'd felt before.

"Mil gracias," I said, cocking my head to either side and letting loose a pop like thunder.

"No hay problema. Also I have a question for you," Carmen said, dabbing the leftover rub onto each shoulder and hitting a quick shimmy as it settled. "So what's the story with 'Purp'?"

"Pues, I told you. It's my favorite color."

"I mean, I get that part." Carmen sucked her teeth. "Pero like not a lot of people just name themselves Periwinkle, y'know? So what's the rest of the story?"

"Well, in a couple years I'm going to be starting at a new school for what we call ninth grade. And to be honest I don't want to have to spend all this time in high school trying to teach people how to . . . well you know, right?"

Carmen blinked at me in the orange light, her shadow flickering behind her.

"I'm just so tired of trying to teach people how to say my name."

"You're tired of teaching people to say your name," Carmen said with a look on her face like when Mami is taste testing habichuelas to see if there's enough seasoning.

"Yeah, it's just, that's what Mira Paredez did . . . kinda. She's a filmmaker, like me. She's my hero! She had a difficult name too and—"

"But Pilar isn't a difficult name?"

Pues, I had to take a beat because normally that's my line. "Yeah, it isn't but—"

"I don't think there should be a but," Carmen mused, picking some dirt from beneath her nails. "I said it right, and we just met yesterday. Why can't they?"

"I don't know, I just . . ."

The rain pounded down louder than before, pues, why was this forest so dang dramatic?

"Look, Pilar. It's fine to have a name you want to be called, pero make sure that it's for you, y'know? It doesn't make much sense to me that *you* changed your name to accommodate *other people's* ignorance."

It was a lot to process, so I just nodded and kept stretching my shoulders. Carmen smiled an old-school Lorena smile, the kind she used to give back before Papi died, before she decided she was the adult between us. Carmen could be cool sometimes, but she gave good advice when she wasn't trying so hard to be a leader también.

"Aight, my turn." I grinned. "Since we doing deep questions, how do you know La Bruja? What's she like?"

Carmen's smile shrank a bit—it looked sad now like a dented mango. "How about we both rest for a bit and I'll tell you after Second Light when we're on our way?"

I felt like Carmen was ducking the question and all the Mira Paredez instinct in me wanted to push harder, but I didn't want to risk disturbing our weird new friendship-alliance thing. I shrugged, winced from the soreness, and lay back on my backpack with Natasha's journal, ready to try and knock out a couple of pages.

3/12/57
Dear Diary,
Mami said something weird today. Pues, I don't know what she meant. Mami has been acting weird, leaving me with Grecia two or three nights a week and saying

she's got a new job, pero there's still not much money for clothes or books. I don't understand what's going on. Grecia thinks that maybe it's a man, pero that doesn't feel right. She still cries over Papi's pictures at night; why would she need a boyfriend?

She won't even tell me what happened to Papi. She says she'll tell me when I'm older, but I think I know, porque she always cries over him after we run into officers. The other day I think I saw two men in SIM uniforms sitting in a car across the street when I got home from Grecia's place. There's so many secrets in this house, why won't anyone tell me anything?

Oh, also the weird thing Mami said! Pues, I keep thinking about it and it doesn't make sense. She said—

And that's when the first claw tore through the top of the tarp.

FIFTEEN

"DOWN," CARMEN HOLLERED AS THE claw continued to scrape through the top of the tarp.

Without thinking I flung myself over my backpack protectively. Carmen leaned back and launched her left foot into the gap in the cloth. The Cucito who had torn through barely got its face to the hole before Carmen's heel caught it directly in the eye. It squealed and fell away. A second later, a high-pitched yowl sounded in the night.

Pues, of course there was more than one.

"Grab your bag!" Carmen called to me. "The rain must have masked their scent, it's an ambush! We're going to have to fight our way out and make a break for it."

Carmen grabbed the hot stone, immediately snatching the orange glow from the awning. It was cold now, pero Carmen didn't look scared, so neither could I.

"Time to kick some mini-cuco butt," I said, slinging my

backpack over my other arm and punching my fist into my open palm. I'd always wanted to do that.

Carmen laughed, a mischievous smile at the edge of her mouth. "We'll make a soldado out of you yet!"

The Cucitos screamed again as Carmen matched my punching motion and walked outside of the ruined tarp. My heart was slamming against my ribs, but I balled up my fists and followed. Pues, I had been itching for a rematch. Anyway, how many could there be?

Many. The answer, it turns out, was many.

It was hard to count accurately with the rain blitzing down into my eyes, pero like if I had to guess, there were at least thirty-five Cucitos arranged across the trees. We were surrounded.

A group of six Cucitos was standing on the broad part of the branch we were perched on, glaring at the two of us. Their drenched fur hung down over their mouths, yellowing fangs glinting behind them. Y también I was kicking myself that we hadn't at least smelled this coming, porque even in the rain the Cucitos still reeked like week-old basura.

"You take left, I take right?" I asked Carmen, pulling on my gloves.

"Something like that," Carmen said, eyes flitting between the trees. "Follow my lead."

And then Carmen jumped off the edge of the branch. The Cucitos growled and started advancing toward me, suddenly alone.

"Wait, how am I supposed to—"

But before I could finish asking, Carmen swung up from beneath the branch and buried both of her feet in the first Cucito's chest. The Cucito's arm flew out, trying to balance itself, and ended up taking down the one behind it as well. I would have laughed as they both plummeted to the ground, but that was when the rest of the Cucitos charged and the trees shook with howls.

Pues, what else was there to do? I jumped.

I caught the underside of the branch, the magic of the gloves sticking to it like magnets, and hurled myself back up, feet first, narrowly missing booting a Cucito in its wide, ugly grille. It bit at me, so I punched it square in the mouth and swung back down.

"This would be mad fun if it wasn't terrifying!" I called after Carmen, who swung down at the same time as me, clinging to the bottom edge of the branch.

"Pues, you get used to it after a while. Just wait till you don't need the gloves!"

Just then a Cucito peeked its nasty head over the edge and barked at Carmen. She grabbed it on either side with her ankles and casually tossed it hissing toward the forest floor.

"Get the girl, le' the 'guapa!" howled a watery voice directly above, staring up at me with its watery demon eyes. "El Jefe wan' the girl!"

What did they want with me? Why was I so important to them? Did this have something to do with Natasha?

For now, all I could do was kick some Cucito butt. Answers would have to come later.

I swung up from below and this time I connected with a Cucito on the first try. Kicked it straight in the nalgas and it went off the edge screaming. Then I knocked out another two with a pair of cross hooks.

And the vice principal said fighting would never get me anywhere but the principal's office! Pues, who's laughing now Mrs. Guttierez? The girl who survived!

Carmen swung up behind me and we stood back-to-back. There were still way too many Cucitos on either side. Similar mutters of "the girl" and "El Jefe" dripped from the little feítos, their wet-dog-born-in-a-dumpster smell making my eyes water as one of them nearly clawed a hole in my shirt. My neck prickled and my heart was still racing as I tried to count how many were left. I was overwhelmed, pues, why couldn't we have had like a training montage before we left the city? It was fun hitting the first few Cucitos, pero who knew if there'd be reinforcements.

"Do we retreat?" I gulped.

"Not until we knock out a couple more," Carmen said bluntly. "*Now* you go left and I go right. Just for fun."

In the fight that followed, the benefit of the branch was that the Cucitos seemed afraid of breaking it with their collective weight, so they could only come at us two maybe three at a time. The rest of them watched from the surrounding trees or launched themselves from above. Once one of them launched from a high branch and I barely ducked in time only to find that another was speeding toward me like a bullet train.

"Pues, not this time," I said.

I exploded into an uppercut that caught the lunging Cucito straight in the jaw. It flew up into the tops of the trees and disappeared. Carmen hadn't been kidding, these gloves really did double your strength.

Pero there wasn't much time to celebrate porque two more Cucitos were running right at me low and hard. I crouched and hit them with a sweeping kick Celeste taught me after taking a few karate classes. They fell as one and I hurled another Cucito like a smelly bowling ball into the ones behind.

I turned to see Carmen, light on her feet as a bachatera, duck under a flying Cucito and catch it full in the face with a kick over her arched back.

"Yo, Carmen, you gotta teach me that move if we survive this!" I laughed nervously, elbowing a squealing Cucito.

"No hay problema. But for now it's time to go." Carmen flicked rain from her forehead and, once again with no warning, jumped off the edge. Pues, mad casual like it was the low dive at the city pool. Carmen really was so bad at giving directions.

"¡Adiós feítos!" I said, and dove after Carmen.

My heart stopped for a moment as I grasped at empty air. I would not go down like this after roughing up a horde of coconut trolls like a badass! I plummeted for what felt like ten years, but was probably closer to a millisecond, before I grabbed a branch, then rocketed up and out toward the next.

And in another life, that might have been the end, pero of course the Cucitos who we hadn't already fought took off after us. I could hear their claws as they scrambled to keep up. They weren't great climbers, pues, they couldn't even catch me, let alone hold a candle to Carmen. Pero like they were still close enough that I could hear one or two barking after me about "El Jefe" and "Get the—" before the wind in my ears ripped away the sound. The girl, they must have meant to say.

They only had eyes, and teeth, and claws for me. Qué suerte.

After a while, the calls and growls grew distant. Carmen yelled "Up" and paused on a springy-looking branch. I swung two more times to catch up, noticing that my chest was on fire again as I hauled myself onto a thicker branch. Pues, adrenaline is really wild when you're running for your life.

"Nice . . . work . . . back there, soldado!" Carmen said, out of breath too for once.

"You . . . too!" I panted back before shooting her a "think we lost them?" look porque I didn't have the wind to ask directly.

"That was a huge number . . . never seen that . . . pero I think we lost them, and the rain should keep our scent hard to track. Y también we aren't very far from La Bruja's and they shouldn't be able to reach us there."

Carmen rummaged in her leather bag and took a deep swig from the water flask before passing it to me.

"What do you think they want with me?" I asked as I handed the flask back to Carmen.

"Pues, yo no sé. When I was younger, I got to go on a few of the raids to liberate new prisoners from La Blanca, back when we still had enough strength to do that kind of thing, but even then . . . they never showed this much focus on one girl. Never said a word the whole time."

I frowned and stared into the distance, trying to ignore how far off the ground we were. I was already being hunted, and nobody knew why; last thing I needed was a case of vertigo to top it all off, entiendes?

Carmen must have seen the worry on my face, porque she rushed to add: "Pero like, maybe they're bored. It's been such a long time since El Jefe fell in your world."

"Over sixty years," I said, still feeling far away mentally, thinking of the army of Cucitos hunting me.

"Exactly," Carmen chimed in, trying to sound chill, though doubt crept into her voice. "There haven't been new prisoners from your world ever since. So El Cuco started coming after our villages, our cities, our homes."

Her lip quivered, a tremor in her voice. Pero she tried to smile anyway, maybe for me and maybe for both of us.

"Pues, I guess what I'm saying is that El Cuco is like every other dictator, he needs a thing to destroy, a new enemy or what is he? Nothing. You might just be a new challenge for him. It's not like we got people from your world dropping out of the sky left and right. Y también, he's 0–2 on catching you, so you're not doing half bad, Pilar."

Pues, I was still anxious, but she made a point.

"The good news is," Carmen said, voice warming as she took the water flask back from me and tucked it into her bag, "once we recruit La Bruja, we'll kick El Cuco's hairy butt and get you home."

She made it sound so easy. Y pues, we knew that it wouldn't be, but it helped to know we both thought we had a shot. We found another wide branch to rest at, this time without the tarp. El Bosque was thick with the heavy scent of rain and moss. With Second Light coming up, we agreed that it would be a bad idea to use the hot stone again, so we slept in shifts with the other keeping watch. I tried to sleep with my head on my backpack, arm through one strap, and used my jacket as a blanket. Pues, it wasn't very warm, pero it kept the rain out for the most part. Mejor que nada.

When it was my turn to keep watch, I crouched on the branch and wondered how many rings were inside this tree. If the ciguapas had been living here for thousands of years, I couldn't even imagine how old a tree would have to be to grow branches like this, wide enough to sleep on.

I looked out at the purpling tops of the trees as Second

Light bloomed over El Bosque. It was mad peaceful, except for Carmen's snoring. I shielded the camera with my purple jacket as I took some panoramic shots. Nobody would believe I had ever been in a tree this high otherwise.

Pues, I thought, using the camera lens to survey the forest as the rain slowed to a gentle trickle, this place could have been beautiful if so much bad stuff hadn't happened here.

I tucked the camera back in my bag and made a mental note to edit out Carmen's snoring if the footage ever made it to postproduction, AKA if I ever made it home. I sighed and thumbed Natasha's journal. I had tucked it into an inner pocket of my bag, caught between wanting to open it and wanting to make sure not even a single page got wet. What had Natasha's mom said that freaked her out so bad? I thumbed the worn leather again. Damn, I really hate waiting.

But there was no time for reading. When Carmen woke we made our way through El Bosque with lightning speed. My muscles were still tired and sore, but whatever had been in that Vaporu really had hit the spot, entiendes? I felt stronger, less awkward in my swings (pero definitely still very thankful for the magical gloves!).

The closer we got to the destination, the happier and more relaxed Carmen seemed to be. I mean the ciguapa was legit doing backflips. Pues, I guess until then I hadn't really thought about how Carmen knew La Bruja. La Bruja sounded like almost more of a weapon than a person to me; a tool to help rescue Natasha. But Carmen was beaming like

I would if Celeste told me she was moving back to Chicago, where she belonged.

"It's just ahead!" Carmen called from a high branch a dozen feet ahead of me. "I'll go down and scout so she knows we're here!"

Without waiting for a reply, she laughed, saluted, and dove down, disappearing into the thin mist that shrouded the forest floor. I followed the echo of her laugh and found a weird smell like . . . ash.

Then a great wail sounded from below.

I landed on a branch, its weight creaking beneath me. I looked down to find Carmen kneeling on the ground at the edge of a field of burnt trees, some still smoldering, cinders hissing as the rain hit them.

And Carmen, pues, she was crying as if it was the last thing she would ever do.

SIXTEEN

AS CARMEN SOBBED, I DIDN'T know what to do with my hands. Pues, there's crying and then there's what was happening below the branch I was perched on. The sound seemed to climb through the branches, like it had arms and legs, entiendes? Birds I couldn't see cried back from high above as if they knew something horrible had happened.

I bit my lower lip as Carmen quieted for a second, shaking like a leaf caught in a fence, and then the sound started again. It was easy sometimes with Carmen's movie-star smile and her punchy "I'm still Carmen from the (Block) Resistance" attitude to forget she wasn't actually a human. Pero I'd never heard a human make a sound like that in all twelve years of my life.

I felt so helpless porque I didn't know if it was better to just let Carmen cry or to go down and comfort her, squeeze her hand just to let her know she wasn't all alone. It sounded like something was cracking inside Carmen.

One time, when I was ten, I tried to comfort Mami when she was crying over Natasha's photo and she just cried harder. I didn't understand, I thought I'd hurt her, pero Abuela told me, "Negrita, sometimes people, even the people you love, are hurt and the best thing you can do is let them ask you for help cuando they decide that they need it, y no antes de esto, entiendes?" So I perched on the branch, como los pájaros still calling from the leaves above, waiting for Carmen and hoping none of those birds were that creepy gray one from the first night.

After another twenty minutes Carmen leaned back on her knees and scooped some soil into her palm. From where I was sitting it looked like dirty February snow.

"You can come out now, Pilar," Carmen half whispered with a small sniffle. "I appreci—just thanks for waiting. I'm, I'm sorry you had to see that." She let the dirt fall through her fingers.

I swung down and landed awkwardly in a puddle and stumbled toward her, trying to look composed. Carmen didn't turn her head to me as I spoke. "You've got nothing to say sorry for." I put a hand on her shoulder; her muscles were tense and rock solid. "You're only—"

I kicked myself as my face grew hot. I was about to say "*You're only human.*" I was totally fumbling this comfort-the-grieving-homie thing. Pues, this is why I only keep one best friend—I'm no good at this emotional stuff.

Pero, Carmen's next sniffle came out as a half laugh. She

wiped a dirty fist across her eyes and looked up at me. There was a diagonal streak of gray across the deep brown of her face, like warpaint.

"I—" She cleared her throat. "I know what you meant, hermana. Mil gracias."

"De nada," I grumbled, looking at the ground.

We both stood there for a minute, the only sound the rain hitting the growing puddles behind us, hissing in the flames ahead. I was burning to know more about what had happened, pero I also didn't want to be rude. Y también, I was worried about the monstros who might've heard Carmen. The fires were mostly guttered out by the rain, pero whatever or whoever had started them, quién sabe how close they still were.

"Pues," Carmen said, standing slowly and dusting off her pants. "We should umm, make for higher ground. I'll explain everything when we get there, te prometo."

We climbed and swung for another forty minutes up and away from the still-hissing fires until we found a spot where a wide tree had cracked midway through the trunk, leaving a space for us to make camp. The thunder boomed high above us as the last of Second Light faded.

"I'm . . . I know you said not to say sorry, pero I still am sorry, Pilar," said Carmen as she began stringing together some broad leaves for shelter. It was more of an umbrella than a tent. "I never expected the enemy might track down

La Bruja . . . I wasn't prepared. And I don't like people seeing me . . . like that, back there." Carmen's lip trembled a bit. "I'm supposed to be in command of this mission. I . . . there's a reason that Yaydil tends to have me work alone, entiendes?"

"Why's that?" I cocked an eyebrow and tried to ignore the bead of water trickling down my neck.

"I guess I just never was good at being an authority figure. I aced nearly every skill task during the officer exams. Yaydil even said nobody had ever passed Hand-to-Hand Combat with higher marks than me. And you know she doesn't give out praise easy."

I couldn't keep my lip from curling a bit. Pues, didn't give out praise easy? Try ever. Una tacaña if ever I saw one.

"But I flunked Strategic Comprehension, Pilar, I flunked it real bad. When Ciudad de Plata fell, I was just a kid. Ever since, I've had faith that I can handle anything on my own. And I always could. So once, in the middle of a drill, I totally abandoned my squad to try and capture the flag on my own."

I nodded, giving her left hand a squeeze between thumb and forefinger porque I read somewhere that it helps.

"You know the ironic part? I got the flag. Pues, the other team never knew what hit them. But it turned out that while I was off playing savior, Yaydil had captured my entire squad. Instant fail."

We went quiet then and the wind whipped hard through the branches. When they clacked against each other they sounded like claves. Carmen took a deep breath.

"It's hard for me to keep my emotions in check on a mission, especially with other people on it. You don't know what it's like to lose your home."

"Yes I do." The words came out of my mouth colder than I expected. I let Carmen's hand go. "Pues, maybe the first thing you need to do is stop assuming you know people, Carmen."

A string of emotions flashed across Carmen's face. Anger, sadness, understanding, envy, then anger again. "Y pues, what would you know? You landed in the middle of a war I've been fighting all my life. The only reason you're on this mission is so you can find a way to leave it."

"What choice do I have? I can't just abandon my home and my family."

"Yeah, well at least you have a place to abandon." Carmen's voice was ice cold now. "At least you have a family who will miss you. Mine's gone. The last of them is ash somewhere below us."

"I'm sorr—"

"Don't." Carmen's voice quivered "Please just, don't. Do you know the hardest part of training under Yaydil?"

I bit back several retorts and shook my head.

"It was that I didn't grow up in Minerva with the other girls. Pues, it wasn't like it is now, it was the capital and they were safer than I ever was. They joined because they wanted to do the right thing. I joined because El Cuco murdered my parents. Do you have a good memory?"

"Umm yeah." I shrugged. "I have a really good memory."

"Well, mine is perfect. But I wish it wasn't. Every day I wish it wasn't."

Pues, having a perfect memory sounded amazing. No more having to study or forgetting to text your friends back. The ability to never lose anything again sounded very lit. I would have traded anything to not have to rewind over and over again during postproduction trying to find the time stamp in an interview!

"Everything that has ever happened to me, pues, it's all up here." Carmen tapped her temple with two fingers. "When your brain is like that . . . como se dice, umm, it's like every day is three days long because there's no breaks, no moments you weren't paying attention, nada. It's all up there. I remember when the fires took the city, I can still smell the heat from the metal. Sometimes all I want to do is *forget*."

My mouth hung open as lightning ripped somewhere above us, harsh beams of pure white light dancing down Carmen's curls like water, then disappearing. I reached for Carmen's hand again, pero she didn't notice. Her eyes were far away.

"I remember La Bruja finding me, this little girl whose mothers told her to run into El Bosque. They . . . they couldn't have known I'd survive, they just knew I needed to escape. La Bruja raised me, she protected me until I was old enough to become a cadet in the Resistance, entiendes? And all through training I knew that every time I closed my eyes, I would smell the scents of my home being destroyed. I knew none of the other girls could understand what I'd been through. Y pues, it all made me stronger, fuerte they said, pero it also made me feel so alone, Pilar. It made me unfit for command."

"It isn't your fault," I said, my voice feeling smaller than usual.

Carmen looked me in the eyes for the first time since we'd finished setting up camp. "I took this mission. I asked you to help. What happens is on me, that's what command is. I have to protect you, but I couldn't even protect the only family I had left. I argued and pushed and we came all this way and . . ."

"Are you sure she's . . ." I searched for the right word. ". . . down there?"

"No," Carmen admitted after a long pause. "Pero that's where she's always hidden. If El Cuco's minions found it . . . I don't know, Pilar. Maybe this was a mistake, maybe this whole mission was a mistake."

"And maybe it wasn't," I said, trying to sound confident. "We came this far. I don't know, Carmen, you're right that I've never been at war. Pues, this whole thing is so scary, but the sisters wouldn't have chosen us if they weren't sure you could do it. That this is—"

"Please don't say 'something worth fighting for.'" For the first time in a while, Carmen's lips formed the ghost of a smile.

"I wasn't going to say that, payasa," I said, side-eyeing her. I was totally going to say that.

"All I'm saying is, we came this far. And I didn't follow you porque you had perfect exam scores. I followed you because . . ." I reached for a reason, y pues, it turned out I had more than one. ". . . porque I know a little about what it's like when someone is taking your home from you inch by inch. About looking at places you loved and it's all crumbling into something new."

I paused and stared at Carmen, who still looked pretty miserable, but at least she wasn't interrupting me.

"Pues, I guess what I'm saying is, I been looking for my cousin. In my world people act like Trujillo never happened, like we just made up the whole thing. Like we're better off just *forgetting*. Pero I knew what was true then. And what I know now is that this thing isn't over, entiendes?"

Carmen looked at me. I knew that look, I'd seen it on Mami's face dozens of times. Determination. It was how I'd gotten to Zafa in the first place. I did what I do best, I stared right in front of me and believed in what I saw.

"It's like you said, we can't just sit around and wait. We have to try."

"You know what, Ramirez?" Carmen said, shaking rainwater from her curls.

I stared, heart pounding and thinking of how I probably was the corniest girl alive for giving an inspirational speech, pues, who does that?

"It's a shame you're from your world. You would definitely be officer material in this one."

SEVENTEEN

WE PASSED THE TIME WEAVING a tight canopy out of broad leaves. Carmen took first watch while I huddled under my olive-green ciguapa jacket y pues, I was knocked out immediately. I don't normally remember my dreams, pero I'll never forget the one I had that night.

It was intense, row upon row of fangs emerging from a deep dark. They chased me, but I outran them, my chest burning as I sprinted. Eventually the fangs changed into the cracked stumps of trees, the tops lit by blue flames. One big flame was in the distance. Pero not stovetop flame blue like the others, but a deep blue like a bruise, gleaming like a jewel. I reached my hand out to it as I climbed over the sharp stumps of the trees and—

"Pilar! Pilar!" Carmen shook me awake. "Wake up, it's your turn, hermana."

My limbs felt stiff beneath the jacket as I wiped the sleep from my eyes and rolled my neck to get the kinks out. We still couldn't use the hot stone porque we lost the tarp, so the light would be visible for miles. Damn Cucitos. Those little rancid coconut trolls really ruin everything.

"¡Oye, da me diez minutos!" I said, waving my arm at her.

"No way, that's how the whole system breaks down. Your shift will only be a few hours," Carmen said firmly.

Pues, Carmen and Lorena can never meet or I may never sleep through the morning again.

I shrugged my jacket on over either shoulder and sat at the edge of the leaf tent, the wind rustling the leaves like maracas. I turned over my shoulder to get in another jab at Carmen, pero, por supuesto, she was already snoring onto her bag.

"Typical." I huffed and sat down to start my watch, blowing my breath into my palms to keep warm as the wind spat drizzle in my face.

I watched the rain fall for a while and then eventually pulled out Natasha's journal to return to the section I hadn't finished because of the Cucito attack.

The other day I think I saw two men in SIM uniforms sitting in a car across the street when I got home from Grecia's place. There's so many secrets in this house, why won't anyone tell me anything?

Oh, also the weird thing Mami said! Pues, I keep thinking about it and it doesn't make sense. She said she needed to take me to the butterflies to find my power. Pues, I don't know what that means, pero her eyes were wide when she said it, like when she really means something but doesn't want me to be afraid.

But I am afraid; everyone is, in our neighborhood. Whatever she meant, I think I just need to go to sleep porque it makes the hairs on my arms stand up to think about it. I hate nights like this the most, where I am afraid even in my own house. On nights like these the wind bends the tree next to my window. Pues, all night, back and forth, back and forth and I know it's nothing, pero when the branches moan, they creak like the new boots of soldiers.

I stared at the last few sentences of the journal entry, trying to will Natasha to write more about the butterflies, about Tía Julia, about this *power*, porque I was just as confused as Natasha about the whole thing. I'd been told that Tía Julia had been snatched by the SIM over "inciting rebellion," pero I never knew how true that was because Mami always folded into a stony silence when I asked about it. But this was evidence that Tía Julia was the real deal, an actual member of the Movement of the Fourteenth of June—the Resistance movement led by the Mirabal Sisters AKA Las Mariposas AKA The Butterflies.

They were folk heroes, pues, even legends, for how many times they defied Trujillo. They fought and organized and were total badasses. Pues, I keep a picture in my locker of the four of them smiling next to a Jeep. I printed it out at the library and put it in a frame from Dollar General. There's many iconic photos of the four of them, but I love that one best porque they look happy together, like they were on the edge of victory and couldn't imagine having anyone else by their side.

That was before, though, before everything went wrong. Later, Trujillo had three of them killed in a cane field and the soldiers tried to make it seem like an accident, pero everybody knew the truth. Pues, I always wondered what happened to the Sister who was left behind; what do you do when all your siblings become martyrs?

But that wasn't even the biggest question on my mind while I fidgeted with the worn leather belt loop of the journal. Pues, even wilder than the fact that Tía Julia had known the *actual* Mirabal Sisters was trying to figure out what they needed Natasha for.

I went over the facts I knew again in my head. Natasha was only thirteen when she "disappeared." After Trujillo fell, most of the records stop cold, de quien disappeared, who was assassinated. And there weren't many records to begin with; just miles and miles of páginas en blanco. I now knew that El Baca had taken Natasha, and Trujillo apparently wanted her pretty bad according to Gray Locks, but there was no smoking gun, no clear reason *why*, just a blank sheet of paper where my cousin used to sit.

Thunder boomed in the distance and the thick smell of

wet moss drifted up from below, climbing up my nose and making me cough and splutter.

"Pues, I am a terrible lookout. I haven't looked up in forever." I sighed to myself, turning to see Carmen totally asleep beside me.

I put the journal in my bag and went back to doing my best impression of Mr. Davis, the security guard at school who takes his job way too seriously. I kept my head on a swivel and spat out into the rain just to watch it disappear. Pero I still felt the question tugging at my heartstrings, like always.

"Oye, Natasha, what did Trujillo want with you? You were my age, what made you so dangerous that there was only enough island for *one* of you?"

The hours dripped by until it was finally time for me to wake Carmen. I shook the wet, heavy curls out of my face and brushed the droplets off my jacket, ready to resume our search for La Bruja . . . and hoping she was still alive.

"Carmen!" I said, shaking her back and forth. "Time to wake up."

"Ay no, we can't, I'm too . . ." Carmen mumbled, then started putting up some very fake-sounding snores. I rolled my eyes and gave her a small kick.

"Oye malcriada, we got places to be before the light changes! ¡Nos vamos!"

After ten minutes of mumbled curses and some totally unnecessary talk of tossing me into the ocean at the next opportunity, Carmen and I were dive-bombing back down toward the forest floor.

"Okay," I said when we arrived at the ashes of La Bruja's former home. "Where do we start looking?"

Carmen took off at a jog toward the cracked stumps of the trees. I was still a little stiff from keeping watch, but I did my best to limp after her at a half jog. Carmen slowed a bit to let me catch up and then pointed her finger in a wide arc around the whitened soil.

"La Bruja and I stayed here sometimes when I was little," she said, voice tight like she was swallowing something sour. "She has a couple of places that she moves between porque El Cuco has been trying to capture her for years. Guess he found this one."

She kicked hard at the ground sending ash and twigs spraying up like seafoam.

"All right so like, besides just dictators being dictators, what's El Cuco's beef with La Bruja exactly?"

Carmen's eyes stopped scanning over my head. She paused and looked at me with her head cocked to the side. "She's the last of her kind. He saw to that the night of the Raid."

"The Raid?"

"Pues, I keep forgetting you didn't grow up here. El Cuco and his cronies have taken a lot from us, pero the Raid is *the Raid*. There have been raids since, but the Raid was how we found out El Cuco was in league with a whole other level of evil. That night, all of La Bruja's people were slaughtered."

My mouth fell open. One night? How could an entire people be wiped out in one night? Pero I didn't ask that question. It felt . . . wrong somehow. Instead I asked, "How many?"

Carmen laughed bitterly; it almost sounded more like a bite. "Two thousand. Maybe more."

"Dios santificado."

"Nobody knows how El Cuco got past the perimeter. The realm of the Bruja nation used to be a notorious secret known only to other brujas. Of all the magical beings on Zafa, they had the strongest connection to La Negra. The things they could do . . . dios."

Carmen's eyes misted over for a second then snapped back into focus just before a clap of thunder dimmed the lights on all of El Bosque.

"That was the day La Negra lost control of the island. El Cuco breached the perimeter during Half-Dawn, and many of the younger brujas fell in their sleep. Pobrecitas never knew a thing."

Carmen snapped her fingers and started speed walking toward a group of stumps jutting up from the ground like fangs as I hustled after her and tried not to think about what all this wet ash must be doing to my kicks. Carmen weaved through the jagged stumps and continued with the story.

"Once the alarm was sounded, the bruja gave that gross furball all he could handle. But they couldn't have anticipated El Cuco's ruthlessness. He was willing to sacrifice his own soldiers. The Bruja nation, all together, was one of the greatest fighting forces in the history of, well . . . anywhere. Pero there were just too many Cucitos, too many Machetes, and finally El Baca came in as the numbers dwindled and took out the rest." Carmen punched deep into the soil. "La Bruja barely escaped. That was centuries before she took me in. Y este comemierda dictador has been on the hunt for her ever since."

I wanted to respond, to ask Carmen if she was okay, pero I felt something move in the ground and my breath froze in my chest. Had I triggered a trap? Was the enemy coming?

It wasn't like anything I'd felt before, more like the patter of faint drums in the dirt. As I listened closely, the music deepened, crying out from below until I couldn't tell the difference between it and my own pulse. I wanted to panic, I wanted to call for help, I wanted to follow the rhythm to its source.

I stepped through the tree stumps, ash nestled at the tops of each like powdered sugar. The rhythm swelled over me as I knelt and pushed my hand into the ground. I didn't know why I was doing it, it just felt like exactly where I needed to be. I dug until I was up to my wrist, then I felt something cold settle in my palm. I gasped and pulled out a thin silver chain with a deep blue gem, a bruise-blue sapphire that gleamed as if there were a church candle inside.

"No me diga." Carmen stared at the little thing in my hand as the drums faded out of my head. "I haven't seen that thing in years. Pues, we have a shot after all!"

"How did I . . . wha—"

Pues, I was freaking out, but Carmen calmly put a hand on my trembling shoulder. Her deep brown features were split by a wild, toothy grin, reckless laughter shaking through her body.

"Like I said," Carmen crowed, "that mangy traitor has been on the hunt for La Bruja for decades. Pero, Pilar, we are about to find her first."

EIGHTEEN

"WAIT, WHAT IS THAT?" I asked, hypnotized by the deep blue gem shimmering inside the jet-black stone frame.

Carmen straightened with a cocky grin that reminded me so much of Lorena with a new report card that I almost rolled my eyes off instinct. Apparently I was even homesick for being annoyed by Lorena.

"This is a resguarda, my old one from before I left for Ciudad Minerva and basic training!" Carmen beamed, cradling the back of the stone. "Did anybody ever make you one of these?"

"Pues, maybe when I was a baby?" I lied.

I didn't mean to lie, pero it's a thing I do sometimes around other Dominican people when they know something that I feel like I should also know but don't. Pues, younger Pilar was the most Dominican girl to ever Dominican. Younger Pilar spoke fluent Spanish but lost most of her Spanish when she had to go to an English-only school. Younger Pilar could salsa, merengue, and bachata, but then puberty came along and now she dances like a payasa. Baby Pilar's first words were Prince Royce lyrics even though my real favorite musician is either Noname or Cardi B. Baby Pilar had a resguarda and knew what it was. Her family always had enough money to go to DR every summer, so she would always know where her people came from.

But now, all I have are Abuela's stories, all I have is a secondhand island. Pues, as much as I love my life and who I am, I'd be lying if I said I didn't wish I were still her sometimes.

I guess I paused for longer than I thought, because I snapped out of it to find Carmen's hand on my shoulder. She squeezed and kept going with her story.

"Well, maybe the rules here are different for what a resguarda can do. When I was little, La Bruja made this for me to keep away bad magic and also to keep track of me." Carmen awkwardly pointed at herself. "La Bruja doesn't love heights and I just couldn't stay on the ground. Couldn't help it, it's my inheritance!"

We both laughed, then shivered as a cold wind passed over us. Pues, what I would have given to be able to use the hot stone, even for a little.

"Anyway, a resguarda uses a wide range of materials but some of the strongest ones have this." Carmen held up the jet black of the stone and made a face that made her look eerily similar to Cardi B. The sapphire winked at me again in the dim light as another wave of thunder shook the trees in the distance.

"So, we can use it to track her?"

"De verdad, hermanita." Carmen smiled. "La Bruja is out there, and this is about to lead us right to her. The gem will glow brighter and get warmer as we get closer to her."

Every hair on my arms rose to attention. I stood up straighter. Sometimes in gym class, when it feels like we've been running forever, I get this feeling, like someone clicked refresh on my lungs. When I asked Lorena about it she called it "runner's high," pero Coach said it's called "Second Wind" and I like that one better porque it's like Second Light in El Bosque.

Okay, I also like that Lorena was wrong, sue me.

I smiled. "Dope. But why the sapphire? They're pretty rare, no?"

Carmen laughed a summery laugh. "¡Pues, esa chismosa! It's a little inside joke from La Bruja porque when I was a baby I thought sapphires were literally made out of fire. So she gave me this one y se fue."

A cold trickle of understanding seeped through my spine. Pues, I had thought all my hairs were standing on end before, but now they were on their tiptoes. The image of the bruise-blue flame from my dream burst into my head and I felt lightheaded, like my brain was floating in soda.

Pues, am I losing it? Can I see the future? Am I psychic? Or is this some kind of jungle madness porque I saw a documentary about that and if I have jungle madness I'm never gonna get Natasha back and even if I get her back pues, how long do you have jungle madness for anyway porque Mami is not going to stand for that tontería at all y también—

"PILAR!" Carmen snapped her fingers in front of my face. It sounded like heels on a tile floor. "Are you okay? Hermana, you looking kinda pale."

I wasn't sure what was happening to me. Maybe I was a powerful super psychic and maybe I was losing my marbles, pero I knew one thing: I had to be strong.

"I'm good," I lied.

Carmen gave me a look like Mami when she knows I'm hiding something, pero just then the sapphire flickered in Carmen's hands and she snatched her finger back like she had touched a stove.

"She's on the move. She's alive!" Carmen grinned a wild wolf-like smile.

She took off at a run, leaping toward a low branch and perching atop it before shouting at the top of her lungs. "¡Oye, vieja! I'm coming for you, te oiste? I'm coming."

Just like that we were off, back on La Bruja's trail!

And maybe it was because we were terrified about what we would—or wouldn't—find, or maybe it was the bad light in that never-ending storm, maybe we were just too excited. Either way, neither of us saw the huge ash-gray bird in steady pursuit behind us, its shadow poised above ours like a claw.

NINETEEN

"I JUST WANT TO SAY that this is some tontería and if I die I'm finna kill you, Carmen!" I hollered at my end of the branch. Y de verdad, I meant every word.

After the resguarda started blinking, Carmen and I had packed up our stuff to head off, pero she hadn't told me where we were going. I was starting to understand how she had failed her ciguapa squad leader training; the whole "just follow me" thing got old really quickly.

We were surrounded by a tight ring of trees. Long, thin branches stretched and weaved together to form a rickety centerpoint where Carmen was standing on the balls of her feet.

"Pues, this is how every ciguapa passes her final combat exam. And it's time you learn how to fight for real. Who knows what will come between us and La Bruja? You did well in the last fight, pero I can help you do better so just stay light on your feet and don't be such a baby." Carmen smirked, which only made me want to fight her even more.

"Pues, didn't y'all have years of training before that exam? And don't we need to be finding La Bruja right now, not doing training exercises a bajillion feet off the ground?" I yelled back over the sound of the rain.

Carmen tapped her chin and walked to the opposite side of the ring like she was thinking, pero I knew she was only trying to get in my head. "I mean, yes to both, pero when we find La Bruja and raid La Blanca you'll be glad we did this, no?"

"Won't we be fighting on the ground?"

"You ask too many questions. Begin!"

Carmen ran hard toward the center, and mad annoyed, I ran to meet her there, ready to swing. Pero, of course, before I could get there she had slipped through a small gap in the branches, leaving me standing alone in the center, fists ready. I barely heard the rustle of the leaves before Carmen swung up through another gap in the branches behind me. I dodged a half-speed punch as my foot got stuck in a gap in the branches. Hair standing on end and heart racing, I jerked free just in time to avoid a kick from Carmen.

"Lesson one, hermanita: Combat is not about who's strongest; the battle goes to the most imaginative. If your opponent is bigger than you, go where size *doesn't* matter."

Sweat beaded on my forehead and trickled along my cheeks. I wiped my fist across my mouth to scatter it. Tan dramatic, I know, pero I was annoyed. I leapt from my spot on the ground and swung hard for Carmen. Her eyes widened a tiny bit before she ducked and swept my leg from under me.

I fell hard on my side into the branches, which were springy like a trampoline but thorny like . . . well, like branches. A number of small cuts opened on my left arm and along the knuckles of my left hand.

"Lesson two," Carmen continued. "Fights are always about balance. You came at me off balance porque you wanted to get even and now you're on the ground. Stay light on your feet and know the terrain so you can keep balance and keep rhythm. A fight will always progress faster than you want it to, so slow down what you can, entiendes?"

Carmen reached a hand down to help me up. I grabbed it with my right. She smiled at me and I smiled back. Then I yanked hard on her arm and swung through her slightly open legs and whipped around to kick her in the butt. I sent her sprawling forward, but instead of falling, she launched into a flip, her long thick curls following behind her like a storm cloud. When she landed lightly on her feet she was smiling.

"Nice one, who taught you that?" Carmen laughed, shaking a few twigs from her hair.

"I taught me!" I said, smiling back forreal this time, not even minding the sting of my cuts.

"Well pues, let's step it up then!" Carmen charged forward, pero I wasn't falling for that trick again. I waited for her to come to me instead, fists ready, but planning to drop through a Pilar-size gap to my right and burst up on Carmen's left. I waited, heart thumping, only hearing El Bosque in spurts between the sound of my breaths.

Inhale: The rain was coming down harder now than when we started sparring.

Exhale: I couldn't hear anything but myself, feel the rain mixing with the sweat and the blood, the breeze dancing through the hairs of my arms.

Inhale: Carmen was closer now, leaping instead of sprinting, maybe eight paces out? I could hear the branches yawning beneath her weight. Pero I could hear . . .

Exhale: . . . my pulse in my throat, thudding like a speaker through the trunk of a car until even the puddles dance, though they don't know the words.

Inhale: Carmen was five paces out now. I felt the world slow down around me. This is what Carmen meant; what a warrior feels when she can fight like a bachatera, when she can win.

Exhale: Nothing but me, nothing in the whole world. I was ready, I could win. I was just waiting for her to come to me.

But then, just my luck, some other tontería came to us first.

When The Child came down from the branches I didn't recognize it as a human shape at first. Pues, I elbowed it away from me porque I was in the zone and assumed it was some kind of booby trap that Carmen had planted to teach me to stay alert. But when I hit the white blur streaking down from above, I connected with something that didn't feel like muscle.

I snapped back to the world, my ears flooding with the sounds of El Bosque and a chill sprinting through my veins as The Child stood up.

It looked no older than eight and came up almost to my hip. It wore a striped gray short-sleeved shirt and raggedy-looking shorts. Its lips trembled as if it were about to cry and its curls were all loose and chalk white. It opened its eyes and looked at me, y pues, my heart stopped porque its eyes weren't human at all. There was no iris, just two orbs the color of a scab.

I didn't know what it was, but I felt dirty from touching it; horrified by this pitiful thing in front of me. I shot a quick look at Carmen, y pues, she was revolted too. She gripped the resguarda and shook her hand like it burned.

"Oh sh—" Carmen yelped.

Pero she never finished that sentence porque that's when The Child started to scream.

TWENTY

I DON'T REMEMBER EVERYTHING THAT happened next,
pero I remember this—The Child's scream didn't sound
like it came from one body. Pues, even now saying "scream"
sounds so gentle compared to the actual sound. It was a wail
that seemed to come from everywhere y también it wasn't
all the same sound, low screams and high screams, pain that
sounded human and agony that sounded almost animal. Its
scab-eyes were unblinking, shedding no tears. Pues, it shook
the trees as if the entire forest was coming apart, until it was
impossible to hear anything else.

The Child rose to its feet and my stomach clenched in
horror as it stepped toward me. I barely remember Carmen grabbing my arm, her mouthing "baca" at me again
and again as pins and needles flooded my palm from her
grip. I don't know how I got my backpack, whether Carmen snagged it or I did, but I felt it settle around my

shoulders. We leapt through a hole in the branches, free-falling, my heart in my throat, as the branches zoomed past us, falling away from that awful scream, racing the rain to the ground.

"Ese hijo de la gran," spat Carmen. "I hate the child-shaped ones. So, so creepy!"

So that was a baca? Thankfully it didn't seem like it was El Baca himself.

"Birds? Fine," Carmen continued, almost hissing with rage and nerves "Lizards? I guess. Cows? Pues, if you must. But children, pues, that's over the line even for el diablo!"

Leave it to Carmen's big mouth porque soon as she spoke, out came that same creepy bird from my first night in Zafa. It streaked down at us like an arrow followed by tons of smaller birds.

"Okay," Carmen said flatly, "maybe the birds are also not fine."

"CARMEN!!" I yelled.

"Oye, I'm working on it. Da me un minuto."

The birds flew faster toward us, and that scream, pues, that scream was coming again. Was it the same baca from before, or were more hiding in the trees?

"CARMEN."

"Y'know, hermanita, this is a lot easier when I. Can. Focus!"

And that's when Carmen grabbed hold of me and her legs stretched out, catching the nearby branch by her ankles.

She swung us both around once, twice, with the whole world spinning above us as that freaky bird and the rest of the baca birds closed in. After the second loop, we fired ourselves like cannonballs toward some very thick branches and Carmen let go of me.

"Catch it!" Carmen hollered, and I put out my gloved hands and caught a branch head-on, whipping up and over it before launching out toward the next branch like my life depended on it. Pues, what do I mean "like," this *was* life or death, and I wasn't planning on dying in a forest because of some ashy dust kid! Not Pilar Ramirez; I had chores to do and an Oscar to win.

I looked over at Carmen, who was moving branch to branch, parallel with me. For the first time since I'd met her, Carmen didn't seem like she was even kinda having fun with this latest chase/life-threatening situation.

Carmen's jaw was tight and she glared dead ahead, not even the ghost of her normal cocky grin. I wanted to ask her where we were going, pero then I heard her yelp like she'd touched something hot. Then two things happened simultaneously.

Pues, thing #1: More child-shaped bacas leapt onto the branches below us. Pale girls in dark gray dresses and little curly-haired boys like some kinda ashy Sunday school choir punching through from below like fangs. They really were so so much creepier than the bird-shaped ones. Pues, even la vaca sounded downright cuddly compared to this demonic group of kindergarteners porque now the howls were 150 percent worse as ten then twelve then twenty surfaced and joined the suffocating yell.

Y también thing #2: Without any warning Carmen swung up and to the left.

"Perfect," I groaned, T-shirt soaked with sweat and rain and more sweat, my arms aching like I was in some satanic presidential fitness test. "Just. Perfect."

I tensed my abs, what was left of them anyway, and hurled myself after Carmen, nearly missing the branch she had just left wobbling behind her.

"CARMEN!!"

I yelled into the rain after her, pero it seemed like she couldn't hear me at all. She kept her same pace, saying nothing as she dipped and swung a jagged left and right like some weird bachata. I was so dog-tired trying to follow her that I didn't even notice the scream of the baca children wither almost to nothing. Y también, so did the thunder.

Finally, Carmen paused on a branch like she was thinking, entranced. Y esa bastarda, the minute I came to that same branch sucking wind like I just ran the Chicago marathon, you know what she does next? You guessed it. She jumps, straight down.

"How. Rude," I said, wishing I had an inhaler, pues, even a balloon would do.

And then, porque what else was there to do, I jumped down after her.

I don't remember the fall; I don't remember seeing Carmen on the way down. Pues, maybe I had an ásthma attack. Maybe I blacked out from the stress. Or maybe it was something else, pero I fell into sudden darkness after Carmen.

When I awoke, I was lying beside Carmen on a thin wooden cot. She was sitting upright, hair flat on one side like she'd just gotten up a second before me. We were beneath a tent, a nice one with sprawling autumn colors. It felt like we were sleeping inside a hot stone. Y también five or six hot stones were floating around us, creating a bubble of warmth and I realized that I was dry for the first time in what felt like a month.

"Where are we?" I asked.

Pero then the flap of the tent flew open and a thick Dominican accent flew in with it.

"Well, well, well, mija, looks like you remembered the password after all."

TWENTY-ONE

"NICE TO SEE YOU TOO, viejita. What's it been? A century?" Carmen stretched her shoulders and spat on the dirt floor of the tent.

"Yes, yes. You're very tough and casual, Carmen." The woman flicked her wrist at Carmen like Mami does when I try to explain that I shouldn't have to be on dish duty because I didn't even eat that much.

So this must be the famous La Bruja. Not exactly the vieja I was expecting, pero *I see it*.

Pues, there's no other way to put it; La Bruja was way shorter than I'd imagined. Like, wouldn't even have been the tallest kid in my grade. She wore an off-white top, a belt of brown rope tied at her waist above matching pants, and a pair of old brown leather chanclas. Her thick braids framed the deep oak brown of her face, similar to Gray Locks, but her locks were only gray at the tips. I had to give it to La Bruja and the others; everybody here looked pretty good for being over one hundred years old.

"It's been ninety-six years by the way. Pero who's counting in the desgraciada army anyway," La Bruja said. Then she turned to me. "¿Y quién es tu amiga? More importantly, what do you want?"

"Isn't it enough for your favori—" Carmen started pero La Bruja just held up a hand and Carmen fell quiet.

"Mija, I know this kind of misdirection is your culture and all yak yak yak." La Bruja talked quickly and used her hands a lot, poking the air so hard between syllables it felt like she was flicking the words over to us. "But I left my dinner on the table, and if you don't tell me what brings you all the way to the heart of El Bosque, I'll assume it isn't important and you can give me back that resguarda and I can go back to my arroz con habichuelas."

And then she hit Carmen with a look every Latinx mom gets in their Mami Starter Pack. Pues, suddenly La Bruja really did look eight feet tall and her shoulder-length locks seemed to crackle with electricity. Everything about her went from "No es nada" to "What's the real story or I'm getting my chancla" in 4.3 seconds. Impressive time even by Mami standards.

Carmen sighed. She looked like it pained her not to roll her eyes, pero to her credit she didn't. "This is Pilar and we need your help to save her cousin."

La Bruja looked at me then for the first time. Her eyes were a deep coal black, dark as the sands of La Negra. Her eyebrows furrowed.

"Is that so," La Bruja said flatly, more statement than

question, not breaking eye contact with me. "And I'm guessing the Galipotes sent you?"

"Yes, they need your help to protect the city so we can mount a strike on La Blanca," Carmen said.

She had pivoted from charm to something more like the voice Lorena whips out when she's trying to show off how good she can fit in with the white kids at her school. If it was supposed to impress La Bruja, pues, she didn't show it. Her face hadn't moved since she started looking at me and I felt heat at the back of my neck.

Please don't tell me Carmen forgot to mention that La Bruja has heat vision on top of everything else.

Just when I thought I wouldn't be able to take much more, La Bruja finally blinked, and turned her head toward Carmen. I exhaled. I hadn't noticed I'd been holding my breath.

"They want my help?" La Bruja said, cocking her head to the side.

"They *need* your help." Now it was Carmen's turn for her voice to drop.

"Well"—La Bruja spread her hands, nails painted deep blue and winking in the light of the hot stones, which made them look almost black—"we all want things."

Something in the air almost seemed to crackle between the two. At some point in the conversation, Carmen had stood up and the height difference between daughter and caretaker, ciguapa and bruja, was even clearer in the deep orange light of the hot stones. La Bruja came up to Carmen's shoulder at best, and it looked like they might actually throw hands. And even after watching Carmen—a prodigy among ciguapa fighters, a woman I had watched punt a Cucito off two trees like a pinball, someone who'd saved my life once—I still didn't like her chances.

There wasn't an ounce of fear on La Bruja's face. Who was this woman? Who had the Galipotes sent us after?

"Ay," Carmen said through gritted teeth. "We don't have time for word games."

"¿Y quién es 'We'?" asked La Bruja. She had two tiny glass bottles full of some twisting dark liquid hanging at her belt. Had those always been there? "Pues, quién sabe that we were all part of this 'We' when El Cuco came and slaughtered my people!? And never helped me rebuild? Never dispatched a unit to help me find the traitor who brought the Raid down on us? And now you *offer* me a chance to fight. Tuh, as if I'm not alive because I fought my way out, alone."

"You know they slaughtered mine too," Carmen whispered.

"And joining the Galipotes' little security force was your choice, not mine. The Galipotes want my help so they send you and this one to persuade me." She flicked a hand at me and three fat beads of sweat raced down the back of my neck. "Well, let me save you the suspense." La Bruja folded her arms, the reflection of the hot stones glinting off her nails like stars. "My answer is no."

Carmen stamped her foot and I flinched. "So you're just

going to keep hiding here? Pretending the problem is everywhere else? You know we need bruja magic to protect the city!"

"Then use it." La Bruja turned for the door, but Carmen caught her arm in a flash.

"You know without you we—"

La Bruja whirled and tore her arm away, glaring at Carmen. "Without me, you still have the bruja you brought with you. What business is it of mine what you pendejas do with your suicide mission?"

Pues, La Bruja kept talking, pero for me, that was when the whole room slowed to a crawl. The thick, steady thud of my blood through my ears drowned out all other sound in the room. Suddenly everything was too bright, my breath felt caught in my dry, dry mouth. Porque when La Bruja said "the bruja you brought with you" she pointed, y pues, I feel like you know where she was pointing.

At a girl far from home, a director in muddy sneakers and a purple track jacket.

I looked at Carmen, whose head seemed to turn almost in slow motion, eyes wide and confused and furious; but I wasn't sure with who. My lips were so parched it felt like they might split, crack, bleed red blood that would look black as La Negra in the light of the hot stones.

"Me," I said, my voice cracking like stale bread. "She means . . . me."

TWENTY-TWO

"WAIT WHAT?!" CARMEN SHOUTED.

La Bruja cocked her head to the side with a "watch your tone" look that Abuela used to give me when I was little and would make too much noise in the front yard running a stick along the chain-link fence.

"Pues, of course she is a bruja. Where on the island is she from?" La Bruja asked, snapping her fingers at Carmen, who was still slack-jawed and looking between me and La Bruja.

"I'm not from the island," I cut in with a tiny bit more attitude than intended. "I'm from Chicago."

I had reached my limit and was determined to stop this tontería right now.

"Chi—what?" Now it was La Bruja's turn to look confused and maybe even . . . afraid? Of me?

"That's what I have been trying to tell you, vieja," Carmen said. "She's from the other side, first in hundreds of years, looking for her prima. Pues, El Baca took her; personally."

There was still a quiver in Carmen's voice, pero I had to hand it to her that she was doing a pretty good impression of her normal sarcastic Dominicana. Pues, if it weren't for her backward-pointing feet, she could have been a regular high school senior arguing with her mom and not a highly trained covert operative for a mythical Resistance force.

"I would also just like to add that I'm from actual Chicago, Logan Square, and not the suburbs."

Nobody laughed. Instead La Bruja was looking at me differently now; before it had been a searching look, her eyes scanning me head to toe, like when Mira Paredez is about to go in for the kill in an interview. Now La Bruja was looking at me with urgent curiosity, and not breaking eye contact. Pues, she didn't even blink.

"Who did you say your cousin was again?" La Bruja said, speaking slowly for the first time.

"Her name was Natasha," I said, trying not to stand awkwardly. It didn't help that La Bruja was doing her freaky immortal being staring contest thing again. Pero I found my bag, fished Natasha's journal out, and handed it to La Bruja.

"This was hers. Yaydil gave it to me. I haven't finished it yet because of all the . . . y'know"—I gestured around the tent as if we were still in the heart of El Bosque—"enemies and phantoms y todo. Pero she wrote that my tía was supposed to take her to the Mirabal Sisters, but I don't know why. She was just a girl, not much older than me, just a girl."

La Bruja weighed the old leather journal in her hands

while I talked, ruffling through the pages, turning it over like a pack of old playing cards, pues, even smelling it . . . before she smacked me in the forehead with it.

"Owww," I said, rubbing the spot. "What in carajo was that for?"

"You aren't 'just a girl.' Pues, disabuse yourself of that notion right now porque it's not going to do you any good as a bruja, and honestly wouldn't do you much good even if you were 'just a girl.'"

"How can you know?" Carmen cut in, seeing my face darken with annoyance. "Pero she's from the other world, she can't be one of your kind, vieja!"

"Yes. She can. And I suspect her cousin must be too. I'm looking at your little friend right now and I'm telling you one bruja *always* knows another when they see each other and she"—La Bruja jabbed back at me with Natasha's journal so hard I thought she might throw it by accident—"has the connection. She's dangerous, and if you want to win you need to start seeing how much that's really worth to you."

They both stared at me; Carmen with disbelief, La Bruja with a strange mix of hype and get off my lawn. Y pues, my head was still spinning, but I had questions.

"Let's say I believe you, for even a second about me having powers," I said, pacing now like an old movie detective. "But if you never met Natasha, how do you know she was a bruja?"

La Bruja straightened her back, scowling at me as if this was such a simple question that it was insulting to even ask. "How many Cucitos did you outrun to get here and disturb my dinner?"

"What does this have to do with my question?" I said, trying to stay calm, but the anger was mounting in my stomach. I could feel it tightening around my ribs like a snake.

"Okay, so you don't know," La Bruja said. "Carmen? Any guesses on how many?"

Carmen just stared at her and waited. Clearly she knew this game and wasn't trying to play along.

"Okay, fine, be that way." She looked between the both of us, Natasha's journal in her hand. "Well, luckily for you two little freedom fighters, the answer, ironically, doesn't matter. However many you faced, the worthless thieving hairball that runs this island commands at least a hundred times those forces. And they swear allegiance to him and him alone."

Silence rang in the tent; the amber glow of the hot stones almost seemed to wilt in the quiet that followed.

"Now, of all these literally thousands of agents, monsters, and abominations that are at Cuco's command, he has only one right hand, one monstrosity he trusts above all others," La Bruja said, spitting hard onto the dirt floor. "El Baca. The beast with a thousand drops of my sisters' blood beneath his claws. The right hand of el diablo himself. Now"—she paused and looked me dead in my eyes with that unending glare—"why with innumerable soldiers, creatures, and syco-phants available to him would El Cuco do this favor for El Dictador and send his strongest soldier out of this world to go pick up 'just a girl'?"

More beads of sweat scurried down my shoulder blades as I stared back, unable to blink. La Bruja spat again on the ground.

"Because she wasn't just a girl, she was a bruja and she was maybe the greatest threat either of those payasos could ever face." She tossed the journal back to me. "Just like you."

TWENTY-THREE

LA BRUJA'S WORDS BUZZED THROUGH my skull, flashing behind my eyes like neon liquor store signs. Words like *power* and *threat* and *monster* bounced around my head as I tried to accept what she was telling me.

Carmen's voice eventually broke through and it was clear that she and La Bruja had a rhythm like Mami and Lorena, using the same hand gestures y todo. Pues, I guess home is weird like that; it can live in a place, pero it can also live in your hands and they never forget.

"Okay so Natasha was a bruja . . . like Pilar? How was she such a big threat to El Jefe and El Furball, though? Porque not for nothing, you're powerful, pero Natasha was just one bruja against an army."

I expected La Bruja to sigh at having to explain, pero instead a wicked grin spilled across her face, like she had been waiting for this part of the conversation. "Pues, finally my dinner getting cold is worth it. Okay, pay attention because I'm only going to explain this once!"

And with that she uncorked both black bottles at her side like a cowboy wielding pistols in an old western. Suddenly black sand streamed out of each bottle like ropes of silk. They formed into the shape of a large flat disc in between the three of us.

Pues, Carmen's face was mostly neutral like she'd seen all this before, pero my jaw was on the floor. The bottles had been so small that I couldn't believe they contained so much substance, pero also this clearly wasn't just any black sand, it was—

"La Negra!" I cheered.

My face burned with embarrassment. Apparently I was the only one who was super impressed by this display.

La Bruja's face was a mask of concentration, pero she allowed herself a small smile. "That's correct, child. La Negra is the keeper of all our stories, all our power. We brujas are chief among all her protectors, dating back generations upon generations long before Cuco built that abomination, La Blanca."

The flat disc of La Negra rippled as if the sand itself were shaking with rage. La Bruja lifted her hands into the air and the disc settled again to be perfectly flat.

"Before Cuco killed my sisters, before the betrayer, the brujas cared for La Negra in many ways; by tending to the land, protecting the trees of El Bosque, and especially by telling stories."

Along the disc of black sand, small figures rose to act out La Bruja's words. Here a tiny stick figure tended to a tree, and on another side of the disc a ring of stick figures danced and acted out some story I couldn't hear. Pues, I'm still kicking myself that I didn't get even one shot for the documentary.

"So y'all were like her . . . priests?" I asked.

La Bruja's mouth turned to a slash as she answered. The little stick figures melted back into the sand without a sound. "It's not really a religion. Consider us La Negra's closest partners. Were we not here, she would still thrive porque she is strong and this island is both hers and ultimately *is* her, entiendes?"

I nodded.

"Vieja," Carmen cut in, "you know I love you pero a veces you get distracted and I'm still waiting to know why Natasha was such a threat. ¿Por favor nos vamos al fin?"

"Desgraciada," La Bruja muttered, along with some other Zafa-specific words that were almost definitely swear words. Either way, La Bruja returned to her story. "Now, your prima must have been one of the rare brujas of your world who has a connection to La Negra without ever having seen her. It's rare, pero it does happen and these brujas have the most powerful memories."

A miniature city slowly emerged from La Negra, a big palace at its center with a dome and even a tiny flagpole out front. The streets were patrolled by tiny soldiers holding tinier guns and wielding small machetes. Even though I knew they were only puppets my jaw clenched, and it felt like my stomach was making a fist.

"The enemy has their knives, their guns, their prisons, the whole long history of cruelty at their command. Pues, they have no shame and want no memory; they lust only for power. Pero that is why they fail, entiendes? They have their weapons, pero there is no weapon more deadly to a dictator than people who refuse to forget."

A small figure emerged from La Negra, a little girl, Natasha, and sent ripples out. Where La Bruja pointed, the sand moved to attack. Now La Negra shook and the dome of the palace cracked. Soldiers were swept away in tides of black sand, pues, it was beautiful; memory fighting against forgetting—and winning.

"This is why brujas tell stories, with and for La Negra, porque memory is our first and last line of defense. A story forgotten or left untold is a machete left in the rain, do you understand?"

"Kinda," I said, still marveling now at the city of black sand where tiny figures in ankle-length skirts carried small pistols and danced with other figures holding guitars and small drums.

"You will understand. It's easier to show you La Negra's power than explain it."

I nodded, both thrilled and terrified. "Pero what does this have to do with Natasha?"

"Everything," La Bruja said flatly, clenching both fists as the city fell away.

"A bruja born with access not only to her own strength, but to the powers of another world and all its memories of a people who yearn to be free was a threat. I don't know how Trujillo found your prima. After all these years there were forces that pendejo was in conversation with that are from neither this world nor that and I don't want to understand them. Pero he knew, and he feared, and he called for Cuco to make his nightmare disappear. Pues, I hear they got him anyway, though?"

"They did," I said, not knowing how to feel and still hearing *monster, creature, power, bruja* on a loop in my brain. "Assassinated only a year or so after Natasha disappeared and Mami and Abuela fled the island."

"Mata dictador," the three of us said together; it wasn't planned pero it sounded like triumph, like a prayer.

"So, that's what you came from. That's what made Natasha dangerous, and it's what makes you dangerous," La Bruja said, looking me right in my eyes as La Negra drained back into the bottles. "Now it is up to you to decide what you want to do with that danger that lives in you."

Dangerous. I'd forgotten about that one, but the sound of it bounced around in my head like a fork stuck in the garbage disposal.

What would Mira Paredez do? I wondered. What would Carmen do?

I looked from La Bruja to Carmen. Carmen's face was mostly emotionless, but her toes were beating a tattoo in the dirt and her eyes looked . . . pues, hopeful but also desperate. Yo no sé if there's a word for that, but there should be.

I bit my lip and tried to push the curve of my shoulders back. I tried to look unafraid like Yaydil, like Minerva, like Mami, like Mira, like Carmen, pues, even like Lorena (nobody tell her I said that).

But I was tired of always comparing myself to everyone else.

"What would I have to do?" I asked.

La Negra snaked out of one of La Bruja's bottles like a long ribbon of black silk. The sand twisted and curled in my direction. When she finally reached me, La Negra wound herself around my palm, warm like sand that had been baking in the sun on a perfect summer day.

La Bruja smirked. "Easy part's over. Let's get you trained."

TWENTY-FOUR

"WHAT'S THE MOST IMPORTANT THING to remember?"
La Bruja sat cross-legged in the middle of the clearing, eating
arroz con gandules from a little wooden bowl.

"That we are partners and we are one. La Negra serves
me no more than I serve La Negra. We are the defenders of
memory, keepers of Zafa, when we move it will be as one
story among thousands, a single drop in . . . ay por favor!" I
said, punching my palm in frustration.

"We've been at this for two hours," said La Bruja, not
looking up from her food. "You're supposed to be a defender
of memory and you can't even remember this?"

I picked up some dirt and mashed it in my fist. The distraction helped me keep my mouth shut. Pues, La Bruja did
have a point, and I wasn't allowed to learn any of the basic
combat skills until I got it right. Some tontería about the
oath being about clarity of purpose, but really it just felt like

hazing. Plus, Carmen just got to nap the whole time back in the tent! Pues, the injustice!

"The rest of the oath?" La Bruja said, her fork finally scraping the bottom of the bowl.

"Umm . . ." I squeezed my eyes shut and tried to think it through again. A light breeze rattled through the trees and I was grateful that it wasn't raining anywhere inside La Bruja's compound.

"Some time today would be ideal." La Bruja jabbed the fork at me, a grain of rice flying off the end. "But by all means, keep moving como una tortuga through the rituals of my people, it's thrilling to observe."

I bit my lip, then took a deep breath. I would get it right this time. Anything to shut the vieja up.

"We are partners and we are one. La Negra serves me no more than I serve La Negra. We are the defenders of memory, keepers of Zafa, warriors when needed and only when needed. When we move, it will be as one story among thousands, a single drop in an ancient wave. We are one rhythm, a beat as old as the first note ever sung, we will move with purpose. We will fight, we will not forget."

When I reached the end, I felt my muscles relax and realized I had been holding my breath the whole time. Pero I could feel other things too, hear the chitter of small insects in the woods, smell the light clingy scent of moss climbing along a branch. I felt connected to everything, like I knew Zafa as well as I knew Logan Square back when it was still mine. That feeling like you know the story of everything around you and porque you know its story, it welcomes you.

"You missed the warriors part the first time, pero that was pretty good. Only my second-slowest student in the last thousand years. Congratulations," La Bruja said, eyeing her bowl for stray rice.

Look, I know she's the last of her people, the guardian of a millennia of tradition and power and magic, not to mention my teacher, pero damn that vieja was such a hater!

"So, do I pass?" I asked, not acknowledging the jab.

"Indeed, let's move on." La Bruja gave up her examination of the bowl and hopped off her stump. "There isn't time to teach you many of the higher forms and spells, but we can go through some basic combat forms."

"But I need more than training to save Natasha—I need *your* help." I tried to catch La Bruja's eye, pero she was having none of it.

"Basic forms. That's what there's time for," La Bruja bit back. "You worry about those. Y también, it won't be so easy to rescue your cousin; don't skirt over that part."

If I hadn't been so annoyed after two hours, I might have noticed that La Bruja's voice sounded sad and wary. Like there was something she wasn't willing to tell me yet.

"Pues, I mean I know it won't, vieja. Pero it will be much harder if we don't step up the training to more . . . practical stuff, right?"

"Fine. Don't listen to me. I've only been successfully

173

navigating this conflict since your abuela was a baby, maybe longer, since time functions strangely between our worlds. What do I know compared with the great and powerful vision of a pre-teen bruja trainee?"

What. A. Hater.

La Bruja sighed and uncorked one of the bottles, allowing La Negra to drift toward me and wrap around my palm in a complex pattern. All the connection I felt to la isla multiplied as each grain settled within me.

"What you're feeling right now, that's tumbao. Every grain of La Negra carries the rhythm of hundreds of stories. Everything that can be remembered since the first of the Tainos inhabited the land resides in her. Your task is to weaponize that memory."

"Okay, how do I do that exactly?"

"Think back to the words, La Negra sits like sand, pero she moves like water. Como el mar, when you strike it will be as . . ."

"A single rhythm."

"There's hope for you yet, Negrita," La Bruja chuckled. "Move in that rhythm, strike the targets as I put them up. Cast your Intention into La Negra and let her lash out at them."

As La Bruja spoke, the remaining sand in her other bottle streamed out and formed a series of targets.

"Close your eyes, concentrate on the tumbao, align your purpose with La Negra's, and strike when you are ready."

I focused on the rhythm of the sand, which felt like a beating heart on my palm. It aligned with my own heartbeat and La Negra warmed against me, like she was saying that we were ready. I opened my eyes and Intended La Negra toward the first target straight ahead of me. Quick as lightning La Negra was guided along my hand in a thick rope and smashed into the target.

"Well, well, well." La Bruja smiled. "A prodigy, in my very own fortress. Ready for another?"

Pero it wasn't a real question porque the second and third targets were already coming toward me on my left and right. I arced my hands out and the rope of La Negra swung through one target, then another like a stream of water. Pues, the corny oath was right; we were moving as one.

La Bruja's sand re-formed into eight smaller targets that advanced on all sides. I cast my hands out and my portion of La Negra formed a ring around me. I flicked both wrists out and the ring spun and expanded, demolishing the targets. I heard a sound, rickety at first like an old tree branch stretching in the wind, pero then I realized that it was La Bruja laughing. I called La Negra back to my palm and glared at La Bruja.

"Pues, there's no need to be rude. I thought I was doing okay!" I stamped my foot, trying to ignore the strange smoke smell in my nose. No time to worry about La Bruja's dinner right now!

"Ay, mija, lo siento," La Bruja said, steadying herself

against her tree trunk. "I'm not laughing at you. Te prometo. I just haven't seen anyone else do these exercises in a very long time y las memorias . . . pues, it warms my heart even if I think your and my daughter's little crusade with the Galipotes is doomed. It just makes me glad to have at least seen it one last time."

"Pues, it doesn't have to be one last time if you come with us!" I said, turning the charm up to "Lorena asking for car keys so she can stay late at the library and not take the L in the dead of the night" levels.

"Not an option."

"Porque, vieja?"

"You really need to stop calling me that," La Bruja dead-panned, and swung her locks out of her face. "You have any idea the kind of suerte you'd need to look this good at my age? And anyway, the Galipotes haven't tried to help me, so why should I help them?"

I was about to answer, pero the smoke smell was getting worse. I waved my hand in front of my face, but it didn't help.

"Pues, can you take whatever you're burning out of the oven?"

La Bruja's eyes went wide, all that playfulness emptying out of her as her body settled into hard lines. It was the first time I had seen her look afraid. I didn't like it at all.

"What do you smell?"

Pero there was no time to answer before a colossal boom shook the entire clearing.

TWENTY-FIVE

"HE'S HERE," LA BRUJA SAID through gritted teeth, already fishing in her bag.

There was only one "He" who could cause this much panic.

Sweat poured down the back of my neck. I clenched and unclenched my fists while trying to breathe deeply. El Cuco, the Dominican Boogeyman, paranormal dictator and collaborator with Trujillo himself, the creature who stole my cousin from my world and forced her into this one, was *here*.

"Take this." La Bruja tossed me what looked like a green leather water flask. "La Negra will be with you . . . if only we had more time I would have been able to tell you more about The Sight. No wonder he . . ."

"Vieja, slow down, how close is he?"

"He won't be able to make it all the way through the barrier," La Bruja panted, some grains of La Negra transferring from her bottles into the flask at my hip. "I'm going to meet him there and—"

Carmen swung down from a nearby branch, flipping twice in midair before landing on one knee like a superhero. Show-off.

"What's going on?" Carmen asked, cocking her head, a wild look in her eyes just like La Bruja's. I wondered if this was how the raid on Ciudad de Plata had sounded when it started.

"He's here. So you two need to leave," La Bruja said flatly. Then she started muttering a few words that I couldn't make out.

"How close," Carmen said, her eyebrows furrowing again as she handed me my backpack. It didn't sound like a question.

"Ask your friend," La Bruja said, still mumbling spells between her English. "She has The Sight."

"What is The Sight?" I asked. My knees shook so hard they kept knocking together like bony tambourines.

"Ancient but rare bruja ability. La Negra sees all and warns those with The Sight, guides them in times of crisis." La Bruja kept on with her spells, and suddenly her chanclas changed into a pair of badass combat boots with blue flames along the toes as she tied her locks back. "Normally doesn't come in fully until your three hundreds. Pues, you're more dangerous than I thought, no wonder Cuco came pers—"

BOOM!

Another explosion erupted, even more massive and closer

than the previous one. Without another word Carmen was off. She sprinted toward the source of the sound.

"Ay por favor esa valiant malcriada!" La Bruja cursed and surged after her at a wild pace for someone with gray hair.

"Y'know, nobody ever seems to walk anywhere on this payaso island unless they're imprisoned," I moaned.

I sprinted after the two of them, the smell of smoke thickening in my nose until it felt like I was choking. When I finally reached them, La Bruja Intended a ring of La Negra to surround herself like I had done earlier in the training exercise, pero hers also had long tendrils like an octopus. Carmen, meanwhile, just had her hands up and a murderous look on her face. They were facing a smoking hole, almost a perfect circle in the trees, branches hanging like stray locks of hair in front of a wall of green light.

And there, on the other side of the light, was El Cuco.

Pues, I'd never seen him before in person, pero it was unmistakably El Cuco. He had splotchy paper-white skin, beady eyes, and a thick black beard that curved in a sharp line down from his high cheekbones. His thin lips were puckered around a stout cigar that hung unlit from the corner of his mouth. El Cuco was shorter than myths had made him sound; pues, I don't know why I was expecting him to be eight feet tall, but he was maybe 5'10" tops.

He stood perfectly still in the little archway his explosions had created. As I took in his clothing, I felt the scowl deepen on my face; he was wearing a filthy old SIM outfit, the light brown military jacket of Trujillo's secret police. If I didn't hate him already, that would've been more than enough to show me he was the villain of the story.

"The famous Last Bruja," he cooed, striking a match against his palm and puffing a few small clouds from his cigar. "I hope I'm not . . . intruding on the festivities."

"You have no business here," La Bruja responded, La Negra's tendrils now rotating around her as if expecting an attack. "Leave or be destroyed. Your choice, furball."

A single wrinkle appeared across El Cuco's forehead, then rapidly disappeared. I smirked. Looked like La Bruja had struck a nerve. Pues, this dude wouldn't have made it ten minutes in *any* Chicago middle school lunchroom, entiendes?

El Cuco straightened his uniform and shook his head at the ground as if La Bruja were turning down a can't-miss deal.

"Fiery as ever, pero I think we'll be coming inside for the little bruja to your right. After all"—I didn't like the way the *r*'s rolled off his tongue, they sounded velvety and hypnotic like poisoned chocolate—"me and my employees have come such a long way, isn't that right, Baca?"

From the shadows emerged the massive dog-man that was El Cuco's right hand. Y pues, he was *exactly* as big as advertised, entiendes? Easily seven feet tall and covered with thick smoky black hair. El Baca's weepy yellow eyes peered out like search lamps. His arms were ropy with muscle, with hands like a human man's, except for the stubby black claws at the end of each finger. He growled and my blood went cold.

I hoped they couldn't see how much I was sweating.

But I was still gonna beat their butts, pues, we had home field advantage *and* it was three on two, classic mismatch.

"Nothing to say, Baca?" Cuco laughed, sounding like a Ricardo Montalban impersonator. He shrugged at us with an annoying grin. "Pues, a creature of few words, not so much like me, but the others tend to like him."

And that's when another one of those creepy baca children dropped down between the two villains before straightening and grinning a toothless smile. Then another dropped. And another. Y también that creepy bird settled on El Baca's shoulder, nuzzling him affectionately, which was somehow even creepier than the baca children.

"You can't have her," Carmen said, putting her arm around my shoulder. Her voice cracked a bit, but she still sounded determined. "I'll die before I let that happen."

"You know," Cuco said, releasing a stream of smoke between his lips, "the old me would have taken this as an opportunity to say something dramatic like 'That's the plan, mi amor' or 'We shall see about that,' but honestly, it was a very long journey and I've already missed out a couple times on catching this brujita porque we sent Cucitos to do a Cuco's job. The whole situation has me feeling un poco weary."

He pulled from the cigar again, the embers flashing in the egg-yolk color of El Baca's unblinking eyes.

"So, let's just cut the banter for once, por favor? We both know you're surrounded. So I will ask one last time, and I will offer you my word, una promesa worth its weight in gold." He pulled from the cigar until it was just a stump he tossed into a puddle. "If you hand over the little bruja, I promise not to make your death as dramatic as I would prefer."

TWENTY-SIX

"**NOT A CHANCE, BLANQUITO, YOU** and este maldito perro can go back to your little clubhouse, entiendes?" Carmen shot back, actually spitting into the dirt between her and Cuco in case it wasn't clear.

"¿Y quién eres tú?" Cuco said, looking unconcerned.

"Carmen Elena Danyeli Del Orbe. You murdered my parents."

"Well"—Cuco spread his pale hands in front of him—"that doesn't necessarily narrow it down now does it, mijita?"

What happened next happened so fast that I still don't know for sure if this is exactly how it went down, pero it's close enough, entiendes? Carmen let loose a grito that I didn't know she was capable of, and by the time I turned my head to her she was gone and sprinting toward what remained of the barrier. The green wall had weakened, and now all that remained of it was a sort of flickering orange energy. On the other side of the trees, I stared at El Cuco's grinning face as one of the baca children sprinted toward the barrier.

"WAIT!"

Me and La Bruja called in unison, y también we moved in perfect sync without saying a word to each other. La Negra poured out as a wall in front of Carmen just in time for two thunderous explosions to knock down another tree directly where Carmen had been headed.

With Carmen safe, La Negra shot back toward me and La Bruja. Pues, we had never covered that in my two hours of training, pero I felt like I was on fire learning the basics!

"Spoilsports!" Cuco laughed sharply, smoke parting like a curtain to find him just on the other side of the even weaker barrier; and down one child-shaped baca. My mouth fell open as I realized what he'd done.

"You sacrificed it?!" My voice came out in a squeak as the horror set in.

Cuco examined his nails with one hand and patted the grubby medallions of his SIM jacket with the other before fishing out a cigar. "Sacrificed, directed. Pues, es lo mismo." He shrugged like he'd just lost a hand of dominoes. "Either way, this barrier is coming down and you're coming with me, brujita."

I didn't say anything, just spat, even farther than Carmen, halfway wishing the barrier would come down long enough for it to hit him right in his beady eyes.

"You have to go," La Bruja grunted, and me and Carmen snapped our heads around.

"We can't just leave you—" Carmen started, but La Bruja silenced her with a look.

"You can, y también you must. I . . . I will hold them off, but the two of you must make it back to Minerva if your little crusade is going to survive," she said, not breaking eye contact with Cuco, who was searching for a match as more baca children dropped down. "He is just going to keep sending those abominations into the barrier. I can only hold them back for so long."

"Why can't you just come with us?" I pleaded quietly, not wanting to alert Cuco to the plan.

"Why can't we just fight him now?" Carmen pleaded, less quietly.

"Because someone needs to keep the back door open. Y because I promised your parents I would keep you safe," she said to Carmen, eyes full of fear and love. "And you." She turned to me. "You, I made no promises, but it looks like you're about to be the last bruja."

Tears pricked the back of my eyes, but I forced them down. Nothing wrong with crying, pues, Abuela says it's a sign of strength, but right now I needed clear vision.

BOOM!!

Another three baca children sprinted into the barrier. No trees fell, but the smoke cleared faster and I could see that the barrier was growing thin in places like an old blanket.

La Bruja, pues, I hated to admit it, was right; it was some of us or none of us.

"Where's the back door?" I sighed, defeated.

Carmen stared at me in disgust, then turned her head to La Bruja, wordlessly begging her to come with us.

"Don't give me that look." La Bruja had a small quiver in her voice as she turned to look at Carmen, as if for the last time. "You know what has to be done. You know what I prom—"

Carmen swept her into a fierce hug, the two embracing like they were trying to pull the other into their heart where they might be safe.

"All right, time to open the back door; listo?" La Bruja said, holding her daughter, my friend, at arm's length.

Carmen nodded and flicked a tear from her eye.

"Well, it's up to you two now. Vaya con suerte." La Bruja knelt and put both hands to the ground.

The forest floor roared open, a midsize hole swelling out and out like the ground had a black eye. Pero it was no black eye, it was La Negra tearing apart the dirt to reveal a tunnel below. My heart thudded in my chest as I flashed one last glance at El Cuco. Y pues, if you can believe it, he was slow clapping. God I hated him!

"Very touching, the sacrifice of the mentor to stall the inevitable defeat of the student." He struck the match, lighting his cigar. "Pues, un poco vieja, pero who am I to argue with the classics?"

La Bruja straightened up and balled her hands into fists.

A second later, Carmen took my hand and pulled me down into the tunnel as a howl that could only be El Baca split the air. I froze, fighting the urge to go back to the surface. My veins ran cold y también my mind was racing a mile a minute.

"It shouldn't be like this," I whimpered, "it shouldn't be li—"

And then the ground closed above just as one final explosion shook the dirt down into my eyes like thick black rain.

TWENTY-SEVEN

WE WALKED THROUGH THE TUNNEL in silence. I held the hot stone in my hands now that we didn't need to worry about the orange glow being seen. Pues, like everything else on Zafa, the tunnel would have been pretty if we weren't in mortal danger; just our luck.

The tunnel stretched for what felt like miles. It was full of earthy scents like rich soil and wet pebbles. La Negra held the dirt of the tunnel back from collapsing, snaking around roots to strengthen them, drawing intricate patterns around the rocks like the exposed brick in one of those hipster restaurants that are always getting set up in the factories that used to employ people around my block.

Carmen wore a grim expression, and even in the amber glow of the hot stone, her face looked ashen. She looked like she'd seen a ghost, or maybe she wished she could see one. Celeste's mom used to tell me that sometimes when a person is sad they need noise, but other times they have enough noise y esto is why they're quiet; de verdad there's only one way to know how much noise they need and that's for them to tell you when they're ready.

That's how I ended up carrying the hot stone. Carmen had carried it for the first mile, pero her hands were trembling and making it hard to see the ground in front of us.

"We should have gone back," Carmen said, finally breaking the silence.

I wasn't sure what to say. Carmen didn't stop walking even though I had. I speed walked to catch up.

"She was the only parent . . . the only family I had left y para qué? So I could abandon her to that glorified bloodhound and his master?"

"You were following her wishes."

"Ay and look where that got us! We're underground and days away from the Galipotes." Carmen let out a bitter laugh. "Pero it doesn't even matter and you know why? Porque we don't even have the one person we spent three days in carajoland to go and find!"

Carmen walked even faster, taking long strides out into the dark and melting into the shadows. I jogged to catch up.

"You didn't have a choice," I said softly, trying to grab her hand.

"And what does that matter?!" Carmen shouted, punching into the wall of the tunnel with all her might as she finally stopped her half jog.

I wanted to say something, pero everything I could think

of sounded mad corny in my head. Pues, what was I supposed to say? "You can honor her by winning this fight"? "It matters to me"? "I'll be your family"?

Pues, even though I meant all of those things, nothing would sound right in this half-lit tunnel. So, I decided not to use words. I put the hot stone in my pocket and offered my hand to Carmen—to the sister I'd found on another island—and squeezed hers while we stood in the dark, the tunnel echoing with the sound of her crying.

Carmen's sobs eventually receded, getting smaller and smaller like waves in a lake, until I saw her straighten and then she pulled me into a full-on, rib-cracking hug.

"Thank you, hermanita. I'm not okay, pero I will be. We—" She sighed. "We have to get back to Minerva and convince the Galipotes that they need to raid La Blanca. Hopefully the fact that you're some brujita who dropped from the sky will help convince them."

I cleared my throat and took the hot stone out of my pocket so that I could look Carmen in the eyes, the orange glow like a furnace turning her brown eyes to black.

"Pues, I want Natasha free same as anybody else. Actually, more than anybody else. But I'm not so sure I'll be enough to convince them. Didn't Gray Locks say that we would get steamrolled if we don't have La Bruja's help?"

Carmen's mouth twitched and I peeped that it was the first time that either of us had said La Bruja's name since the tunnel had closed above us.

"Pues, even with her, we were up against bad odds. Pero if they're going to take the city anyway . . ."

"We might as well hit the payasos where it hurts."

"Yup, hit them right in the prison!" Carmen grinned for the first time in hours as she punched her own palm. "Now, if only we were closer to the city . . ."

Her grin faded a bit, the half-light pulling her frown into long lines of shadows down her face. I felt the touch of La Negra along my arm, the beat of the tumbao pulsing against my palm until it felt like my own heartbeat. As I inhaled and exhaled in time with the warm black sand, I began to see things, not full images but like the starts of ideas and memories; the first syllables of words I guess La Negra expected me to finish. It felt like trying to watch a movie, but somebody kept hitting skip at all the wrong scenes.

"What are you trying to tell me?" I muttered, but in the small tunnel the words echoed so they sounded like three other Pilars were begging *tell me, tell me, tell me.* The tumbao picked up, faster now until I could make out individual images. A young bruja riding a wave, an avalanche, hands moving together, a maze of tunnels, another wave of that strange white ocean.

"Pilar, are you okay? What are—"

"Da me un minuto." The echoing Pilars called back *da me, da me, da me* and the tunnel sounded for a second like I was killing it on the dance floor. I never am killing it on the dance floor, pero maybe someday.

Bruja, wave, hands, wave, cart, avalanche, butterfly, butterfly, butterfly.

"WEPA!!! I understand!" I yelped, throwing my hands in the air and smacking a knuckle against a jagged rock. I sucked the cut with a wild grin on my face and looked at Carmen triumphantly.

"Hermanita," Carmen said, "I'm just going to say that if you go crazy on me in this tunnel, yo no sé que."

"I just used The Sight like a straight-up bruja! I know how we're getting back to Minerva!"

"Um yeah . . . me too," said Carmen, side-eyeing me. "We walk until eventually the tunnel is over y después de eso we walk some more."

"No, hermana." I laughed, a wicked grin spreading across my face. "I had, como se dice, something else in mind."

TWENTY-EIGHT

"IF THIS IS SUPPOSED TO be revenge for not giving directions when we were in El Bosque, lo sientoooooo!" Carmen cried out as we raced through the tunnel at breakneck speed.

"Pues, I'm not that petty. But thank you!" One of my arms churned back and forth in time with La Negra, pushing us forward with extraordinary speed, while the other arm held my camera on night mode. We zipped through the tunnels faster than a North Side white boy jumps into Lake Michigan when it's thirty-seven degrees in Chicago!

Once I'd worked out the initial kinks in the plan, it was actually really easy! La Negra was the heart of Zafa, so as La Blanca's corruption had begun to loosen her hold on the island after the prison was built, she created a series of underground tunnels in order to avoid being wiped out entirely. Pues, end of the day, La Negra was like Mami and Abuela and Carmen and any other Dominicana; a survivor to the very end, entiendes?

With the tunnels holding such a concentrated amount of La Negra's body and power, it was possible for me to use my bruja connection to churn the sand to propel us forward, like a boat on water. La Negra didn't tell stories with words, but feeling the tumbao between us I could see images of the tunnels ahead and could help steer the swirling black sand to the left or the right. Pues, we were moving at maybe triple the speed that we had when we were climbing and swinging through El Bosque and I was loving it!

"AHHHH, Pilar, I swear one of these rocks is going to take my head off! You gotta be more careful on the turns, hermanita!"

It was safe to say that Carmen was *less* of a fan.

"Y también how do you even know where we're going?" Carmen wheezed, narrowly ducking another rock. "At least when we were in El Bosque I knew where everything was!"

"Tranquilo, Carmen, La Negra knows the way and we'd never be able to move this fast aboveground!" I laughed.

And it was true, La Negra was honestly doing most of the work. We'd been at it for only a couple hours, but we'd already made a full day's progress back toward Ciudad Minerva! Was it also like my stomach was riding two different Six Flags roller coasters at the same time? Yes, pero no me importa! Every twist and turn of the tunnels brought us closer to the city and making a plan to save Natasha and get me home!

"You gotta just lean into the turns, hermana," I called back. "Pues, it's like riding a bike!"

"Riding a what?!" Carmen shouted as she crouched behind me.

Okay, bike was definitely the wrong word, and not just because Carmen didn't know what a bike was. It was more like being a wave, just like La Bruja had taught me, moving as one with all of La Negra's power and memory. The power that coursed through me was like nothing else in the world; like remembering every great summer day at once but for like, generations! The power, the speed, it was all carrying us on.

Pues, I get warm thinking on it even now; if that was what memory felt like when it's a weapon, I understand why every dictator ever fears it. For the first time, I felt dangerous and happy, and we zoomed through the dark toward the city, cutting through the distance like a knife.

TWENTY-NINE

"Y'KNOW, THIS CITY IS WAY more scenic when you're not a captive," I said as me and Carmen walked behind Gray Locks through Minerva, the sunlight on our backs.

"Pues, you weren't a captive the first time either, you know," Gray Locks said with a wink.

"The machetes said otherwise."

"Shouldn't have arrived in such dramatic fashion," Gray Locks said. "Either time."

Me and Carmen exchanged a quick glance, pues, she had us on that one. A couple minutes earlier we had erupted out of La Negra's tunnels at the city gates and been surrounded by machetes, again. The ciguapas thought the city was under attack, but luckily for them it was just us.

"Well next time we arrive I hope that I have less sand in my mouth." I sulked and spat a couple of grains out, then blushed when I saw a small boy staring at me like I was eight feet tall with electric blue hair.

He wasn't the only one, though. As we made our way up the main street of Ciudad Minerva, I could see how many people lived in the city, and how many of them knew immediately that I wasn't one of them. The air was heavy with the cries of vendors and the smell of fresh pastelillos floating out of colmados. Little children ran through the streets playing tag, but they stopped to stare as we passed. Pues, as rude as it was, so did other adults and even kids my own age. I mean one girl even stopped mid-bite on a pastelillo when she saw me walking by!

Were these all the children and grandchildren of people who had been stolen by the Trujillato? It felt so weird to think about how many people lived here purely because El Jefe had been afraid of some of these kids' abuelos or cousins. Did they still think of themselves as Dominicans even if they had never seen the island?

I mean, I guess I've never seen the island either, and I was also born in a strange place because Trujillo set his sights on Mami and Abuela and they made it out. If they hadn't, quién sabe who I would be?

Y de verdad, if Ciudad Minerva was a city of survivors, how many more were still in La Blanca? It made me feel a little like crying and a lot like fighting, and I walked even quicker behind Gray Locks, gritting my teeth and thinking again of what I would say, what I was asking the city to give up.

When we finally reached the Hall of the Galipotes, the

doors were already flung open as if they were expecting us. The four sisters stood before their high-back chairs as Gray Locks led us inside and down the long hallway to their stage. I was grateful the door was open; having a warm breeze at my back made me feel a little more confident, like the island was pushing me forward to pitch a plan that was feeling more and more like tontería with each step.

We finally stopped in front of the stage and gave a brief salute. I made sure mine was extra crisp, just like Carmen's. Gray Locks nodded in approval and stepped up to her normal spot next to the Galipotes, all of whom had black wings with silver patterns today. I wondered if they changed their wing colors every day or if they already knew the worst part of the coming news and were dressed for the funeral.

Minerva stepped forward first with a weird look on her face. She was smiling warmly, that always-wind moving through her shoulder-length curls, but her eyes were all fire, all fight, and her brows were furrowed like Celeste's get sometimes when she's trying not to cry. Minerva's face was holding three emotions all at once and she hadn't even heard my plan yet.

"Pilar, we're all so happy to see you again. I'm assuming . . ." She trailed off.

"La Bruja se murió," a small voice choked out to my right, and even though she was the only one who could have spoken, I still had trouble recognizing it as Carmen's; it sounded like she was saying it from the bottom of a well.

The Galipotes didn't gasp in shock or cry, but each of them bent their wings and bowed their heads sadly.

"I know, I know we had an agreement," Carmen continued. "I know the city will be in danger without her magic to help us keep it protected." She was shaking now, so I took her hand and gave it a squeeze to let her know I was there.

Carmen took a deep breath. "La Bruja died protecting us from El Cuco. She died protecting me, her only daughter." The sapphire on Carmen's resguarda flashed brightly in the sun above the collar of her uniform jacket. "She would want . . . she would want you to know the mission wasn't a total failure. That she didn't just die protecting me, she died protecting our only hope of bringing down El Cuco and taking back the island."

Tears were falling quickly down Carmen's face now. I wanted to hug her, I wanted to tell her this could all wait. I wanted her to have days and days to cry, but we were at war and there wasn't time to rest.

"What is this hope?" Galipote Dede said, smoothing her black dress and looking at us warily. But behind that worry her eyes carried the same fire as Minerva's. So did Maria Teresa and Patria. That's when I knew, they were ready for a fight too; they'd always been.

I picked up where Carmen left off, giving her hand a squeeze to let her know I could take it from there. "My name is Pilar Ramirez. I came from the other world, from my city, to rescue my cousin and destroy La Blanca. El Cuco has stolen my family, and Carmen's family, and the families of all the people living in this city. My cousin was a bruja and Trujillo feared her power, so El Cuco stole her before I was born, and nothing has ever been the same."

I let a stream of La Negra flow out of the bottle and settle along my arm in an intricate pattern like the wings of the Galipotes. Their mouths opened in surprise.

"I am Pilar Ramirez. I am a bruja. And I will rescue my cousin and bring El Cuco to justice, with or without your help."

THIRTY

I LET A SMALL SMILE twitch at the corner of my lips before trying to make my face blank again, como un soldado. Pues, I had enough trouble getting adults back home or even Lorena to listen to my plans seriously and they were only years or decades older than me, not centuries!

"La Bruja gave her life to save us, so that we could continue the fight. And she also handed us what could be the key to our victory. The only reason we escaped is because of a system of hidden tunnels that La Negra created under the island. This is how we turn the tide of this war. If we can use these tunnels to bring a small team to attack La Blanca, we can bring the prison down from the inside." I cleared my throat, then looked fiercely at the Galipotes.

Gray Locks nodded solemnly, which felt encouraging since if anyone was going to be the first to poke holes in the plan it would probably be her.

The Galipotes' expressions were more of a mix. Minerva's

eyes were glittering like when she'd first heard that some Cucitos had spoken to me in El Bosque. Her eyes flitted back and forth as if they were drawing an invisible map, counting troops and possibilities, but overall just excited for an opportunity to swing first for a change. Patria and Maria Teresa looked excited, but a little more reserved, like they were waiting for someone to agree with me before they could let themselves feel fully on board with the plan. Dede had a deep crease in her brow, the wind twisting and curling the silver strands of her hair.

"Did La Bruja tell you what awaits in La Blanca, Pilar?" Dede sounded far away. "Don't you think we've tried to bring it down before?"

I opened my mouth to answer, but Maria Teresa cut in.

"La Blanca is surrounded by acres of a razor-sharp cane field."

"We've sent patrols; some escaped, some didn't. None have ever even made it to the walls of the prison. Good people were lost." Dede shook her head at the floor.

"Good people were also lost trying to hold on to what we have, and more is lost by the day, by the hour," Minerva cut in. "If La Bruja believed Pilar was fit to lead this mission, believed in this plan, then we must try!"

"If La Bruja believed Pilar was fit to lead this mission, she would have said so," Dede bit back. "Has anybody said such a thing? No. I am willing to fight, I am no coward, but we have lives to protect beyond our own."

"And how much longer can we protect them? The fall of the city grows an inch closer every day that El Cuco sits atop that monstrosity poisoning the island. Our people know they cannot go beyond the walls; they love the city, pero, hermana, the city is becoming a cage," Minerva snapped back.

"And still, it is their home." Dede fought to keep the emotion out her voice. "Our home. Would you so easily give it up to the enemy? Without La Bruja the city can't be protected. Am I supposed to accept the deaths of a sister and my city all at once? For a suicide mission?"

"It's not a suicide mission if we work together!" I said, stomping my foot, sick of being ignored.

"One of us has already died pursuing this foolish plan!" Dede replied.

"La gente will accept our plan; do you honestly believe that none of them want to take up arms, that none of them have grown tired of living in fear? Don't you want to join them?" Minerva said, her face calm, her words hard.

"Of course I do!" snapped Dede, her wings fanning out behind her, huge and impressive. "Of course I do, but I won't allow you to get yourself killed. To get Carmen killed. To get Pilar killed."

"That's my choice to make!" I growled.

"Mine too," Carmen said angrily, wiping the last of her tears away.

"You see," Minerva said, wings spreading to the same size as Dede's, "we are out of options."

Patria finally broke her silence. "La Blanca's cane field likely goes deep into the ground to protect that abomination. So the tunnels can only get a squad *close* to the cane field undetected, rather than under La Blanca. Still, we'd have the element of surprise if our main force attacked from the opposite end while Pilar's strike team infiltrated the prison. A two-pronged attack . . .," Patria said, brow furrowing. "It would depend: If the strike team can't get past the patrols in the cane field then they are doomed; if they can then we stand a chance."

Patria crossed her arms matter-of-factly. Minerva's mouth crinkled with a grudging smile. Dede wasn't budging, though. I was mad that she didn't have faith in the plan, pero I could see how she was just trying to keep everyone safe también.

"Every day the enemy closes around us like a noose. We have lived either in retreat or under the fist of this tyrant for centuries. No más." The fire behind Minerva's eyes blazed as she turned to me. "Young bruja, you have my vote in this fight."

"And mine," Maria Teresa added.

"Yo también," said Patria.

"If we must fight," Dede said, her shoulders sagging with worry for her sisters, "then Pilar deserves to *know*."

"Know what?" Carmen said, looking confused.

Dede swept the silver streak of hair at the front of her face from right to left and stared around the now quiet hall. I clenched my jaw to hide the fact that I was afraid, pero I was.

I looked from sister to sister, each looking sorry, each saying nothing.

"Pues, what aren't you telling me?"

"We—" Minerva took a deep breath, like she was bracing herself. "The power that allowed Cuco to travel to your world . . . it's unique. We've never been able to replicate it by ourselves."

A trickle of understanding began to raise the hairs on the back of my neck. It couldn't be.

"Most of our strength, even now while we're talking to you," Patria started, "goes into reinforcing La Negra's barrier around the city."

"With La Bruja dead . . ." Minerva trailed off.

"We're afraid you may be stuck here, Pilar," Dede finished, looking drained and *sad*. "Forever."

The dread started in my stomach. Gray Locks and the Galipotes continued talking, but I couldn't hear any of it. I could feel Carmen at my side squeezing my limp hand. All I could think about was the knot in my stomach that made me want to bend over and vomit. Dede's voice echoed in my head, *forever, forever, forever*.

I could be stuck on Zafa forever? Y de verdad they'd known the whole time?

White-hot anger prickled under my skin as I felt Carmen squeezing my fingers again. I snatched my hand away from her—had Carmen known too? Would she really have let me risk my life knowing I might never get home anyway? I glared up at the dais, clenching my jaw so hard I was afraid my teeth would break. Tears pricked the corners of my eyes. I felt light-headed, but too angry to pass out también.

"I . . ." Pero nothing else came out of my mouth.

"Pilar, we—" Carmen started, but I was already sprinting through the huge double doors, tears streaming down my face until I could barely see.

I didn't know where I was going; this wasn't my city, wasn't my island, wasn't my world. All I knew was that I couldn't stand to be there another minute. I could barely inhale a full breath, my chest ached, but I didn't stop, couldn't stop, as I bolted out into the sunlight on the island I might be trapped on forever.

THIRTY-ONE

I FINALLY RAN OUT OF breath near a panadería. I curled up against the wall, hugging my backpack between my legs, the zippers rattling like tiny bells as I heaved. The smell of freshly baked bread drifted out of an open window above my head, the wet slap of dough hitting the table every few seconds. My chest was on fire, pues, who knew how long I'd been running or how far. I hiccuped a little from trying so hard to catch my breath.

What if they're right? What if I never get home and Mami thinks I ran away?

I remembered those nights after Papi died. There had been days that Mami wouldn't leave her room and the house was so quiet it was hard to breathe. Nights Mami would sit at the dinner table after I was supposed to be asleep and she'd cry very quietly into Abuela's shoulder so she wouldn't wake me and Lorena. Mami seems like she knows everything, pero I don't know if she knows that I saw that, that I notice how even now she stares at the door for a long time like Papi will walk in and kiss her and call her Mi Amor, just walk in as if nothing has changed, as if nothing will ever have to change again.

My eyes came back into focus a bit as another wave of dread snaked through my chest. I looked at the sky on the island, cloudless and blue like nothing was wrong. More tears fell down my face and I could feel the snot oozing onto my upper lip, pero I didn't care. I hugged my backpack tighter and kept looking up at that perfect blue sky. On the other side of it, Mami was waiting for me to come home and now I never would. Just like Natasha, I'd become a picture she looked at and cried over when she thought no one could see. Just like Papi, I'd become another pair of missing shoes by the door.

"It's all their fault!" I yelled, another wave of angry tears falling as I buried my face in my backpack. "It's everyone here's fault! Why didn't they—why couldn't they—"

Laughter, straight from the belly, interrupted me. Someone in the panadería had made a joke I didn't catch.

I clenched my jaw, full of anger. How dare anyone be happy when I felt like this? It made me so mad I could scream, I could unleash my powers and bring the whole building down and then another and another. I could, I had the power to, but I knew that I wouldn't.

What right did I have to take away all these people had ever known porque I was mad? That's what El Cuco would do and I didn't want to end up like him, no matter how sad I was.

"¿Quieres jugar?"

The voice caught me off guard and I scrambled up immediately prepared for a fight, pero it was just a little boy. He couldn't have been older than seven, with baby fat cheeks and wearing a faded blue-gray shirt and green shorts with no shoes. The boy held out a brand-new baseball, white as a tooth. He seemed to notice all at once that he had spooked me, and his shoulders sloped in.

"Lo siento," he mumbled. "I didn't realize you didn't want to play."

"I . . ." I opened my mouth trying to find my words. It was the first sound I'd made since I fled from the Galipotes' hall and still the words wouldn't come.

A shadow passed over both of us, quick like a seagull over the lake, and just like that Carmen was standing next to the boy. His face split into a big grin at the sight of her and I could see the pink of his tongue through the gaps in his teeth.

"Carmen!"

"Tomasito!" She grinned back, one eye still on me. I realized my fists were still up and slowly unclenched them. "¿Cómo te sientes?"

"¡Bien, tengo una nueva pelota!" He held it out to her like it was the coolest thing in the world.

"¡No me diga!" Carmen smiled at him the way grown-ups used to smile at me when I was a kid and would pretend to take their picture. "Well, Tomasito, we'll have to play sometime when I get back."

"Are you going away again?" Tomasito frowned.

"Yes." Carmen nodded and crouched to his level. "But one way or another, it's for the last time. Te prometo."

"Okay!" he said. "Should I have Papi make you a basket?"

"Not this time, mi amor." Carmen stroked his stubby black buzz cut. "Pero make sure he doubles up on the best pastelillos in Zafa when I get back. Right now I need to talk to my friend here, sound like a plan?"

Tomas did a pretty strong impression of a ciguapa salute, nodded at me briefly, and ran off, tossing the ball in the air ahead of him and running to catch it before it hit the ground.

Carmen turned to face me, muscles tensed like I was about to run off again. Y pues, it crossed my mind, but my legs were so tired y también I had nowhere to go, so I plopped back down in the street with my head resting against the wall of the panadería. I heard Carmen sit down next to me, but I still didn't want to look at her.

"Did you know?" I asked, surprised by how far away my voice sounded.

It was quiet between us for a moment, the wind whipping the fresh baked bread smell away from the alley.

"No, pero I . . . had my suspicions," Carmen finally said. "But, Pilar, I need you to understand."

Anger surged through me, white hot all over again and itching beneath my skin.

"You need *me* to understand!?" I snapped my neck sideways to face her. "I may be trapped and separated from my family on this island, forever. Pero you need *me* to understand?!" I let out a quick bark of laughter even though nothing was funny. "Please, this ought to be good. You tell me what you *need* me to understand about you lying to me so I would help you with your revolution."

"I didn't lie," Carmen said, voice sharp. "I am a spy and a ciguapa, look at me! I'm designed to mislead people, to be hard to follow. Pero I promise you, Pilar, hermanita—"

"Don't call me that," I hissed. She didn't feel like my sister anymore. Lorena may be . . . well, Lorena was just annoying, she never would lie directly to my face.

"Fine," Carmen said, blinking twice like she'd just been slapped. "Pilar, I know you're mad and I may never be able to make it up to you. But can you please just hear me out on this, por favor. After that, you never need to talk to me again, deal?"

I didn't say anything back, but I didn't leave either.

"There hasn't been a new arrival on Zafa for decades," Carmen said, pushing each word out very slowly like she was afraid I might bolt at any moment, "and then you came along y pues, I didn't know you were a bruja, but I knew you must be special if the Cucitos were after you."

Carmen paused for a second and looked at me like she was asking for permission to keep talking. I gave the tiniest nod I've ever given, and she continued.

"Every day that we are here, the island is snatched a little farther away from us. Every day we get a little closer to losing this war and nobody seemed willing to make a run at cracking open that monstrosity Cuco has been poisoning Zafa with for as long as I've been alive." Carmen sighed. "I don't know if you have this effect on people in your world, but you make people want to fight."

If I'd been in a better mood, I would have pointed out that I do, technically, have that effect on people in my world. But the vice principal calls it a "disciplinary issue" and a "deep-seated problem with authority."

"Once you arrived, the Galipotes were *finally* willing to let me find La Bruja, all of them. You know how long I've been trying to get them and La Bruja to make amends? That was all because you fell out of the sky. And I'm just a spy, not even a unit commander, so what do I know about the limits of the Galipotes' power except that they're not willing to leave the city and its people vulnerable? I figured maybe with no threat left they wouldn't need to use so much energy to protect us, maybe they'd be able to get you home."

"And what if La Bruja had survived?" I snapped. "What if she'd survived and still refused to help? I would be stuck here, caught up in your war."

"Pilar, I'm going to say something you might not like, pero maybe you need to be reminded. It's not just my war, it's our war."

"*Our* war?" Blood thudded through my eardrums. "I wasn't in this when the week began in my world."

"But you were," Carmen said, taking a deep breath. "I wasn't completely honest with you when the mission started, and I'm sorry for that, pero you need to admit that you wouldn't have taken the mission if you didn't know in your heart that this is your war too. Hermana, they stole your island like they are still stealing mine, they stole your cousin like they stole my parents, your life is different forever because they chose to do that. Like it or not, this war is yours too. You might be stuck here for good, only you can decide what to do with that; but you must decide before the enemy decides for you, so what's it gonna be?"

I thought about Natasha, her cramped handwriting in her journal, how she slept always afraid that the boots of soldiers would kick in her door. How they took her mother, then they took her.

When my mother had been a child on her island, there was nowhere safe for her to be a daughter, and now the same was true on Carmen's island. I was still mad she hadn't told me the whole truth, mad that I may be trapped, may never see Mami or Abuela or my room ever again. But Carmen was right; I was born in America because Trujillo and El Cuco took a shot directly at my family. I couldn't imagine living under the boot of El Cuco, always scared that today would be the day he found me.

"All right," I said, standing up slowly. "If you promise never to lie to me again, I'm in."

"Are you sure? This plan might kill us all," Carmen said.

And I knew she meant it, that I could walk away and she would understand.

Pero I didn't want to walk away. I wanted to make El Cuco pay for what he had done to my family, for every tear Mami and Abuela had shed over Natasha and every tear they might shed over me. I shivered, cold sweat beading down my neck, thinking of him in his dirty SIM uniform. I wanted to break everything he owned, piece by piece.

"You're right, the plan might kill us." I reached out my hand. "But if we don't stop them, the dictatorship definitely will. So let's go kick his butt and free my cousin."

"Now that"—Carmen grinned—"sounds like a plan."

THIRTY-TWO

ONCE I RETURNED TO THE Hall of the Galipotes and told them I was down to help with the raid on La Blanca, the four sisters thanked me and nodded at Gray Locks, who gave a crisp salute and sprinted out of the hall to sound the alarm. Pues, didn't even take five minutes before a siren rang three short bursts. Three of the Galipote Sisters flew up to their quarters to get dressed for battle without a backward glance, but Minerva stuck around for a second.

"Gracias, Pilar, I don't know if we will all survive this, pero you've given us a chance to fight. I'm sor—"

Pero I held up my hand, then threw it into the strongest ciguapa salute I could manage. Minerva nodded and flew up after her sisters, dark black wings beating the wind back against my face.

I went outside to see all the citizens of Ciudad Minerva rushing and zigzagging around one another. I pulled out the camera to capture a few scenes, pues, quién sabe if we would ever get to see the city again, or if I would ever get home to show people what I'd seen. Pero this was what Mira Paredez would do, y también it's what Pilar Ramirez would do; capture the truth until you can't.

To my left two men held their son as they rushed to stuff a bag of rice into a raggedy-looking suitcase. Up the street a woman who sold mangoes was hurriedly handing them out to anyone who passed by. A young girl hustled after her parents with one shoe half on. Everyone had looks of terror stuck on their faces, brows knit together, arms shiny with sweat. Pero the kinda freaky part was that nobody looked like they were panicking; they knew where to go and what to do.

"The Galipotes run drills every three months to keep everybody sharp," Carmen said, putting a warm hand on my shoulder. "Y también, many of the adults come from fallen cities and have been through one of these evacuations before."

Pues, I hoped I'd never become that practiced at leaving my home because the enemy is coming.

Twenty minutes later we were in the armory. A ciguapa with a buzz cut named Dilcia tossed me a dark green jacket made of thick material and some black pants with a belt built in.

"The cane field that guards La Blanca is razor sharp," Dilcia explained. "This material will keep it from cutting you, entiendes?"

I nodded and slipped the jacket on. It was pretty light and fit really well. I made a note to see if I could get a couple more if we made it out of this.

All around the armory grown-ups were getting outfitted with the same gear. Some looked nervous, but most looked like they were ready to pounce. Yo no sé what I looked like, pero I hope I looked half as fierce as them.

"Oye, Brujita." Dilcia knocked hard on the table to get my attention, then handed me a package. "General says this is for you. The sisters had it made special while you and Carmen were in the forest."

I opened the long oak box and found a machete perfectly sized to my hand. I took it out and weighed it in my palm.

"Unsheathe it." Dilcia smiled, running her hand over her dark brown head. "Pues, it's some of my finest work."

The blade was polished like a mirror with a black edge along the blade. Immediately I felt the tumbao pulsing through my blood. Carmen whistled over my shoulder.

"Pues, que guapa, I haven't seen a blade like this since . . ." Carmen trailed off.

"That blade will put down a baca in seconds, estoy tan orgullosa de esto. No chance it hurts anyone on our side también, a perfect blade if I do say so myself! They only give those out to the bravest among us," Dilcia explained while handing another woman a pair of steel-toed boots and a machete. "You see the inscription?"

I turned the blade over to one side where it read *Recordamos*, and on the other side *Catorce*.

"Why 'Catorce'?" I asked, letting the light move over the words. Dilcia blinked as if she didn't understand.

"Porque that's your code name; you're an honorary ciguapa now. All of us got code names."

I looked at the blade again and thought about how the Mirabal Sisters fought for the Movement of the *Fourteenth* of June. They didn't have special powers; their magic was that they refused to live in a cage any longer. And the Galipotes had given me the name *Catorce*.

Holding that machete, I felt powerful, I felt loved. I thought of how Mami called me "Negrita," how Carmen called me "hermana," how me and Celeste called me "Purp." I guess that's the cool thing about love, your parents name you the big time, pero when you're loved you can get named again and again.

I sheathed the machete. It slid in easy and made a sound that hummed like a song.

"Okay, so is everybody good on the plan?" I said to the people huddled in the quiet.

I stood in front of hundreds of mothers and husbands and children, and I felt twelve again for the first time in hours. Pues, what if they didn't trust the plan that a seventh grader from another land was asking them to risk their lives on? Tomasito's eyes were locked on me, huge and orange in the glow of the hot stone.

The ciguapas and I had agreed with the Galipotes that it made the most sense for the citizens who couldn't or didn't want to fight to hide in La Negra's tunnels. But we were asking many others to risk their lives for the cause.

An older guy walked forward. He couldn't have been older than Papi, sporting a big gut that pulled his guayabera close against him.

"I think," he spoke slowly, slicking down his mustache, "I speak for everyone when I say, they took our daughters and abuelos and tíos; about time we took something from them."

The people behind him nodded in agreement.

"I need to stay back here to look after Tomasito. Pero I hope you kick that monster right in the teeth!" The man crossed his arms and a huge cheer rattled the walls of the tunnel.

"¡Mil gracias!" I nodded before adding, "And I will!"

I knelt before Tomasito who held tight to his new baseball.

"¿Tienes miedo?" I asked.

Tomasito shook his head.

"Good, porque I need you y tu papá to look after these people. And I have a special mission for you, can you handle it?"

Tomasito nodded this time, eyebrows arched like he was wondering what I meant by "special mission." I handed him my backpack.

"Inside here is the most important thing in the world to me. You have to be very gentle with it. Think you can keep it safe for me until I get back?"

Tomasito nodded one more time with a huge grin and ran off to find his father.

I turned and sped down the tunnel to where Carmen and a squad of seven ciguapas lay in wait to ride La Negra's tunnels toward the cane field. It felt strange not having the backpack, the camera; pero we were headed into the fight of my life and there was no time to look back.

THIRTY-THREE

THE RIDE THROUGH THE TUNNELS to the edge of the cane field passed mostly in silence, pues, even the tumbao seemed quieter. The ciguapas sat with grim looks on their faces as we slid left and right. One ciguapa, even younger than Carmen, who everyone just called Fina, sharpened her machete and hummed a song to herself, but even that petered out a few miles in.

Eventually the tumbao faded more and a string of images shot through my head. *Razor, sky, knife, knife, cage* and then in full HD an image of a field. The field stretched for miles in every direction with stalks easily twice my height. Abuela has shown me black-and-white pictures of the fields where Abuelo used to work. In one, he's smiling while standing at the edge of the field with a basket and a bottle of water. She says the top of the cane fields can be as green as an emerald; so green it hurts your eyes. Pero there was no green in my vision, just acres of white. I wasn't there, pero I could smell the memory, and it smelled like death.

"Why'd we stop?" Fina grunted from the back as La Negra slowed to a crawl.

"Oye tonta," said another ciguapa. "Let the brujita do her job so we can do ours."

"I'm just saying," Fina started up, voice cracking.

"We're here," I said. "This is as far as the tunnels can take us."

"Then we go up," said Carmen, speaking for the first time since we entered the tunnels.

I thought in sync with La Negra and pulled open a hole above us. Each ciguapa climbed through, except Fina who insisted on jumping. According to Carmen, she was a prodigy just like her. She even looked like a younger version of Carmen, with dark brown skin, her mouth always pulled a little to the side with a cocky smirk. Fina had refused to take no for an answer on being part of the strike team. While we infiltrated from below, the main force of the Galipotes would press toward La Blanca from the opposite side of the cane field to create a distraction.

After the last ciguapa had gone through the hole, Carmen reached back to pull me up with the other seven warriors.

"Everyone stick tight, head on a swivel, and communicate where you are. Nobody goes silent, then nobody gets left behind, bueno?" Carmen said, voice tough and curt like Gray Locks. Everyone nodded so Carmen continued. "We've waited for a shot like this for centuries; let's teach that furball and his damn dog some manners!"

Twelve minutes later we were at the edge of the cane field, y pues, call me a liar if you want, but the stalks seemed even taller than the memory. You couldn't even see La Blanca, just the huge stalks swaying in the wind.

"Catorce." Fina tapped me on the shoulder. "Can you use your machete to carve us a path?"

"I could, I think," I said, mulling it over. "Pero stealth has to be the priority. The main force is trying to buy us some time to try and bring down the prison from the inside and I think they'll notice if part of the field starts falling on the opposite side."

Everyone nodded and followed my lead as we put up our hoods and checked one another one last time for any inch of exposed skin that the cane might cut.

"Recuerdas," Carmen said, facing the group. "Nobody goes quiet . . ."

"Nobody gets left behind," we all responded as one.

I ran point of the group, hand on my machete as we quietly moved through the tight openings in the cane stalks and toward the prison where Natasha was waiting.

The first thing that struck me about the cane field was how I immediately lost sight of the rest of the squad. The stalk pressed in tight on either side like it was rush hour on the L. It was hard to fully inhale without snagging the protective jacket on some cane. I could hear the footsteps of the ciguapas behind me, sticking in a tight formation, and hear Carmen muttering to my left, pero other than that, the cane was all I could see. Something was very wrong about this place; the air was filled with a sickly sweetness like rotting fruit. Pues, it was just like La Negra's memory—the whole place smelled like death.

I shifted my right hand to grip the polished wood handle of the machete and felt a powerful urge to whip it out and slash the whole field down. It pulsed in me, not the tumbao, but just a need to kill whatever was making it so hard to breathe.

"Pilar, you okay, hermana?" asked Carmen.

I took my hand off the machete, stopped walking, and craned my neck to face Carmen.

"Yeah." I shook my head to clear away the haze. "But there's something . . ."

"Wild ugly about this place?" Fina offered, glaring at a stalk of cane like it had insulted her entire family.

"Pues, not even that, pero also yes?" I said, trying to put my finger on it.

"I've heard rumors about this," said a deep voiced ciguapa to Carmen's right. She adjusted her hood until all you could see were her gray eyes. "The field has some kind of curse on it to drive people mad. Pues, nobody ever confirmed it porque the scouts we sent in the early days of the war . . . never came back."

I felt a bead of sweat trickle down my neck and my vision narrowed. My chest felt tight and I gripped the handle of the machete again just to feel a little more balanced.

"The curse starts by making you feel like you're completely alone. Eventually it wears you down until all you can think about are the worst things you've ever done. Enemies of El Cuco feel more and more isolated until eventually they lose the trail out, y se fue." She drew her finger across her neck and winced when one of the sharp leaves pricked her.

We all stood there, perfectly still, while dread sat like a lead ball in my stomach and I started to hear my pulse in my ears.

"All right," Carmen called out, trying to re-center everyone. Pero at that exact moment three things happened:

1. A massive explosion boomed from the other side of the field, signaling that the main force of the Resistance had arrived.
2. The shriek of a baca child ripped through the air as we clamped our hands down over our ears.
3. Something cut through the cane to my right and tackled me screaming to the ground.

THIRTY-FOUR

PUES, JUST WHEN YOU THINK you've seen everything, you get pinned down and look up to see the face of a skeleton glaring down at you. Deep brown eyes leered out of its skull as the skeleton screamed in my face. Its breath smelled like five dumpsters having a kickback at an onion convention, so gross!

I wrestled one of my hands free and clocked the thing clean across the jaw and sent it sprawling backward into one of the cane stalks.

Thank god for ciguapa-strength gloves.

I scrambled to my feet as another enormous boom sounded and I looked around. The ciguapas, including Carmen, were all locked in fights with at least one baca child who had leapt down from the top of the stalks.

I reached for my machete and then remembered I had a problem of my own, 206 bones worth wearing the tattered remains of a SIM uniform charging right at me. I dodged and tried to roll to the left, but the skeleton clipped my shoulder and I hit the ground hard as the machete bounced off my belt and out of reach. I looked up and pues, I swear I saw the skeleton grin, and if you've never seen something grin at you without any lips . . . let's just say I don't recommend it.

"PILAR!!" Carmen called out, voice cutting clear through the howls of the baca child she had forced into a headlock. "I'll be right over, just give me a sec."

Pero, I didn't have a second as the skeleton drew an enormous machete from behind its back and charged a third time.

"I'm getting really sick of this," I grunted, and uncorked the bottle of La Negra slung around my back and took a deep breath.

I imagined I was back in the jungle sparring with Carmen, focusing on my breath and letting the scene before me slow down.

Y pues, I could count the skeleton's steps as it charged, see the curve of its blade. I Intended La Negra out in a concentrated stream like a whip that smacked the skeleton's machete hand clean off its arm!

Moving as quickly as I could, I cast another rope of black sand that tripped the thing and it crashed into the dust. As a baca child was hurled over my head with a yelp, I directed La Negra to where my machete lay on the ground. The black sand responded immediately and tossed my machete perfectly into my outstretched hand. I plunged it into the back of the skeleton, which howled as steam poured from its eyes.

There was no time to celebrate, though. I looked up and saw the rest of the squad still locked up with the baca children. La Negra was wrapped around my left arm, leaving my right arm to wield the machete as I yanked the blade free from the skeleton. I sliced through one baca child as it turned to face me, reducing it to ash as I charged toward my squad.

Pues, I'd need to remember to thank Dilcia if we got out of this! This machete was amazing!

"PILAR!" Carmen called as a baca child had her pinned to the ground. "Heads up."

Carmen hauled herself forward, narrowly avoiding a stalk of cane cutting her face. She somersaulted over the baca, catching it squealing by the head, and hurled it toward me. I smacked it with my machete like a baseball.

Within five minutes, me and the squad had cleared out the rest of the attacking baca children. The shadow of that massive bird passed over our heads, briefly eclipsing the sun as it streaked off toward the prison.

Carmen spat on the ground and dusted herself off. "So much for the element of surprise."

"Pues, I'll say," Fina groaned, working her shoulder in a circle.

"More troops will be converging on this spot soon. We'll need to move to avoid more of . . . this," said one of the ciguapas, who sported a nasty cut above her left eye. She kicked a skeleton in disgust.

"What was that thing?" I panted, pointing my machete at the skeleton.

"Dios santificado," whispered the gray-eyed ciguapa. "I didn't want to believe it."

"Pues, more rumors?" Fina winced.

"Hush, Josefina!" said the ciguapa nearest her. "Go on Yami, qué es esto?"

Yami walked over to the skeleton and kicked it over so the front of its uniform was visible. The deep brown eyes that had glared at me out of its skull were gone, replaced by two dark holes where all that hate had been. A name tag on the left side of the uniform read *Rubirosa* in black thread.

"These are The Machetes," Yami said flatly, mouth curling in disgust as she read the name. "The worst of El Jefe's personal entourage guard this field and La Blanca. Their souls are bound to this abomination by the agreement between Trujillo and El Cuco. So long as La Blanca stands, so do they."

"Why would anyone agree to that?" Fina piped up.

"Pues, mija," Yami said with a half shrug, "men do strange things to their souls to feel like they hold the world in their hands even for a moment."

"Y también," added another ciguapa, "El Jefe probably didn't tell them this is where their deal with the devil would lead them."

Panic flooded through me as the conversation continued. I dropped the machete to the ground. I looked between Carmen and Yami, who were mouthing words to each other that I couldn't quite catch. I was too zoned out to hear them.

"Pilar, are you okay?" Carmen asked, staring at me with a worried look.

"I . . . killed someone?" I finally sputtered out.

Pues, even if he was an evil human being, I felt a surge of guilt. It had all happened so quickly, and I hadn't thought twice about it because I assumed it was just another type of baca. What was war making me into?

"No," Yami said firmly. "These men are bound here by their deaths for as long as La Blanca stands. You sent his soul to El Odio, pero it will find its way back to this . . . thing." She kicked it again.

I felt a bit of relief at that, pero still, I didn't like how this made me feel. I shook my head and tried to focus.

Carmen's hand squeezed my shoulder. "It was him or you, and we would all choose you too. Are you going to be okay to finish the mission?"

I looked in her eyes and saw it was a real question.

"Yes, we have to do this. For Natasha. For the people of Zafa. For all those we've lost. We only get one shot at this thing. That bird will be on its way to snitch to El Baca, so let's get moving before those reinforcements show up."

"You heard the bruja," Carmen called out. "We don't have

much time, so let's hustle forward and see about bringing this place down!"

I picked the machete off the ground and walked to the front of the group and swung through a stalk of cane and watched it fall.

"I'm coming, Natasha," I said under my breath. "Even if I have to cut down this whole field, I'm coming."

THIRTY-FIVE

IT WAS A LONG MARCH through the cane fields as the sun rose higher in the sky and sweat dribbled into my eyes, stinging like needles. The going was easier now that we didn't have to worry about moving stealthily around the cane and it felt good to push the machete through that evil place, even if my arm was getting tired. It'd been mostly quiet since the two explosions, which made me nervous porque ever since I had gotten to Zafa, quiet had only brought bad news.

I think Carmen felt the same way because every twelve steps she did an elaborate call-and-response whistle to make sure the whole group was still with us. It made me feel better, knowing they were there watching my back, pero I could still feel the curse of that lonely cane field pressing against my temples. How many more miles was this place?

"Hermana," Carmen whispered so only the two of us could hear, "you look like something's bothering you, qué fue?"

I gritted my teeth and swung through another stalk as we marched closer toward La Blanca. Then I sighed; if I was asking Carmen to always be honest with me, I had to do the same.

"I'm worried about how easily I stabbed that Machete. Killing shouldn't be so easy."

Carmen gave another whistle and the squad whistled back.

"Pero you didn't kill him you just—"

"But I thought that I did," I muttered. "I thought that I did and I—"

"Don't know what that means?"

"Yup." I hacked down another stalk. "I don't want to be a monster like them."

"You're not," Carmen said firmly.

"How do you know?" I asked.

Carmen whistled again and another seven whistles came back in sequence.

"Porque I know you," Carmen said under her breath, "and there's a difference between killing un inocente and putting down a demon who was trying to murder you, hermanita."

I could see the logic in that, and it made my head hurt a little less.

"Mira," Carmen continued, "I know war is new to you. I know it feels terrible not to have many choices. Pues, I don't even know if fight or die really counts as a 'choice,' entiendes?"

Another whistle, another seven responses.

"Pero I need you to trust me, Pilar, you are doing the best you can with the choices you have and there's honor in that."

I nodded and hacked down another stalk and switched hands to give my right arm a break. "Are the Galipotes expecting me to kill El Cuco?"

Carmen was quiet and I turned my head to look at her, brow furrowed in concentration.

"I don't know, hermana, are you expecting you to kill him?"

I paused for a long time. "I'm not sure," I finally said.

"I won't tell you what to do," Carmen said slowly, like she was holding back something she wanted to say, "pero just make sure he pays."

I nodded as I hacked down one more stalk.

And just like that there was no more field in front of us, only about six yards of bleached sand and then a wall so white it hurt my eyes to look directly at it.

"There it is." Carmen grimaced, all color draining from her face. "We made it."

In front of us, huge and windowless like a grave, stood the prison. La Blanca.

THIRTY-SIX

TRY AS THEY MIGHT, THE carvings in the Hall of the Galipotes didn't do justice to how massive La Blanca actually was.
Smooth, windowless white walls reached hundreds of feet into
the sky. Looking right at it made my eyes water like I was
staring directly into a flashlight. The walls of the prison were
ringed with barbed wire, and we could see, even at a distance, that each barb was red hot. I imagine by night that they
would glow like the ends of cigars, a red bloody crown in the
dark. And punching into the sky above it all, a single tower
glared down at the entire island.

Pues, I knew Cuco must be up there, and a wave of anger
ripped through me as I thought about kicking his butt for all
the pain and misery he'd caused. He had to pay for what he'd
done. There needed to be justice. There was just one problem.

"How do we get in?" Fina questioned.

"Dang it." I spat, lowering my hood as if that would make
a door suddenly appear. "There has to be a way in."

"¿Pero dónde?" Yami grunted. "This abomination is nothing but walls."

We all walked closer, poised for a fight, so we could inspect closer, but no dice. We could hear the clash of the Galipotes with El Cuco's army on the other side of the prison, the occasional massive boom rattling the cane behind us, pero at this point we didn't know whose side the explosions were on.

I kicked at the sand in frustration. La Blanca wasn't just guarded by the cane field or bacas or even by The Machetes; the prison itself was a barrier.

"If prisoners can enter, there has to be a way in," Carmen said, punching one of the white walls with all her might.

I was about to suggest we either dig under the wall or join the fight with the main force and hope for an opening when we all heard a rumble coming from the walls.

"GET BACK!" Carmen hollered. "BACK TO THE FIELD!"

We sprinted back to the field and peered out from between the stalks as the wall in front of us opened wide as a mouth with a sound like ten thousand sheets of paper ripping at once. A troop of maybe forty-five Cucitos was waiting on the other side, jaws dripping with saliva and led by another of The Machetes. The Machete spoke with a dusty voice, like it hadn't sipped a drop of water in a hundred years.

"We take the Mariposas from behind," The Machete said,

teeth clicking together after every word like a fistful of dominoes. "We break them here and bring the maldito sisters to El Cuco."

"Well, I say we can kill two bacas with one stone here," Carmen whispered loud enough for only the squad to hear. "Yami, let's ambush their ambush. You'll take down that bag of bones while Pilar and I slip inside."

"Hermana"—Yami smiled—"you read my mind. Pilar, you like the plan?"

"No," I said, smiling. "I love it."

"Wepa!" Fina punched her hand into her palm.

And just then the massive Bird baca dove from the wall of La Blanca, soaring directly toward us. The Machete's head snapped around 180 degrees.

"Y'know," Carmen sighed, cracking her knuckles, "just once this mission I'd love to *keep* the element of surprise."

"INTRUDERS!" The Machete cried. "SEIZE THEM!"

And with that the battle was on! With a howl of rage, ciguapas and Cucitos charged toward each other as me and Carmen sprinted toward the opening in the walls of the prison. Cries of pain rung out as teeth met armor, fists found bone, and all I wanted was to turn and fight, pero there was no time porque Carmen wouldn't let go of my arm.

"Hurry, Pilar!" she shouted.

Twelve yards ahead of us, the wall of La Blanca was closing back up. We might not get another chance to slip inside.

I forced more oxygen into my lungs as white sand flew up from the battle occurring all around us. Ten yards. The wall was still knitting itself together as I felt a stitch open on my left. Five yards.

"SLIDE!" Carmen gasped and we both dove through the hole, away from the noise, and then it was silent, so silent, as the wall sealed behind us.

THIRTY-SEVEN

INSIDE LA BLANCA, HUNDREDS OF stark white cells were stacked on top of each other. Pues, I wish there was a metaphor, a way to make people truly *see* the horror of this place; pero there are no metaphors for a wall of cages full of stolen people. Each cell held a person inside, some pacing and others merely sitting in a corner, staring at nothing. I looked at Carmen, she looked back at me. We were inside, and we were on our own now.

"We have to get to the tower." Carmen frowned, breathing hard like she'd just sprinted three miles.

"How do you know?" I gasped back, wishing I had packed some water.

"Pues, I don't." Carmen winced. "No ciguapa has ever made it this far and not been caught. Pero, if the place only has one ridiculously big tower, I have a feeling that they probably keep something important in there."

"That's real, maybe there's a key so we can free these poor people," I added. "And find Natasha."

"There's fewer guards than I thought; the majority are probably all out fighting the main force."

"Pues, let's make it count. If we're going to bring this place down, then we need to make sure the prisoners are safely out of here first."

And we were off, jogging down the hallway past the cells and searching for a staircase. The prisoners of La Blanca stared out from their cells as I looked left and right, hoping one of them was Natasha, but none were. I saw a balding man staring at me, but not *seeing* me. Another woman with thick eyebrows kept picking at a spot on the wall of her cell.

"The curse of the cane field must go double for them here," I whispered to Carmen as we hit a fork in the hallway and headed left. "I can't imagine spending an hour here, let alone years, even decades."

As we navigated the cells, I felt my vision flicker with The Sight again, pero it was all wrong like a bad TV signal. Pues, of course La Negra was full of static and pain in La Blanca. I gripped my flask of La Negra and the images settled. I saw that they were all the same this time. *Key, key, key.*

"Pilar?" Carmen said, gripping my shoulder. "You stopped walking, you okay?"

I nodded distractedly. I understood what La Negra was saying, but I didn't understand how she expected me to open the cells. I didn't have the key. The key image flickered from sight like a dying candle. Pero right before my vision went back to normal, I saw one last image, a few grains of dark sand falling down. Pues, I understood, but I wished that I didn't.

"We have to let them out," I said through gritted teeth.

"I know, that's why we have to beat El Cuco. That's the whole plan."

But I shook my head; this needed to be handled immediately. I walked to the nearest cell, where a woman about Mami's age gazed dejectedly at the wall. I reached my hand out toward the cell door and a few grains of La Negra floated out of the flask.

"Mil gracias for your sacrifice," I whispered to the grains, to La Negra.

As soon as La Negra touched the cell door, it wrenched open with a shriek that echoed in the clammy half-light. My palm seared with a wave of pain, like warm needles moving beneath my skin, up my arm. And then it stopped, but I could feel La Negra weaken, like a part of her had died. The grains of La Negra fell to the ground, small and gray as ash.

"How did you . . . ?" Carmen asked, mouth a perfect O.

"La Negra. I don't all the way understand, pero she does. This is how we open the prison. We have to help them remember if they're ever going to get out of here."

We turned to the woman in the cell, who was now cowering in the corner. Pues, not the reaction I was expecting. Was this a trap? Could the prison's evil magic have fooled La Negra and given me a false vision?

"What's your name?" I said as softly as I could, pero the woman even flinched at that.

"Not again," she muttered. "You won't fool me again!"

"Quién?" Carmen said, pero I knew immediately that the haze poisoning this lady's mind had to be Cuco's work.

"What's your name, Doña?" I repeated, spreading my hands.

"Yessica. You talk . . . more than the last one. Pero I won't be fooled again." She shivered.

"We're not trying to fool you," Carmen said calmly. "Do people often come here to fool you?"

"Not people." Yessica snapped and then softened again. "Those things, they aren't people. Just smoke and mirrors. Smoke and mirrors."

I was confused, but a look of understanding was spreading across Carmen's face like she'd swallowed something bitter.

"Yessica." Carmen's voice was just above a whisper, but Yessica perked up at her name like it was the first time she'd heard it in years. "Do you think Pilar is a baca?"

My stomach turned to rock.

"So-sometimes," Yessica stammered, "they come and tell us that we're free. They disguise themselves and you . . . you just want to believe so bad. But the door always—" She stood and her whole body trembled against the wall.

"We promise," I said, "I'm Pilar and this is Carmen and we're here to rescue you for real."

I stepped into the cell and my head was full of a horrible

buzzing, like a wasp nest on full blast. Pero I reached out my hand, and led Yessica out into the hallway and the buzzing stopped.

"Yessica." Carmen tapped her shoulder. "I need you to find somewhere to hide. We're going to take down the whole prison and when that happens, I need you to be ready to run, entiendes?"

Yessica seemed to gain strength with each use of her name. She was still shaky, and her eyes had dark rings around them, y pues, who could sleep with that buzzing in your head? But she nodded, her eyes watery as if she couldn't believe her luck.

"I tried to leave, I was supposed to leave the island the next day, pero they found me. I won't let them find me again."

Carmen and I went from cell to cell, freeing people with La Negra's touch, and each of them was distrustful of us at first, just like Yessica. Pero as more came out, they told us fragments of why they were in La Blanca.

"My prima caught the eye of a soldier, but I wouldn't let them take her."

"I made a joke about El Jefe."

"I didn't do anything, I just ran a colmado."

"I fought with the Mariposas. I helped after Johnny Abbes and his thugs killed them. I just wanted my family to live in a safe place."

"They thought I was Haitian, and I heard what the SIM did to Haitians, so I tried to get to America, pero they found me."

Pues, that's how they all ended. "They found me."

Finally, we arrived in a hallway with a massive white column in the middle and a door to a staircase.

A girl around Lorena's age stood inside a cell close by. She wore a twitchy expression, as if she was being followed. I did the ritual with La Negra to open the door. My vision swam before my eyes and I understood this was the last door I could open on my own and still have the strength to fight. I pointed the emaciated girl in her dirty yellow dress down the hall and she jogged away. There was only one way to open the rest of the cells, and that was to win.

It was a desperate hope, especially because we still hadn't tracked down Natasha.

Carmen's eyes skittered around the hallway, examining each cell in turn as they searched for a trap.

"My mind will never be rid of this abomination now." She scowled. "I had imagined before, everyone does, but now I will *never* forget this cruelty. Let's destroy this prison once and for all."

I felt the same anger and paranoia as we charged toward the stairs, porque we'd been running for at least twelve minutes and seen no guards. No bacas, no Machetes, pues, not even a Cucito. Everything had been quiet and quiet never brought good news.

Right on cue, I saw one clawed foot covered in thick black fur descending the stairs and then another.

There emerging from the opening in the column, easily

seven feet tall, was El Baca, coal-red eyes red eyes gleaming at the two of us, claws leaking smoke into the air.

"Pues," Carmen grunted, cracking her neck to the side, "nothing's ever easy, is it?"

"Tell me about it." I sighed, summoning a stream of La Negra to my palm. The tumbao was even weaker than before, a faint pulse where there should be a hundred drums. Had I given too much away freeing the prisoners?

"So, you go high, I go low?" I said out of the corner of my mouth.

Carmen shook her head, eyes not leaving El Baca for a second.

"No, I go high *and* low and you go for the stairs."

"But—"

"It wasn't a suggestion." Carmen grimaced. "If this monster is here, then his beloved master is upstairs probably working on something nasty for the Galipotes, and you're the only one here with a strong enough connection to La Negra to bring that payaso down."

I lowered my head, knowing we didn't have time to argue. El Baca snorted out some ash like he was laughing as ten long black claws extended from his fingers.

"Plus, this mutt burned my city and killed my mentor." Carmen cracked her knuckles. "Honestly, I've been waiting on this rematch for a hundred and fifty years."

El Baca bellowed and charged forward.

"Buena suerte, hermana. See you on the other side." Carmen sprinted toward El Baca and leapt into a strong roundhouse kick that caught the demonic dog right across the muzzle.

I rushed toward the stairs, hating myself for every step I took away from Carmen. I bounded up the stairs two at a time for what felt like forever. Out of breath, I finally made it to the top and came face-to-face with a polished oak door. I forced a calming breath into my lungs as I dabbed sweat off my face. I drew my machete and pushed my mind to that space Carmen had taught me, that La Bruja had taught me, where the world slowed down—where La Negra and I could fight as one.

Everything would come down to this. Here goes nothing.

I kicked the door as hard as I could and it flew open.

There he stood, sucking down one of those nasty cigars; El Cuco himself, with no more barriers between us.

"Ah, the little brujita arrives at last. Pilar, wasn't it? I was starting to think I would have to watch your little alliance's last stand fail all alone. Please, step into my office. I must admit, I've been waiting for this."

THIRTY-EIGHT

EL CUCO LOOKED DIFFERENT THAN he had in El Bosque de las Tormentas. He was still wearing his uniform, but it was even dirtier than before y también there was a big rip above his shoulder where thick dark hair was poking through. Actually, the hair was poking through from everywhere—that was the big difference. When I'd seen him in El Bosque he could have passed for a hairy, middle-aged dude with a thick beard and hairy forearms, but now it was way more of a "general from *Planet of the Apes*" kind of look. And despite the tough talk about crushing the rebellion, he had a wild look in his eyes like he hadn't slept in days.

I pointed my machete at him, ready to take him down.

"Where's my cousin Natasha, Cuco?"

He raised an eyebrow but didn't move. "Ah, finally a little clarity of what brings the little brujita from the world beyond to my humble island."

I clenched my jaw. "It isn't your island if you stole it." I sliced the machete through the air, the whistle emphasizing my point.

Cuco's eyes followed the blade but he didn't flinch. "Pilar—"

"Don't say my name." I stepped forward. "You tell me where Natasha is. I won't ask again."

Cuco blew a cloud of smoke and tossed the cigar at one of the floor-to-ceiling windows that ringed the top of the tower. "You can put the butter knife away. I think we both know you won't use it."

"Do we?" I took a step to the side, trying to keep the open door away from my back in case it was a trap.

"We do. Because I'm the only one who knows where your cousin is. I'm the only one who's known since dearest Abbes sent word from El Jefe that the little bruja needed to go. What's it been, forty years in your world?"

"Fifty," I spat.

Cuco spread his hands, fanning out his long, clawlike nails. "My, my, how time flies. Well on *my* island, in *my* prison, dearest Natasha has been here for hundreds of years." He patted his pocket for another cigar and shook his head when he couldn't find one. "And here she will stay because if you kill me, y pues, I don't think you have the mettle to do it even if you could, Johnny Abbes is leading his Machetes on a counterstrike as we speak that will, ahem, end this Mariposa Rebellion once and for all. So I would say you have the same options as your beloved mentor, La Bruja. You can surrender, or you can die. The choice is yours, pero I would choose quickly; Johnny never was known for his merciful instincts."

"Look, you Great-Value-Ricardo-Montalban-sounding furball, your time is up."

Cuco fished another cigar from a pants pocket and clamped it between his yellow teeth, which looked more like fangs. He went to strike a match, pero before he had the chance, I hit him in the chest as hard as I could with a whip of black sand. He stumbled back and snarled, his eyes yellow like a wolf.

I ran forward, machete in hand, and dodged a swipe of his huge, hairy forearm by sliding under it.

Heart pumping a mile a minute I whirled to face him, pero he was too fast and tackled me to the floor. The machete sprung out of my hand and bounced across the room. El Cuco roared in my face as we wrestled on the ground. A string of images shot faintly through my mind from La Negra: *blindfold, sand, tears, a single yellowing eye.*

"You think you can kill me?" His rancid breath rolled over me with each word. "You think I built this prison so some little brat could—"

A stream of black sand shot out from the bottle fastened to my hip and wrapped itself around his head, covering his eyes. Cuco took his hands off me and screamed as if somebody had thrown boiling water on his face. I kicked him in the chest as hard as I could with both feet and rolled away.

"You talk too much," I said, spitting out a little blood and trying to find the machete.

Pero I was already too late. Cuco ripped the sand off his eyes and it turned white in his hands like ash at the end of a lit cigar. I felt it in my chest, just like when I'd freed the prisoners, as though something had withered, all that memory lost in an instant.

"Pathetic," he crowed, letting the corrupted grains dribble from his hand like sand through an hourglass. "You know who throws sand in the eyes of their enemies? Children." He marched toward me, seeming to grow taller by the step. "You're outmatched, little bruja. La Negra has no power here."

As I frantically searched for the machete, I finally saw it at the other end of the room. I tried to dodge around him, but Cuco grabbed the hood of my jacket and yanked me before taking me by the throat.

"This is my world."

He slammed a fist into my ribs. The ciguapa-made jacket took most of the force of his punch, pero it still drove the breath from my lungs.

"This is my island, my history."

Another punch, the coppery taste of blood flooded my mouth. The tumbao growing fainter.

"So long as this prison stands, I'm eternal, entiendes?"

I thought of the prisoners, their hollowed cheeks in their miserable faces. I thought of Mami and Natasha separated for decades porque Trujillo and Cuco wanted power. It wouldn't end like this. I wouldn't let it.

I thought back to my sparring training and heard Carmen's voice echo in my mind: "Lesson one, hermanita: Combat is not about who's strongest; the battle goes to the most imaginative. If your opponent is bigger than you, go where size *doesn't* matter."

Time for some imagination.

With all my might I slammed my head into his. Cuco screamed as blood streamed out of his head like a bandera and he released me. I dropped and rolled away from him, casting a stream of La Negra toward the machete. It zipped back to my hand and it felt warm, like a small sun, like something better was coming.

"A headbutt? What kind of bruja are you?" Cuco snarled, wiping blood from his face.

"The kind who survives," I said, charging forward. "The kind who remembers."

His claws met my machete in a hiss of smoke, our teeth bared. Pero I saw in his eyes that the pain was worse for him than for me. La Negra *did* have power here, and we both knew it.

"We are partners and we are one. La Negra serves me no more than I serve La Negra." I huffed as I pushed Cuco back into a stumble.

"We are the defenders of memory, keepers of Zafa, warriors when needed and only when needed."

Another swing of the machete as I ducked under a right hook. Fabric tore and Cuco howled in agony.

"When we move, it will be as one story among thousands, a single drop in an ancient wave."

Cuco was a fragile beast now, like all dictators. Slobbering and wounded, swinging wildly like my old bullies, y pues, just like them he was going down hard. I sent a rope of La Negra swinging into his gut like a fist.

"We are one rhythm, a beat as old as the first note ever sung, we will move with purpose."

I smacked Cuco aside with the butt of the machete and held the blade to the tip of his throat, a single line of smoke coiling up where blade met fur.

"We will fight, we will not forget. Ever," I finished, glaring down at him.

Pues, I was a warrior, a bruja, I was alive porque I was more beast than this beast.

"So, is this it, little bruja?" Cuco groaned. "Is this where you kill me?"

I gripped the machete harder and stared into yellow watery eyes. I had won, pero was this justice? Was this really the only way?

BOOM!!!

A massive explosion rattled the tower and the entire prison. Cuco's grip slackened for just a second and I summoned all my strength and kicked him in the chin and pushed off just in time for a second enormous BOOM!! to shake the foundations of La Blanca.

I twisted my ankle as I landed. "Ahhh!" I shrieked as the pain shot up my leg.

"WHAT WAS THAT?" Cuco shouted at the top of his lungs, scrambling to a window.

Y pues, if I hadn't seen it with my own two eyes through the windows, I wouldn't have believed it. A golden comet the size of a Jeep was twirling in the sky, then slamming into the prison like a yo-yo. But where bricks should be falling, instead pages flew everywhere, thousands and thousands of blank sheets of paper. Daylight burst into the prison as holes were smashed into the walls by the golden comet.

It dawned on me all at once: This was what La Blanca was made of. Not truly bricks, but hidden pages full of forgotten names, unfinished stories just like Natasha's.

Those same stories had brought me to Zafa.

A hole had formed on the floor of the tower, and I could see below into the main area of the prison. The prisoners I hadn't freed earlier squeezed their way through newly formed craters in their cells, sprinting toward freedom.

"No!" Cuco roared, almost like he'd forgotten I was there. "Impossible!"

The comet zoomed past the window, y de verdad, it was no comet. Inside a field of yellow energy were hundreds of butterflies.

"I was sure, we checked, we burned the whole damn sanctuary to the ground," Cuco pleaded, mouth frothing with spit.

And as the golden wrecking ball looped back for another round, I saw it. Five women sitting in the air, hands locked as if in prayer. Four with wings, one without. My mouth fell open. It couldn't be, pero it was.

La Bruja had survived.

"YOU! You opened the cells?! Nobody can escape or the whole prison will collapse–YOU WILL PAY FOR THIS! NOBODY ESCAPES!" Cuco snarled, lunging at me.

But another rumble sent the floor sloping downward as part of the tower bent from the force of the magic wrecking ball. He tore my jacket off my back but missed the rest of me. I wheeled and sprinted toward the door, pain screaming through my foot as I hurtled down the stairs. One way or another La Blanca was coming apart and I could only think of one thing.

Natasha.

THIRTY-NINE

AS I SPRINTED DOWN THE steps, more pages from the
upper tier of the tower fell around me. My ankle was killing
me, pero there wasn't any time to let it slow me down. When
I finally got to the base of the stairs my heart stopped as I saw
Carmen on her knees, clutching her shoulder.

"CARMEN!" I hollered as another earth-rattling wave
sent more chunks of the prison barreling down from above.

Streaks of sunlight blasted through La Blanca in huge
golden columns. The prison tried to knit itself back together
in several places, but it was outmatched by the wave of
destruction. Tons of cells previously occupied by gray-faced
inmates were empty, only the light was left behind the bars.

"¡Gracias a dios!" Carmen smiled wide, then winced. "Are
you okay? Where's Cuco? I think the whole place is coming
down!"

"I sprained my ankle, but I'm fine. More importantly,
we have to find Natasha!" I reached out a hand and hauled

Carmen to her feet with her good arm. I winced as another bolt of pain shot up my leg.

As we ran through the hallways calling for Natasha, another few reams of the prison crashed down to our left.

"I don't understand what's bringing down the prison!" Carmen shouted. "This wasn't in the briefing! Pero whoever it is has an amazing sense of timing porque I think El Baca broke my shoulder and he was coming at me hard. I had him dead to rights, pero the minute the prisoners got loose, he teleported away in a cloud of smoke. Coward."

I stopped running, lungs screaming for air. I had no idea where to search. Even with the sunlight coming through, La Blanca was still a maze. Had Natasha gotten out? Had she been recaptured? Was she safe? And, maybe worst of all, what if La Blanca itself had crushed her? The thought was too awful to hold so I pushed it away as Carmen looked at me with concern. A smaller rumble signaled that even more of the prison was falling somewhere else.

"So to recap, both El Cuco and El Baca are missing, we don't know where Natasha is, and La Blanca is collapsing around us," I said, bitterly.

"Pues, the good news just keeps rolling in." Carmen laughed sourly. "I thought you'd killed Cuco and that's why the prison started breaking."

"Nah," I said, "but man, have I got some good news for you!"

Pero telling Carmen about La Bruja would have to wait

because a massive hole exploded on the wall to our left. Sunlight poured in as I looked through the hole and saw hundreds of men, women, and children sprinting away from La Blanca toward the field.

"Pilar, maybe Natasha is with them. We might not get another chance before La Blanca collapses," Carmen yelled as dust and pages and white sand rained down all around us.

"But what if she's not?!" I yelled. "I can't leave her here, not after all this!"

"And I can't leave you here, hermana! Mira, the wall is closing up." Carmen pointed to the gap in the wall, which was slowly knitting itself back together. "If Natasha is out there and you die in here, what good are you to her? If you stay then I stay, pero we have to choose." Carmen stomped her foot and her face was a mask of pain as she grabbed her shoulder. "Leap of faith time, Pilar, nos vamos o no?"

I looked at Carmen, I looked at the hole, I looked at La Blanca and felt my chest tighten. It shouldn't be like this, I shouldn't have to choose, I should just know. Pero I didn't. I did have to choose, and I chose to run. Tears filled my eyes and the pain climbed farther up my leg like a hundred lightning bolts. Beyond the wall the field was a golden haze, every person ahead was blurry, out of focus like a camera lens zoomed too far out.

Then I saw her.

About eight steps ahead of me, crystal clear as if the whole world were happening in soft focus around her. A girl, smallish for her age, with a curtain of dark black curls. It had to be her, it just had to be. I forced myself to move faster, not even caring about my ankle, just determined to reach her. We were parallel to each other, two lenses in the same camera, mirror images. I gunned it even harder, pues, I'd never gone so fast.

Until I saw a huge chunk of the prison falling downward toward the girl. She saw the shadow of it swelling above her. The girl tried to sprint to the side but tripped over the skeletal hand of an unconscious Machete. Everything slowed as she fell hard into the dirt and clutched her elbow in agony. I kept hustling toward the fallen girl, forcing every desperate breath into my lungs.

Not like this.

The massive chunk of prison dropped toward the girl, shedding pages like some kind of horrible meteor entering the atmosphere. Moving at a speed nothing can survive.

Not like this.

I felt my heartbeat intertwine with the tumbao of La Negra once again. No Sight, just an avalanche of drums surging in me, like a second pulse.

It was all I needed. This isn't how I'd let the story end.

Barely thinking, I shot a huge wave of La Negra toward the falling pages of the prison. The chunk exploded above us both, casting debris to either side. The girl looked back, stunned, and our eyes met as I felt tears prick like hot needles.

It was her.

Unmistakable, her eyes big as saucers looking at the pages coming down, maybe the closest thing she'd ever seen to snow. I opened my mouth to call out to her, to hold her close, but another chunk of La Blanca crashed to the ground, hurling dirt and dust into my eyes. I fought to see again, but I couldn't find her. I clawed through the dust screaming her name until all I could feel was the thick red hurt of Natasha's disappearance.

"PILAR!" Carmen hollered from behind me. "Don't slow down, hermana, I promise we are almost—"

And then we were out, the sun dancing on our skin, as we sprinted forward until I wasn't running anymore but was *lifted* into the sky. The freed prisoners became dots as I soared higher and higher. I searched for Natasha in the crowd, which moved forward and *away, away, away* from La Blanca. Just like Abuela; after years of being trapped, they knew freedom meant anywhere but here.

They got smaller until they were like ants, and finally my brain understood I was flying. Someone was holding me around the waist as if they might never let go. I looked up and saw Minerva's shining face, her hair whooshed back not just by the force of her own always-wind, but by the actual wind. To my left Dede was laughing, crying, laughing next to her sister as she held Carmen who looked as confused as me. I looked down one last time at La Blanca, just in time to hear a crack like a whole forest falling at once as the prison collapsed into the sand.

"Does this mean?" I looked up at Minerva, but my throat was too sore from screaming for Natasha to finish the question.

She grinned and her mouth was a wide, sharp moon.

"Yes, Pilar, we won."

FORTY

THE GALIPOTES HAD SET UP a camp a mile or so to the north of the cane field, which had wilted to acres of faint brown nothing the minute La Blanca collapsed. Cheers erupted from all the former prisoners as Minerva and Dede landed delicately and we were rushed over to a medical tent. My head was ringing from the applause, from the prison's buzzing, and over and over again I heard Minerva's calm voice in my head.

We won.

I felt like I should be relieved, crying, over the moon. *We won.* But instead I felt exhausted, so bone-tired and sore I didn't know which way was up, entiendes? All I could think was that there were so many people who got out of the prison, pero I still had no idea where Natasha was.

"If Natasha is lost, I think we lost," I said mostly to myself as I waved off the nurse who was fussing over me and trying to offer me some food. I downed a jug of water in one gulp and pushed back into the camp to look for my prima.

After saving her from being crushed by a piece of broken wall, I *had* to believe she'd survived.

I limped through camp, shouting Natasha's name until my throat was raw all over again. I marched past old men embracing small children, while women who'd fought with the Galipotes called out for their tíos and cousins. Brothers huddled together under green jackets just like the one I'd had to leave behind as I fled La Blanca. Nobody was alone anymore; freed prisoners and soldiers and nurses cried and laughed and even sang the names they'd been whispering for centuries. It was a whole chorus and my voice felt so small and tired among them. I was afraid I might not find Natasha, if she was even alive at all.

Just then, I heard huge wingbeats and the crowd ahead of me parted as Maria Teresa descended, butterfly wings outstretched and golden like a crown.

"Ah-ha!" Maria Teresa crowed, a huge smile lighting up her face to match her wings. "I was starting to think we'd lost you again! Been looking all over camp!"

The exhaustion had me almost seeing double, but I noticed that the Galipote was carrying someone.

She was smallish for thirteen, with nut-brown skin. A baggy military jacket was draped across her shoulder like a cape, and below it she wore a gray prison uniform. Her loose black curls framed her face in a shoulder-length bob. Pues, she was so skinny from years of imprisonment it looked like a strong breeze might carry her away at any second, and when she smiled it looked like even that small gesture cost her something. But it was her, no doubt about it. She survived.

"Natasha!" I yelped, relief flooded my chest as tears pricked my eyes, turning the setting sun to rainbows. "I—"

And that's when I felt the blade at my throat. A grizzled beard against my neck. Natasha's and Maria Teresa's eyes widened in horror as I heard that voice in my ear again, *his* voice.

"Well, little bruja," crooned El Cuco, pushing back the hood of my jacket with his free hand, "it seems we are . . . how you say, at an impasse."

FORTY-ONE

THE CURVE OF EL CUCO'S machete held close to my neck, vibrating in his shaking hand. The cigar stench of his breath wafted over me. Just seconds before it had been a huge party. But while celebrating the end of La Blanca, no one had noticed its warden skulking past the inmates he'd promised to keep miserable and isolated forever.

"Cuco." Maria Teresa fought to keep her voice steady, though her face twisted with rage. "Think about what you're doing. You're surrounded, La Blanca is dust, you'll never make it out; it's over."

"This brat has taken everything from me," Cuco rasped, jerking my head back and holding the machete even closer to my neck. "EVERYTHING! You think I care if I make it out of here? And do what? Become a fugitive? Live in the shadows like a common rat? No, no, Mariposa; I won't go back to that. I WON'T!"

Everyone flinched as he barked out the last of his sentence

and jerked me around, the blade still at my throat. It was so close I couldn't move an inch, couldn't clear my head enough to ignite my connection with La Negra and hopefully knock him out before he slit my throat. Cuco cackled in quick bursts of tobacco-drenched laughter, lapping up the fear of the crowd like a feral dog.

"No, no, no, no, Mariposa, I don't want to escape anymore than you and your wretched sisters want to let me walk even one more step on Zafa. My fate is sealed; you have no idea what you've done! All I want is to die seeing the helpless look on your faces as the life drains from this little bruja's eyes."

I was trapped, and to make it all worse, Natasha looked so afraid. I didn't want that to be the last thing that I ever saw.

I tried to take deep breaths, calm my nerves, find a way to reach out to La Negra, but my mind was consumed by the machete and the cigar breath and the heavy smell of smoke in the air.

Wait, smoke? Where was the smoke coming from?

Y pues, I'm paid to believe in what I can see, pero I still barely believe what I saw next.

"A life for a life," said El Cuco as I felt his hand grip tighter on the blade.

Just then, four thick, charcoal-black chains shot toward Cuco, hissing like snakes. They curled around his wrists, cuffing him, and wrenched his blade hand up and out until something popped. Cuco screamed as if he were being tortured and dropped the machete and his hold on me.

Within seconds Maria Teresa zoomed over to me, grabbed me around the waist, and shot back to where Natasha stood and pushed us behind her massive wings like a bodyguard. The gold of her wings turned clear like glass as we watched what was happening. The twisting chains wrapped tighter around Cuco, forcing the filthy general to his knees with a desperate look in his eyes.

Pues, if you didn't know who he was you might have pitied him.

With Cuco detained, I let my eyes follow the chains, and a wave of confusion washed over me as I stared at none other than El Baca.

"I thought they were allies," Natasha whispered next to me, eyes wide as saucers.

"Me too," I muttered, still confused.

"Cuco," El Baca's voice boomed, deep like a massive drum, "you have failed in your alliance."

Cuco merely screamed in response. Whatever those chains were doing to him must have been twice as bad as La Negra's effect on him, because it seemed like he couldn't even see us anymore. Drool pooled at the corners of his mouth and his head jerked side to side as his face grew hairier with each scream. He looked, well, like a giant Cucito.

"La Blanca lies in ruins and prisoners walk free! You! Have! Failed!" Baca snarled.

"The price must be paid."

Among the surrounding crowd, jaws fell open and parents shielded the eyes of children as El Baca roared, his chest parting like a gate to reveal a hypnotic crimson vortex. I saw Minerva and Dede hovering in the sky, watching with horrified expressions, but poised to strike when the time came.

"What kind of tontería is th—" I started, but Baca's voice boomed again, silencing everyone nearby.

"Per the contract, you are sentenced to El Odio," Baca growled. "You may never return. May your agony be a lesson in your shortcomings for all lives to come."

Cuco squealed and now he didn't even resemble a man at all aside from the uniform he wore, which was bursting at the seams with bristling black hair.

Pues, so this was what had been lurking underneath his face. Que feo.

Cuco was hauled kicking and screaming, frothing at the mouth, into the energy field. El Baca snarled and fell to his knees weakened and trembling.

Out of nowhere, La Bruja charged out from the crowd. I'd never been so excited to see that vieja hater! A pair of her own magical black and gold chains sprung from the ground and held the massive demon in place.

As Cuco disappeared into the void, Baca turned and snarled at La Bruja, teeth bared.

Pues, she didn't flinch. La Bruja cocked back her arm and

punched El Baca clean across the jaw with a sickening crunch. Just like that the demon dog who helped murder a nation fell silent in his chains.

For the first time in centuries on Zafa, quiet brought good news.

FORTY-TWO

"WAIT, WAIT, WAIT! START OVER and tell me again, her-manita, and don't leave anything out this time!" Carmen beamed.

Me and Natasha exchanged a look and laughed. Me holding my ribs, her covering her mouth with one hand.

"Pues, I've told you the story like six times already and we'll be landing soon!"

I rolled my eyes. After the hostage incident with El Cuco, the Galipotes had insisted that they carry us back to the city in a tarp above the ground. Minerva and Dede said something about the air giving them home field advantage. I was too exhausted to tell them no, y pues, after a week of sprinting, climbing, swinging across vines, tunnel surfing, and hand-to-hand combat, sometimes it's nice to be driven.

"Yeah, you told me, but I still can't believe I missed it! Plus, seven is my lucky number, sooooo quit stalling and make with the story. Paint a picture in my mind!" Carmen smiled sweetly.

"Fine." I rolled my eyes again. "One last time.

"Pues, so there we were after Cuco got taken to El Odio. La Bruja looked good for someone who was supposed to be dead. Then she cocked back her arm and slammed her fist right into his eye. Then she spat and said, 'That was for my sister, and for Gabriela.' Y se fue. Baca was taken away to be guarded by Gray Locks, Patria, and Maria Teresa."

"I still don't know how La Bruja survived," Natasha said quietly. "When El Baca took me . . ."

She shook her head and didn't finish the sentence. Natasha was quieter than I had imagined she'd be from her journal entries, pero prison will do that to you. Celeste's older brother had been in prison once for stealing a TV. When he'd gotten out, she said the most important thing she and her family did for him was to let him know they were there for him and he could speak when he was ready. And Ramon had come home after three years.

Natasha had been gone for fifty years in our world, all alone, never aging because of La Blanca's curse. It was going to take some time before she was ready to talk, and me and Carmen had an unspoken agreement not to rush her. Y de verdad, we still didn't know how La Bruja had survived either. When me and Natasha had asked her the question while Carmen wept and hugged her like she may never let go, do you know what La Bruja did?

"Can't tell you all my secrets, now can I?" She had laughed, a mixture of mischief and pure joy. "I'll teach you someday, pero today we celebrate!"

The nerve.

"We're going to be landing soon. Hang on to something!" Minerva smiled. She hadn't stopped grinning the whole flight back.

Until we arrived in the city; that wiped the smile off everyone's faces.

Without the Galipotes there to protect the city, we'd expected Minerva to be hit hard by hordes of Cuco's bacas. Pero as we saw the citizens emerging from the tunnels, we realized it wasn't just that the city had been hit hard, it's that there wasn't even much of a city left behind at all.

The plan with the tunnels had luckily worked to perfection, no casualties, pues, not even a broken bone by all accounts. But the forces that El Cuco had watching the city must have struck not long after the evacuation, and pues, it was even worse than I had imagined. Nearly every home, storefront, and stall was ash and splinters. Smoke still rose in plumes from some of the fires. Stairs were cracked, ragged banderas turned in the ashen streets like tumbleweeds. And there in the center of the city, the Hall of the Galipotes was beaten and dented like an old pop can. One of the huge double doors hung off the frame, the other crushed entirely, leaving a dark space in the silver walls like a tooth punched clean out of its gum.

"It . . . will take years to rebuild even part of this," a woman around Lorena's age murmured behind me, trying not to alarm her little sister fast asleep on her shoulder.

"Then," Minerva said, wind sweeping her hair back as she stood on the cracked steps of the hall, "I guess we start today. Who will help?"

There were murmurs of worry and wonder, and then Tomasito's father stepped forward. And then another person and another until the whole crowd was raising their hands. Lifelong citizens and those who'd just gotten free from La Blanca stood in the midst of their ruined city, their city of smoke and memory, and said they would rebuild.

And then, Natasha stepped forward.

A lead ball grew in my stomach like when Celeste had told me that she was moving to Milwaukee. My face grew hot, my skin prickled as Natasha stared back at me with a look that said *Sorry* in at least two languages.

"Natasha," I started, taking her wrist gently. "La Bruja survived. We can probably go home. Don't . . . don't you want to go home? And see Mami and Abuela? They miss you . . ." I trailed off, not knowing what to say. I was upset and angry and even betrayed that it felt like she was choosing Zafa over her own family.

Natasha smiled sadly; she was getting a little better at smiling the farther she got from La Blanca. It looked less like she had a cramp and more like she'd just gotten a paper cut now.

"And I've missed them. Every day, no matter how many days it's been." Natasha looked over her shoulder back toward where La Blanca had been as Gray Locks started dividing citizens into teams to salvage food and water. "But, where you live, pues, even the time you're going back to, isn't my home anymore, entiendes? It'd be like . . . traveling nine hundred years into the future and only knowing three people. What good can I do there anymore? Here I can be a bruja, I can help rebuild the city. La Bruja might even teach me and we could rebuild her family too. But our world, your world—that belongs to you, prima. I hope you can understand?"

It was the most words in a row that Natasha had spoken since we flew away from La Blanca. I opened and closed my mouth like a payasa, but I had to admit she was right. This was Natasha's world more than ours was now. And maybe that could change, but it never would if I tried to force it now.

"I feel you." I squeezed her hand. "What am I supposed to tell Abuela and Mami, though?"

Natasha dragged her finger across her chin just like Lorena does when she's genuinely stumped. "I don't know. I wish there was a way I could say goodbye to them. Show them what I have here, why I can't leave."

I was about to respond when I felt a small tug at my sleeve, then a more insistent one. I looked down and saw Tomasito sporting a big grin on his face as he held my backpack out to me. Plus two cold but still very, very good pastelillos.

"I did it!" He beamed, handing me both the backpack

and the pastelillos. "I kept it safe the whole time. Porque I promised."

Before I could even respond or say thank you, he hit a crisp ciguapa salute and ran off to join one of the salvage teams.

I gave Natasha a small smile. "I think we just found the end of my movie after all."

FORTY-THREE

"ALL RIGHT," I SAID, KEEPING the camera steady in my palm as I adjusted the light settings, "you ready to do this?"

Natasha nodded, the last of the day's light highlighting the red undertones of her hair so it looked like she was crowned by a halo of fire. Pues, not for nothing, but it looked badass, just like Mira Paredez. Mami will never let me dye my tips, pero a girl can dream, right?

I tipped my finger to let Natasha know we were rolling. In the background, teams of people, ciguapas and humans alike, hauled up shelters and handed out food and water. The city was rebuilding itself behind her; Natasha, la Virgen del Trujillato.

"Can you state your name?"

"Natasha Violeta Maria De Jesus."

"How old are you?"

"Thirteen and three months, pero, I've been here for way longer."

"How much longer?"

"Fifty years in your world, hundreds here. It's hard to tell; La Blanca erased time when we were taken inside. Pero either way, too long to not see the sun, too long for joy to be a memory."

"Why were you taken?"

"Because they took Mami, porque I was a threat, or at least somebody believed I could be."

"Are you a threat?"

"Not now, but I hope to grow into one; just like you."

We both laughed at that. It was going to be weird going back to a world that didn't see me as a threat, or it did but just not in the same way.

"Last question: Do you have anything you want to say to the people in our world?"

Natasha cleared her throat and took a sip of water. The sun's light slipped down her face as a shelter collapsed behind us and the team went right back to putting it up.

"Gracias, Grecia, gracias, Tía Daniella, for all the years you remembered me. I lost a lot of my life in La Blanca, pero I lost even more not getting to spend those years with you. It's funny, I've had centuries to think of how much I miss you, pero it still won't all fit into words. I hope there's a heaven, I hope we all get to meet again there, but right now I'm doing what you always taught me, Tía Daniella, what my mami taught me, and, Grecia, maybe you most of all; I'm where I'm needed. Gracias por los recuerdos, mi hermana, mi familia."

I shut the camera off and threw my arms around her until both our shoulders were wet with tears. We stayed like that for a long time. When we finally separated, the last of the sun had dragged itself over the horizon.

"So, how exactly is this going to work again?" I asked, moonlight silvering all the women around me.

"You ask a lot of questions; anybody ever tell you that?" La Bruja grunted.

"All the time," Carmen chipped in, "pero it's who she is and who she is is . . ."

I smiled at her.

"¡Mejor que nada!" Carmen finished.

And there goes the smile.

"Well, it's supposed to be pretty simple to explain, but umm . . ." Natasha trailed off nervously.

"But very hard to actually manage," the Galipotes said in unison.

"Great," I said sarcastically. "So, now that we're done talking in riddles, does somebody want to help me understand why this might work and not accidentally . . . oh, I don't know, trap me in El Odio with Cuco and who knows what else?!"

"Tranquilo." La Bruja yawned like she was bored. "You're the one who wants to go back so badly."

"Or, y'know, you could stay," Carmen pointed out. "I'm going to be commander of the entire spy unit now and I could always use a talkative little bruja to run missions with! You know there will always be a place for you on Zafa. You're the hero of the entire island!"

"Guys. The plan." I side-eyed the whole group.

"Okay," Minerva started. "We know now that La Blanca was made out of sheets like this one."

She gestured at a blank page weighed down by four black resguarda stones in the middle of the circle.

"We'll call those 'Forgettings' to keep it simple," Dede added. For some reason, all of her hair was now silver instead of just the normal swoop in the front.

"El Odio is a powerful force, a negative hellscape from which all the Fuku that made Cuco's reign possible stems," La Bruja said, now a little eager to show off since we were done playing "Keep the Plan from Pilar." "La Negra is infused with the opposite, the positive charge of all Dominican memory dating back to the dawn of the island and the Tainos in your world."

"When you touched the page in your world, you must have tapped into the curse energy the Trujillato likely used to convey messages from their world to our world and transport Cuco and Baca back and forth with captives." Maria Teresa flapped her wings agitatedly.

"That same energy is what transferred you here. To us. And why we have never succeeded in being able to reverse the polarity of one of the portals on our own. We would need a bruja of uncommon strength, one from your world," Patria said, screwing up her face like she was doing a math problem.

"And that's where I come in," Natasha said meekly.

"Bring it home, little one." La Bruja jabbed her with an elbow. "Once more, with feeling, you can do it now!"

Natasha stood up a little straighter and smiled like she meant it. Like Carmen, she had a weirdly strong connection with La Bruja's gruff demeanor. As much as I appreciated La Bruja saving our butts, I couldn't say I was going to miss her style.

"The people of Zafa have memory, but no experience of *our* world, Pilar," Natasha said clearly and calmly. "But I do, so with my help we should be able to work with La Negra to reverse the polarity of this Forgetting and make it into a portal, like the one you fell through, and take you home. I'd say there's maybe like a three percent chance you end up in El Odio."

My eyes widened.

"Which are good odds! Lo siento, I should have added that."

"I know I said you were a prodigy and all," La Bruja said to me, though she beamed at Natasha, "pero like, *that's* a prodigy! Picked it up in less than a day!"

I twisted my mouth but didn't say anything. It was good to see Natasha already looking so at home, and if I had to get roasted in the process, it was whatever.

I stood before the Galipotes, their wings all deep silver for the occasion, as they spoke in unison to me.

"Pilar Ramirez, bruja, soldier, artista. You have helped liberate our island. Zafa owes you a debt it can never repay. Wherever you go, go with our love, never forget your strength."

I hit a salute that they returned and then nodded.

"I give you a hard time," La Bruja started in, "but you gave me a chance to avenge my sisters, and you brought back my daughter, Carmen. And you freed my new protégé, who will surpass you if you don't keep practicing your brujería in that other world you like so much!"

We both laughed as I patted the little container of La Negra's sand that I would bring back to practice with in my spare time.

"Anyway, I love you, kid. You're a true bruja. I hope your world knows how lucky they are to have you."

I looked at Natasha, who just pulled me into a huge hug. We didn't need to say anything, we already knew.

"Okay, well, I guess I'm up last since I don't have any magic or whatever," Carmen said, pulling me into her own massive hug. "Pilar, que te puedo decir, you gave me back my life. I'd said goodbye to so much . . . thank you for helping me find so much of it again." Her eyes shone with tears until her irises were half-moons in the silvered light and we hugged again.

"I've said goodbye a lot," Carmen repeated into my curls,

"and I think this is a good time to change that; so I'm going to say 'see you later' porque our story isn't over, entiendes?"

"You know it."

I stepped into the middle of the circle. Each woman took a palm full of La Negra's black sand and walked to the center to press it onto the page of the Forgetting. It glowed a deep purple, then blue, then a column of purple light blasted into the sky. A huge breeze came off the page, like we were in a wind tunnel. I smelled the ocean breeze and the warm sand of Zafa.

"Does this mean it's working?" I yelled.

"Ninety-seven percent sure!" Natasha smiled. "But only one way to be certain."

I smiled at each of the women with their palms pinning down the page. At Carmen, who mouthed something that looked a lot like *You better visit* and grinned when I nodded my thanks. And without another word I hitched up my backpack and stepped into the warm purple light. I was yanked up high behind my chest, then squeezed like I was going through a straw.

Everything went dark, and when I opened my eyes, Zafa was gone.

FORTY-FOUR

PAGES RAINED DOWN ALL AROUND me like huge, blunt snowflakes. I blinked and found myself back in Professor Dominguez's office. I fished my phone out of my backpack. 3:08 P.M. Pues, only a few hours had passed in this world since I'd entered Zafa. My phone buzzed and I saw a text in the family group chat. Lorena, of course.

HIIIIII, hermanita, Professor Dominguez emailed me that he had a faculty meeting run long so he's a little late, but he should be on his way soon! Hope you haven't been waiting too long. Let's catch up before you leave campus to head back up north?

A little late. I almost laughed aloud as I stuffed my Galipotes Resistance jacket into my bag and put on my purple track jacket that I had been wearing when I left the house.

I thought back on the week-long whirlwind of my time in Zafa and realized it would make a great game of two truths and a lie someday.

1. I have escaped a prison.
2. I have gone to an office hours and the professor was one week late. Oh, and I ended up on a dang magical island in between!
3. I hate cheese fries.

Okay, I'm still working on a more believable lie. Pues, who hates cheese fries?

I texted Lorena back: **Sorry, hermana, the ride over here ended up taking a lot out of me and I told Mami I'd be home to help with chores, pero maybe we can get lunch once a week?**

Mami sent a heart, Lorena sent a GIF of a dancing penguin. Damn, it was great to be home.

As I exited Professor Dominguez's office, I saw a thin man hustling up the hallway toward me. He had his beige sport coat thrown over his shoulder, and the glistening bald patch swirling at the front of his head gleamed like the eye of a hurricane.

"Excuse me! Excuse me! Are you Pilar?" the man said hurriedly, little notes of a Dominican accent leaking out between gasps.

"Umm yes. Are you . . . ?"

"Yes, I'm Profesor Dominguez. I met your sister the other day! I am so, so sorry I was late, I'm still"—he wheezed and used a pocket square to dab sweat from his face—"finding my way around. And clearly working on my cardio, no?"

I laughed a little too loud, thinking of all the running I'd been doing. Pues, I felt for the guy.

"Oh, that's okay! I'm sorry I accidentally knocked some things over in your office. I thought you were inside and I umm . . . tripped into some papers."

And the award for understatement of the century goes to . . .

"No hay problema, honestly it's such a mess in there right now, the whole place is full of surprises."

"Tell me about it." I laughed, and Professor Dominguez cocked his head to the side. "I mean . . . umm . . ." I scrambled. "Maybe you could tell me about it soon? I think your research is so fascinating and would fit really well into this documentary I've been putting together."

"Ah yes, your movie!" Dominguez's face brightened and split into a warm grin, the hairs above his bald spot swaying like little palm trees caught in a storm. "Lorena has been telling me all about it, quite a superstar that sister of yours!"

Normally this would be my cue to roll my eyes, to be annoyed at another opportunity to talk for a long time about how perfect Lorena was. But de verdad, it rolled off my shoulders easy as rain. Lorena *is* pretty amazing, a dork of the highest order, but pretty amazing! And me? Pues, I'm becoming pretty amazing.

"Totally, and she and I are going to be having lunch once a week now! Maybe I can join you as a research assistant or something? Help you put some of those papers I knocked over back in place! It's the least I can do."

Dominguez stroked his chin for a second and dabbed at his forehead again like he was thinking. "Pilar Ramirez, I think you've got yourself a deal!"

He grinned and we shook on it. I didn't even mind that his sweat made my hand all wet.

As I waved goodbye to Professor Dominguez and hustled off toward the L, I thought for a minute about the fence by my house, *my* fence, the one I'd been looking at all my life, with its glistening steel beneath the paint chips. How the blue paint is maybe less like the sky and more like a four-dollar lottery ticket from Jewel-Osco that nobody has rubbed all the way through yet. How the women in my family, here and in Zafa, are like that—made of unexpected luck and power, women of faith and ceremony who never give up. Natasha and Mami, Carmen and Lorena, Abuela and La Bruja y todo, and me all alive because we believe, because we remember always what it is to be powerful and free and make home wherever we find each other.

Pues, the way I see it nothing could be luckier; and I'm paid to believe in what I can see. I see that I come from lottery women with quarters in hand, remembering and dreaming of what they might win, everything they will finish, tomorrow.

AUTHOR'S NOTE

Dear Reader,

Like Pilar, I grew up fixated on a tragedy that most of my teachers couldn't even pronounce. Part of the loneliness I felt as a young reader was to know that once Rafael Leónidas Trujillo had dominated the Dominican Republic for thirty-one years and yet nobody I asked outside my family could point to that hurt on a map, could point me to a book for my reading level that spoke to kids who had parents and grandparents who couldn't return to the Dominican Republic for years. It's why I wrote this book, one that deals in the mythos and memory of that regime, the Trujillato.

The story of how my own abuelos had to flee the island is not uncommon. My abuelo, like many others, chafed at the oppressive tenets of Trujillo's regime: how, whether by broad daylight or cover of dark, friends and neighbors could disappear at the hands of Trujillo's secret police, the Servicio de Intelligencia Militar (SIM), for so much as a whisper of discontent. He saw the genocidal moves that Trujillo made against the island's Haitian population—Trujillo would eventually slaughter twenty thousand men, women, and children. My abuelo feared for the daughters he would one day have, one of whom grew up to be my mother. He went to secret meetings about the need for regime change, though nothing would come to change the island until Trujillo's assassination by CIA-backed rebels in 1961.

My abuelo was a loudmouth, he said the wrong thing about Trujillo among the wrong people. The SIM came looking for him. Where our story is less common is that my abuelo escaped and went on to raise four daughters. Like the Mirabals and the Galipote Sisters, who share their names in tribute, my mother was born with three sisters: all equal parts brilliant and brave. The difference (all that separates any of us) in my family's past is that my abuelo and abuela survived to tell the story of that trauma for which there were seemingly so few books.

I set out to write this novel in a way I might have understood as a young reader, with a voice I might have felt seen and heard by; some confirmation of both the strangeness and the magic of being Dominican. Dearest reader, I hope if nothing else you felt a little of the joy I felt in helping bring Pilar and her friends into this book and, however briefly, into your hands!

With gratitude,

Julian

ACKNOWLEDGMENTS

Books are, like Zafa, never merely the work of one solitary imagination. My undying gratitude goes to so many in creating this book. I owe a special debt to Noel Quiñones, George Abraham, Nicholas Nichols, Itiola Jones, Miriam Harris, Joshua Nguyen, keepers of my memory, I love each of you so very much. Where there was silence, you sowed music. When I feel lost, every time, you gift me back to myself!

To my wonderful family, my mom and dad, thank you for so many years of knowing a world with both of you in it. I would choose no other life but the one we've built together! To my sister Marin, brilliant friend, artist, and hero, thank you for every lesson in grace, which is to say thank you for every minute we have spent in each other's company. My nephew Dominic, my favorite story, you're a superhero and I've loved all the time I've spent watching you become who you are!

To the staff at Holt and especially my brilliant editor,

Brian Geffen, it goes beyond thanks! Brian, you've shown me every day of our working together just how much of a gift thoroughness is. Thank you for seeing this book and for seeing me, from word one! To my Sister and Role Model, Liz Acevedo: gracias hermana. More than maybe any other writer, you showed me that I was capable of writing this book. Thank you for always believing I had something to say and being so generous with whatever questions I had as I stepped down the path you're making, every day, for all of us. And to my brilliant agent, Patrice Caldwell, without you there is no book. Thank you, on one muggy and otherwise belligerently sad week in July for making my dream come true and becoming my agent. Here's to the first thing we ever did together, may there be many more!

I want to thank every teacher and mentor who encouraged me to find some productive way of reconciling the many people in my head. Without you, I am not myself. Thank you, Kiese Laymon, Derrick Harriell, Aimee Nezhukumatathil, Vievee Francis, Jericho Brown, Morgan Parker, Greenie, Mary Dilg, David Fuder, Jeff Stone, George Drury, Michael Moos, and so many more.

No matter how great the effort I can never thank the full spectrum of writers and friends and who help make me better every day. But to thank a few, all my love and gratitude to Daniel José Older, Kwame Mbalia, Julia Alvarez, J. C. Cervantes, Safia Elhillo, Hanif Abdurraqib, Nabila Lovelace, Clint Smith, Paul Cato, Aurielle Marie, Janelle Viera, Afaq,

Raych Jackson, Shanel Edwards, Xavier Velez-Perry, torrin a. greathouse, Tarik Dobbs, Bradley Trumpfheller, Tiana Clark, Britteney Black Rose Kapri, John Murillo, Daniella Toosie-Watson, Jamal Parker, Perry 'Vision' Divirgilio, José Olivarez, Nate Marshall, Danez Smith, Franny Choi, Fatimah Asghar, Jamila Woods, and Sam Stevens.

Mad, bright, unreasonable, endless love to the City of Chicago and especially the Logan Square that I loved and will always love. Thank you for being home, thank you for letting me come home.

MORE MAGIC AWAITS ON PILAR'S NEXT ADVENTURE.

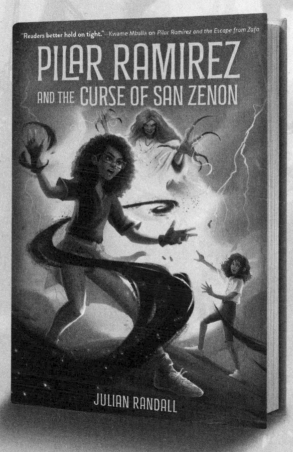

Keep reading for an excerpt.

ONE

I STARTLED AWAKE FROM THE DREAM.

"Ay, not this tontería again," I muttered, pulling my hoodie down farther over my curls and shifting in my window seat on the plane.

Lately, my dreams have been full of teeth. It's been nearly a year since I came back from my adventure on a magical island called Zafa, pero the island still lives on in my dreams. And my nightmares. I dream of baca dogs, demons running wild over ruined villages, while coconut-shaped Cucitos tear down anything they can get their gross, yellowing nails into. Storm clouds curl around the eerie white towers of El Cuco's prison fortress, La Blanca, like a ghostly hand. The jaws of a dog-demon snap against its chain, El Baca's howl swallowed by thunder.

It's not like the dreams come every night, but they're coming more often lately. I think it's just nerves though—after all, today's one of the biggest days of my life.

Pero this time was different—this time the dream took place in *my* world. A man in a Trujillo-era military outfit had sat in total silence, laying out goat bones in constellation-style shapes, etching symbols and figures into the bones. The man had continued his creepy ritual under the yellow light that hung from a chain in his room. Pues, I hadn't known who this dude was, pero anybody in that uniform spelled trouble, whether it's El Cuco, or just some random member of Trujillo's secret police, the Servicio de Intelligencia Militar (SIM). Ever since they'd kidnapped my cousin Natasha fifty years ago.

I had no idea what the dreams meant, but it couldn't be anything good.

I was about to try to squeeze out some more sleep, but then I felt a sharp, insistent pain in my right shoulder. I pried one of my eyes open to see what could possibly be attacking me. Pues, I should have known.

Lorena's bony little fingers were jittering into my shoulder like a hummingbird.

"Ay por favor, Lorena, what is it now?"

"Don't take that tone with me, baby sister! I'm trying to help you!"

"By severing my right arm?"

"No, genius," Lorena huffed. "For your information, the pilot just said that we'll be landing in thirty-five minutes."

"Lorena," I growled, "that's thirty-two more minutes I could have been asleep!"

"Look, you little malcriada, I put a lot of effort into making you these flash cards and the least you could do is look at them! How are you going to do work on your movie if you can't understand the language?"

She had a point, pero you can't really give Lorena an inch on these kinds of things, so I faked snores until she gave up and just tossed the cards in my lap.

"Desgraciada. I can't wait until this moody teenager phase is a thing of the past!"

I tried to get my sleep rhythm back, pero it was a lost cause, and already the dream was fading from my memory. A couple of weeks ago I'd come home from school as fast as I could porque Mami said Lorena had big news and a guest on the way. Normally Mami is always good to roll out the red carpet whenever Lorena has a new girlfriend, pero this time things were different. Lorena's guest was Professor Dominguez, the professor whose office had stored the magical sheet of paper that I fell through into Zafa last summer.

Turns out, Dominguez got a massive grant from some organization, The United Hispaniola Research Fund, to take the whole family on a trip with him to DR. The pamphlet looked super legit y todo, a shimmering silver medallion at the top with a proud goat looking out from the top of a mountain. After thirteen years of never seeing the island, all the delays, all the times our plans had fallen through at the last minute, today's the day I see the Dominican Republic.

I was still a little annoyed at Lorena for interrupting me while I was trying to remember the dream, even if she'd just been trying to help in her Lorena way. Details started trickling back in. The man in the dream had been pale and sported a mustache so thin it almost looked like a trick of the light. He had moved a bone in the middle of the elaborate constellation display, causing a broad crimson line of light to flit from one bone to the other like the most depressing pinball machine ever. A smile had finally flickered across the man's face, sweat pooling in the deep creases around his mouth.

And then the light had vanished.

The man's smile had sputtered like an old car and

died. His mouth had twisted with rage. He'd slammed his hands down on the display, sending the bones flying into the air where they hung, suspended for just a moment, before exploding with red light, leaving only the outline of the man. When the dust had cleared, there stood a different man in the rags of a uniform, hands clawing at his eyes. Or where his eyes should be. Pero when he'd looked up, his face had no eyes, no nose, only a mouth ringed with tiny fangs.

Minutes later, that image still gives me the creeps.

I couldn't shake the feeling that I knew that faceless dude. Pero, on the other hand, wouldn't I remember meeting a dude with no face? All these dreams must have been making me paranoid, entiendes? I squeezed my eyes shut tight to try and remember more of the dream, but it was no use; The Mystery of Spoonface and the Explosion would have to wait. I opened the window and let the glare of sunlight hit Lorena in the eyes just in time for the captain to announce that we were beginning our descent.

I looked out the window to see the first blue spots poking through the thin stretches in the sea of clouds below us. Pues, it looked like the ocean at the edge of the beach in Zafa. I smirked a bit remembering how much seeing the bleach-white waves with blue crests had freaked me out when I'd first arrived. I'd thought that would be the worst and most confusing thing I'd see, pero it barely cracked the top five.

Then the clouds thinned, the smirk fell off my face, and my mouth formed a perfect O as I saw the Dominican Republic, Mami's island, for the very first time.

The ocean stretched out and out to what seemed like the edge of the world. I'd never seen an ocean before and now it made sense that the sky would be blue, like it was jealous of the sea. Beneath us I could see Santo Domingo, and even hundreds of feet in the air I could feel that it was everything I had dreamed and more, entiendes? The thin, winding streets sprawled out like a labyrinth, and even from our great height cars winked in the bald, yellow sunlight like sea glass.

I could have looked out at that moment forever. Pero then—

"Oye, hermanita, scoot your big ol' head to the side!" Lorena whined. "You're not the only one seeing this place for the first time!"

I responded with the peak of maturity and stuck my tongue out at her. "Shouldn't have chosen the middle seat if you wanted to see."

"You know I get carsick!"

"Pilar Violeta Ramirez, let your sister look out the window!" Mami whisper-shouted from across the aisle. "People are staring, yo me muera."

Darn, we haven't even been in the country 5 minutes and Mami already called me by my full name.

I bit my tongue and leaned back trying to ignore Lorena's big smirk as she leaned over me with her ~~equally~~ even bigger head.

I looked at Mami across the aisle to see if she had cooled off and was excited to be home. Pero she had a far-off look in her eyes, and her mouth cut a slash across her face as Abuela squeezed her wise, calloused fingers around Mami's own.

I tapped Lorena's shoulder. She looked annoyed until I pointed at Mami and Abuela huddled over each other, eyes closed and whispering as if they were trading prayers. Lorena frowned.

"I was afraid this might happen," Lorena muttered. "She hasn't been home in a very long time and I think she's a little freaked out is all. Last time she left here, cousin Natasha was kidnapped and . . ."

I felt my gut clench at the mention of Natasha and fought to keep my face neutral. Because I was hiding a big secret. A your-cousin-has-come-back-from-the-dead kinda secret. And an

I-traveled-to-a-magical-island-and-squared-off-with-demons kinda secret. Truth was, I still hadn't told my family about Natasha and Zafa. Even with the footage I had to prove it, and Natasha's video to Mami and Abuela explaining what had happened to her, I just couldn't find the right time to completely upend their lives like the news had upended mine.

"You know how Mami doesn't always . . ." Lorena tapped her chin ". . . answer questions about the old days?"

I nodded. Pues, not for nothing, but it was really like pulling teeth with Mami and Abuela to try to get them to break their silence about that time in their lives.

"It's just the way trauma is sometimes. Trujillo's been gone fifty years, pero to Mami that danger will always be a little realer and nearer than it ever could be to us, you understand?"

I did. As I watched Mami, I thought about my best friend from Zafa, Carmen, and her perfect ciguapa memory, and how it was a curse as much as a blessing to remember where you came from and everything that might be waiting for you there. Pues, Mami has always been like a superhero to me, pero it is easy to forget that before she was anything else, Mami was a daughter, and sometimes a daughter needs her mother's hand more than anything else.

The plane's wheels screamed across the tarmac and immediately the plane was filled with thunderous applause. I joined in, and a wide smile split my face. We were here! I eyed Mami and Abuela to see if they were okay, and they were both clapping as well, even if Mami's eyes were still far away. Pero we'd made it! After fifty years, Mami was finally home.

TWO

WHEN WE STEPPED OUT OF the airport to call a taxi, the heat smacked me in the face like a wall. Pues, no wonder Mami was always complaining about the winter in Chicago. I knew a little bit about heat from being on Zafa, pero this was on another level.

"¡Bienvenidos a Santo Domingo!" Professor Dominguez crowed at the top of his voice. "Ay dios santificado, there really is no place like home!"

"It was Ciudad Trujillo when we left," Abuela muttered, staring around as the leaves of palm trees swayed in the light breeze "After all these years . . ."

Abuela trailed off and I reached out to squeeze Mami's hand, pero Lorena's was already there. I hiked my backpack higher on my shoulders and patted Abuela's arm.

"There's a lot to show you, Negrita." Abuela smiled dimly at me. "If it's still there anyway."

"Much has changed." Dominguez patted his bald spot dry and smiled apologetically. "Pero it's not all for the worse. Let's call a taxi and then we'll head over to where you'll be staying."

We all piled into a bright white taxi and pulled out onto the street with the airport shrinking in the distance on our right and the long stretch of ocean glistening in the sun to our left. Pues, there wasn't a cloud in the sky, and it seemed to bring out joy in everyone we zipped past. As Lorena chatted excitedly to Professor Dominguez about the itinerary for tomorrow, I learned that we were going to be staying in Dominguez's older cousin's apartment since he was away most of the year and Mami wouldn't hear of an Airbnb. Why? Who knows, pero Mami had put her foot down about it y se fue.

Pero none of that was on my mind, porque my face was smashed up against the glass taking a long tracking shot of the island with the camera. The documentary may have been "finished," pero a director's work is never done, y también I wanted to always remember what it was like the *first time* I saw the island. It was nothing like where I lived.

Chicago, at least the one you see in postcards, is

all steel, concrete, and windows. With buildings that tower and shimmer even in the winter, Chicago is a place where, when the sun goes missing, we build our own. Pero with the sky visible for miles, Santo Domingo was built like a place where the sun never sets. Bright paint layered over dusky yellow buildings with rectangular roofs; it looked like art to me.

The traffic was super different as well. Cars were either old or brand-new and sparkling. Pero the biggest difference was how many motorcycles there were gunning it down the highway next to us in groups of three, five, sometimes more. Weaving through the traffic like schools of mismatched fish. Pues, there was even a guy riding along in the back of a pickup truck casually tossing and catching an emerald-green aguacate that was as big as Lorena's head, and that's saying something, entiendes?

I felt something building in me like the tumbao that connects me to La Negra. I wanted that moment to stretch forever. I understood a little better why Mami's rhythm never seemed all the way right in America, why she could love this place I'd never seen as fiercely as I love Chicago. There are different magics to these lands, and maybe there's nothing worse than being separated from the magic you love best.

I swiveled in my seat and grinned at everything and nothing in particular. Old salsa wheezed through the speakers of the taxi while a motorcycle rider, his girlfriend in back, bobbed in and out of lanes like a needle and thread, sewing the traffic together. I loved the flags streaming, and the sky with only one cloud, pitch black with unspent rain.

"¡Nos necesitamos preparar por la reina!" I announced, and smiled broadly at the car.

Crickets.

"¿Pilar, qué te dijo?" Mami's grin slid half off her face in confusion.

"The . . . the cloud?" I pointed, turning off the camera. "There's rain coming, no?"

Everyone in the car looked at me like I had three heads until . . .

"Oh," Abuela said. "Pilar, you mean *lluvia*. *Lluvia* means rain, 'reina' means queen."

My heart sank. We'd only been on the island for an hour tops, and I was already making rookie mistakes? Where was Zafa's auto-translate feature when you needed it?

"It's a common mistake, hermanita!" Lorena patted my knee. "But anyway, it's a gorgeous day, there are no clouds in sight!"

"But what about that one?" I jabbed at the window again, pointing at the pitch-black cloud.

Pero nobody else seemed to see it. They all just looked at me until Lorena broke the silence with a joke. I shook my head and stared out at the ocean, that one cloud curled in on itself like a knuckle. It was there, why couldn't they see it?

The cloud felt almost alive, glaring down at me like a warning.